PLACES
WE'VE
NEVER
BEEN

ALSO BY KASIE WEST

The Distance Between Us

Pivot Point

Split Second

On the Fence

The Fill-In Boyfriend

P.S. I Like You

By Your Side

Love, Life, and the List

Lucky in Love

Listen to Your Heart

Fame, Fate, and the First Kiss

Maybe This Time

Moment of Truth

Sunkissed

West, Kasie,
Places we've never been /
[2022]
33305250162736
ca   08/31/23

WEST

PLACES WE'VE NEVER BEEN

DELACORTE PRESS

This is a work of fiction. Names, characters, places, and incidents either are the product of the author's imagination or are used fictitiously. Any resemblance to actual persons, living or dead, events, or locales is entirely coincidental.

Text copyright © 2022 by Kasie West
Jacket art copyright © 2022 by Ana Hard

All rights reserved. Published in the United States by Delacorte Press, an imprint of Random House Children's Books, a division of Penguin Random House LLC, New York.

Delacorte Press is a registered trademark and the colophon is a trademark of Penguin Random House LLC.

GetUnderlined.com

Educators and librarians, for a variety of teaching tools, visit us at RHTeachersLibrarians.com

Library of Congress Cataloging-in-Publication Data
Names: West, Kasie, author.
Title: Places we've never been / Kasie West.
Other titles: Places we have never been
Description: First edition. | New York : Delacorte Press, [2022] | Audience: Ages 12 and up. | Summary: While on a cross-country RV trip with her family, aspiring video game animator Norah reunites with an old friend, prepares for her college interview, and encounters unexpected romance and revelations.
Identifiers: LCCN 2021014397 (print) | LCCN 2021014398 (ebook) | ISBN 978-0-593-17630-6 (hardcover) | ISBN 978-0-593-17631-3 (library binding) | ISBN 978-0-593-17632-0 (ebook) | ISBN 978-0-593-57254-2 (int'l edition)
Subjects: CYAC: Recreational vehicles—Fiction. | Automobile travel—Fiction. | Drawing—Fiction. | Universities and colleges—Fiction. | Dating (Social customs)—Fiction. | Family life—Fiction. | LCGFT: Novels.
Classification: LCC PZ7.W51837 Pl 2022 (print) | LCC PZ7.W51837 (ebook) | DDC [Fic]—dc23

The text of this book is set in 11-point Adobe Text Pro.
Interior design by Cathy Bobak

Printed in the United States of America
10 9 8 7 6 5 4 3 2 1
First Edition

Random House Children's Books supports the First Amendment and celebrates the right to read.

Penguin Random House LLC supports copyright. Copyright fuels creativity, encourages diverse voices, promotes free speech, and creates a vibrant culture. Thank you for buying an authorized edition of this book and for complying with copyright laws by not reproducing, scanning, or distributing any part in any form without permission. You are supporting writers and allowing Penguin Random House to publish books for every reader.

To *my* Skyler, who is thoughtful, kind, funny, and resilient. Love you!

CHAPTER 1

"NORAH, BREATHE," WILLOW SAID WITH A LAUGH. "I swear I've never seen you this excited in my life. I'm starting to get jealous."

I swatted her arm with a folded blue sweatshirt, then added it to the open suitcase on my bed. "You *should* be jealous," I teased. "He was my best friend for most of my life. You only just passed three years."

"I think *was* is the key word there."

She was right, of course. I hadn't seen Skyler since the summer before eighth grade. That's when he and his family moved across the country to Ohio. We'd Snapped and messaged and texted a lot that first year, but every year since, we'd drifted more and more apart until we basically had zero communication. Now all we did was occasionally like each other's posts on Instagram.

"I was kidding," Willow said. "Bring back your super-cute excited face. Tell me more about taking over Pokémon gyms and gummy worm dioramas and video game marathons and how you did all this without kissing this boy, not even once."

I laughed. "He left when we were thirteen."

"And?"

I dug through the top drawer of my dresser and scooped up a handful of socks. I threw them in the air like confetti. "And now he's coming back!"

"For three weeks," she reminded me. "Where you will be crammed in an RV together. Sounds"—she picked up a sock ball from where it had landed on the floor next to her and half-heartedly threw it in the air—"fun?"

"This trip is going to be amazing. I get to see my childhood best friend. I get to visit my future college. It's like my past"—I held up my left hand—"and my future"—I held up my right—"are coming together!" I joined my hands in a dramatic clap.

"What did you just do with your hands? That didn't look good. Are you getting in a major traffic accident on this trip?"

I frowned at my hands, which were still clasped, fingers intertwined. "No, it represents a magical combination where magical things are going to happen."

"It looked like a major collision—glass and twisted metal everywhere."

I rolled my eyes. "You really are jealous."

"Yes, I am. He will not take back best friend status from me. I will fight him to the death for it."

"Weapon of choice?" I asked, collecting the socks, then dropping them in my suitcase.

"Probably a long sword. Or a throwing ax. It depends. Is he tall?"

"He wasn't four years ago."

My phone buzzed on the bed with a text. Behind me, Willow's phone buzzed too. It was a message from Leena in our group text. *Who's going to the party this weekend?*

My initial instinct was to type, *Not me, I'll be in a magical collision with my childhood friend.* But that was dumb. Nobody else would get that and I'd sound ridiculous. I only said stuff like that around people I felt perfectly comfortable with, like Willow . . . and Skyler. I never worried about how I sounded around Skyler; he was just as weird as I was.

I looked out the window again, my anticipation almost unbearable now, but the street was still empty. My phone buzzed.

I'm in, Willow had answered. She wasn't one to analyze everything she said.

I'll be out of town, I finally typed. A perfectly normal response.

"You won't have to fight him," I said, back to our conversation. "Like you said, it's only three weeks. And technically we won't be crammed anywhere together. He's going to be in an RV with his mom and siblings, and I'm going to be in our RV with Mom and Ezra." But Skyler was coming to see me! Well, not specifically to see me, but it felt that way.

"Why now?" Willow asked.

"What?" I studied my suitcase and the backpack beside it, trying to decide if I had remembered everything I'd need. I had my sketch pad and pencils. Skyler would want to see all my drawings. He'd be surprised at how much better I'd gotten. I hoped he brought his sketch pad, too, so we could draw together like we used to. I'd even brought the charcoal pencil he'd loaned me before he left that I'd forgotten to give back.

Willow's voice drew my eyes out of my suitcase. "You said your moms have been talking about doing an RV trip since they were in college."

"Yeah."

"So why spring it on you now? After all these years?"

"They miss each other. Apparently, they've been planning it for months. They wanted to surprise us." I pulled my stack of flash cards from my back pocket and held them up. "Plus, I told you, I have my college interview thing."

"That's a weekend trip, not a three-week, multi-stop, bring-two-families-together-who-haven't-seen-each-other-in-years kind of thing."

"It's just another good excuse to do it now. That's all I'm saying."

"Truuue . . ." Willow crawled over to my bookshelf in the corner and started running her finger along the spines of books, pulling several out as she did and setting them aside.

"Why did you say *true* like that?"

"That's how I say *true*."

"That was a suspicious *true*." I pocketed my cards again. "Speaking of my college tour and interview, what do you think of this outfit?" I grabbed the hanger from my closet that held the pencil skirt, button-down, and blazer my mom had bought me the week before.

"Are you applying to be their librarian? Or maybe just run the school?"

"I'm serious, what do you think?"

"I think no wannabe video game animator I know would ever wear that."

"How many do you know?"

"Just you. And you don't wear that."

I laid the outfit flat across the contents of my suitcase. "You want me to wear a T-shirt and leggings to the interview?"

"Yes, your *Super Mario Bros.* Princess Peach shirt would be perfect."

I didn't even wear that to school. Besides, this was an interview. I needed to be professional, show I was serious. "Maybe Dean Collins hates *Super Mario.* Maybe she's more a *Street Fighter* fan. I can't create controversy from the very first impression."

She rolled her whole head to show she disagreed, then pointed to the stack of books she had created. "Can I borrow these while you're gone?"

"Yes."

"Cool." She stood and slid the books into her bag by the door. "And you were right about my *true.* It was suspicious."

"I know. So talk."

She looked in the mirror above my dresser and patted her dark curls. Willow was beautiful, dark brown skin, full lips, intense eyes, and curves for days. "I just think that there's probably another reason for this sudden RV trip that doesn't include husbands."

"You consider something that took at least six months to plan 'sudden'?"

"They told you two weeks ago."

"That's what a surprise is," I said. "And I've heard about this plan pretty much my whole life. It was always supposed to be husbandless. Believe me, my dad is not offended. He's been on plenty of RV trips."

"You're probably right. You know me, always suspicious. But prepare yourself for some big news in the next three weeks, just in case this trip has some hidden agenda."

"Like what?" I asked, my brain suddenly creating possibilities at her suggestion.

"As long as they don't tell you that you're moving to Ohio to join your ex–best friend, I'll be okay."

"*You'll* be okay?"

"Yes."

I picked a stuffed animal off my bed and threw it at her.

She caught it and studied the embroidered eyes of Donkey Kong. "Maybe take him to the interview?" She turned him to face me. "Is he the one that climbed a building to save that woman in distress?" She chucked him toward my bed, and he landed perfectly in my suitcase.

"You're thinking King Kong, and I'm pretty sure he *caused* her distress. But Donkey Kong is no prince either." I tossed him back in my pile. "If I were to take anyone to my interview, it would be Ms. Pac-Man. She's a baddie."

"Like you're going to be in that interview."

I took a deep breath. I hoped she was right. I would just have to focus, not go off track like my brain sometimes did, and stick to my rehearsed answers. I'd be fine.

Before I realized what she was doing, Willow had snatched my flash cards from my pocket and started flipping through them. "These are the questions you're studying for it?" She had her back to me and I reached around trying to get the cards back. "Who has influenced your art the most? Why animation?"

"They'll ask those," I said.

"Why do you look like you want to be our librarian?" she said, pretending to read off a card.

"You're such a brat."

She turned around with a big smile and handed me the cards. "There will be some questions you didn't write on these cards, too, you know."

I *did* know. And that was the thought that had me adding questions to the cards every day. I needed to think of everything. Even the unexpected.

"Norah! Ezra! They're here!" Mom's voice rang out from the hall.

My eyes shot to the window, where an RV now blocked my view of the road. I smiled. "They're here!"

"Go," Willow said, shooing me. "I'm going to leave some notes in your suitcase for you to find later that will remind you of your loyalty."

I hugged her and ran out the door, nearly colliding with my older brother, Ezra, as I did.

"Today's the day!" I said, grabbing hold of his arm and shaking it.

"It's this kind of attitude that made Mom think three weeks

in a rolling box is something we actually want to do," he said dryly.

"You know you're excited."

"Three weeks, Norah. Only weirdos like you can spin that into anything but torture."

And Skyler. He'd be into this, I was sure of it.

I took Ezra's hand, pulling him toward the front door, where I could now hear voices. "You get to see Austin." Austin was Skyler's older brother, and much like me and Skyler, Austin and Ezra had been inseparable when they lived in Fresno.

Ezra shook his head. "Literally haven't said a word to him in about three years."

"So."

"Just saying, it will be weird."

"Only if you make it weird."

"I will," he joked. "I totally will." Unlike me, Ezra never made anything awkward. He had been the King of Cool in high school. Mr. Popular. Star football player and class president. Nearly everyone I met knew of my brother.

We came to the end of the hall and rounded the corner into the living room, where laughter and hugs were being exchanged. Mom had her arms tight around Olivia, tears in both of their eyes.

"Best friends shouldn't spend four years apart," Mom said.

Olivia nodded.

My gaze searched the room, landing first on Paisley, Skyler's younger sister. When they moved, she was only ten. Now, at fourteen, she had long dark hair and was almost taller than me.

Austin looked like an adult, which technically, at nineteen now, he was, complete with face scruff, neatly trimmed dark hair, a filled-out frame, and jeans instead of basketball shorts. My dad was shaking his hand. When he backed away, Austin saw us.

He smiled. "Hey, guys."

Ezra, who seconds before had pretended not to be excited, was the first one forward. They exchanged a quick hug, slapping each other on the back once, and then laughed.

"Oh, Norah, look at you," Olivia said, free from my mom's hug. She walked toward me and I met her halfway. "You're all grown up and beautiful." I didn't feel much different, at least looks-wise. I still had my long wavy brown hair, my same burns-easily-in-the-sun white skin, my same average height and build.

"Hi," I said, hugging her. "How was your trip?" I asked when really I wanted to yell, *Where is Skyler?* Because he definitely wasn't in this room.

"We flew in last night and got our rental RV about an hour ago," she said. I had forgotten how calm Olivia was. Where my mom was loud and animated, Olivia was slow and measured. "So far it's been great. But now the real adventure begins."

Ezra cleared his throat. "Where's Skyler?"

I wanted to hug my brother for asking, but instead I stood very still so I wouldn't miss the answer.

Olivia looked around the room as if realizing for the first time that he wasn't here. "I . . ."

"He's in the RV," Paisley said. "On the phone."

Olivia rolled her eyes toward my mom. "Not everyone thinks this is a dream vacation like we do, Miranda."

Ezra raised his hand and when Mom shot him a look, he said, "Oh, we weren't talking about me?"

Austin laughed.

"We will convert everyone by the end," Mom said with a smile.

My heart seemed to drop to the floor. Skyler didn't want to be here.

CHAPTER 2

"YOU ALL PACKED?" MOM ASKED ME.

"What?" I'd been staring at the front door while everyone chatted, wondering if once Skyler got off the phone, he'd come in and show that even if he didn't want to be in an RV, he at least was happy to see me. "Oh, yes. Just let me get my stuff."

Willow really was tucking notes into my suitcase when I got back to my room. "Well?" she asked. "How was the grand reunion?"

"Um . . ." I put a hand to my forehead.

"What is *that*?" Willow pointed at my wrist. "I haven't seen that in years."

I twisted the bracelet. A faded letter on each of the blue beads spelled out *best friends*. "It's funny and nostalgic. Me and Skyler were going to laugh about it together."

"And did he think it was funny and nostalgic?"

I pointed out the window. "I haven't seen him yet. He hasn't come in, but he will."

Willow's brows popped up. "Oh."

"What?"

"Nothing."

"No, what?" I zipped my suitcase closed and hefted it off my bed.

"Here I was worried he was going to steal my best friend. I guess I didn't have to worry. He's grown up into a bona fide jerk. Did we see signs of this early on? Are we proud, or no?"

"Funny."

"It wasn't a joke."

I waved a hand through the air. "No, Skyler is . . . was . . . the nicest, funniest boy I knew. Whatever. It's fine. He's just on the phone. Maybe he's getting summer homework or something. It's obviously important."

"Ooh, maybe it's his parole officer. Or maybe he's talking to a sick relative or is learning he really can get the demon horn on his forehead removed."

"Demons have *two* horns."

"He's a single-horned demon, trust me on this."

I shook my head with a smile. "Well, I'm going to load this on the RV and then we're taking off."

"Hey, Norah?"

"Yeah?"

"I'm sorry."

"For what? It's fine. I'll be sending you goofy pics of me and him soon."

Willow took me by the shoulders and looked me in the eyes, straight into my heart like only a best friend could. "I know this wasn't how you thought this would go down. And I know he represented a part of childhood for you that you've never fully told me about, but if his present self turns out to be a jerk, his past self can still be really important to you. You can still have that magical collision thing, okay?" She clapped her hands together.

"Thanks," I said, and gave her a hug.

"Now, I expect you to bring me home a couple souvenirs from this trip, so choose wisely."

"Don't get into trouble while I'm gone."

"Where's the fun in that?" She swiped up her bag and followed me out of my room this time and through the house. The living room had emptied into the front yard, where my dad was helping load luggage and my mom was walking around the outside of the rental RV, obviously checking it out. It was early June, but the hot summer of Fresno had already descended. The weeds growing in sidewalk cracks and orchards were already yellow instead of their spring green.

I wheeled my suitcase to my dad and he lifted it into the side storage compartment along with the other luggage and ice chests and toilet paper and all the other things Mom had stocked up on. "Jeez, kid, what did you pack?"

"Three weeks, Dad."

"Fair enough." He pulled me into a hug. My dad was short, so our cheeks met in the embrace. "I'm going to miss you."

"You too."

"Hi, Willow," Dad said around me.

"Hi, Mr. Simons. I know you'll miss me, too, but I have faith in your survival."

"I appreciate the vote of confidence." Dad turned to close the storage hatch. "Anything else for down here?"

"No, I want my backpack with me."

Something over my shoulder drew Dad's attention. He lifted his hand in a wave. "Good to see you, Skyler."

My heart sped up and it felt like I was moving in slow motion as I turned.

"You never kissed *that*?" Willow mumbled beside me.

"I'm going to pretend I didn't hear that," Dad said before he joined Mom.

Willow covered her mouth, muffling her laugh.

Skyler waved to my dad and then our eyes locked for a brief moment before he looked away.

He was the same, yet very different. He was much taller and broader than before. But he had the same relaxed expression, the same thick blond hair, the same light brown eyes. And because of all the sameness, a memory flooded my mind of the last time he'd come home after a long trip. He'd spent a month at his grandma's one summer, and that month had felt like an eternity to me.

The day Skyler was coming home, I had sat on his porch, too excited to wait for him at my house. The sun was setting and the sky was bright orange. His mom's car pulled into the driveway and he'd flung open the passenger door before the engine was even off.

"Norah!" We'd collided in a hug.

"You were gone forever. Ezra refused to work on my *Minecraft* world with me, so I hope you didn't play too much in Oregon or you're going to be so bored this week."

"Can a person ever play too much *Minecraft*?" He took off his backpack and sat on the grass. "I have something for you."

"Good to see you, Norah," Olivia had said, patting my shoulder as she walked by. Skyler looked nothing like his mom. She was tall and lean, with dark hair, like her other kids. Much to his annoyance, Skyler looked more like his dad, even though their personalities were completely opposite.

"You too." I plopped down next to Skyler.

"You have something for me?" I asked.

He dug into the front pocket of his backpack and pulled out a beaded bracelet. "It was my grandma's."

"You stole it?"

"What? No! You think I would steal from my grandma?"

"You *are* kind of shady."

He grinned a gap-toothed smile. "Shady like a fox."

"Isn't it *crazy* like a fox?"

"Is it? Are foxes crazy?"

"Are they shady?" I asked.

"So shady." His eyes got big and then he laughed. "Here, look. She gave this to me." He pointed at the beads and to the letters on each of them. "I guess it's from when she was a kid." He picked up my hand and slid it on my wrist.

I played with the beads. "Vintage." Then my eyes popped up to his. "Where's yours?"

"Mine?"

"It's a best friend's bracelet. I wear one and you wear the other."

He shrugged. "I guess whoever her best friend was at the time has the other half."

"Should we try to steal it?" I asked.

"Of course we should," he said, that playful glint shining in his eyes because we always found each other's jokes funny, never odd.

"What are you going to do?" Willow's voice brought me out of my memory.

Skyler had shut the door to the RV and was walking to where my brother and Austin stood, still catching up.

"Skyler!" I heard Ezra say, and then they hugged.

"Is he really not going to come over here?" Willow asked. "I take back my implication that he is hot. He is no longer hot."

Hearing her say he was hot was strange to me. I mean, I wasn't blind. He was attractive. But I couldn't think of him as anything other than the kid I'd spent so much time with.

"His brother, on the other hand," Willow said, assessing Austin. "Can I call dibs?"

"He's nineteen," I said.

"And?"

"And gay."

"You should've led with that one," she said.

"Probably true. Come on, I'll introduce you to everyone before you leave." Because like I'd told Ezra, this was only going to be weird if we made it weird.

"Okay."

Austin turned toward us first as we walked across the grass to join the group. "Hey, Norah." He switched into a high-pitched voice, obviously imitating his mom, and added, "You're all grown up."

I pointed at the hair on his chin. "Is this *your* attempt at being grown up?"

Skyler laughed and my first bit of hope returned. I wanted to give him a hug, like my brother had, like we always used to, but I hesitated and the window of time where it wouldn't have been awkward passed.

"This is my friend Willow, guys. Willow, this is Austin and Skyler."

"Hello," she said.

"Nice to meet you," Ezra said, and Willow punched him in the arm. My brother grabbed her fist in his hand to keep her from doing it again. Willow was one of my only friends who had never been starstruck by Ezra and his high school fame status. She had never been giggly or silly around him and I loved her for that.

"How did Norah talk you into three weeks in an RV?" Austin asked.

Willow shook her head. "Oh, no, that's not happening. I just came here to help Norah pack and check out my competition." She gave Skyler a hard stare. "Now that I'm sure I have none, I'm taking off."

I elbowed her and she laughed.

"Call me," she said. After a hug for me and a wave to everyone else, she climbed into her car and drove away.

Ezra and Austin were rehashing memories from freshman year like they talked all the time—laughing and finishing each other's sentences. Skyler and I stood silent, listening, as if we'd never met before this moment.

"How are you?" I finally asked him.

"Yeah, I'm good, thanks." That's all he said, no goofy quip, no knowing smirk. "How are you?"

"I'm okay." I nodded toward the rental RV. "Are you ready for this?"

He scoffed. "No."

"A forced participation, huh?" Then, because we had just as much shared history as Ezra and Austin, who were still going strong, I added, "Like sixth-grade science fair? I think I still have dried crickets in my teeth."

He gave what I remembered as his courtesy chuckle, which had never before been directed at me, and said, "Yeah."

I blinked, my hope from before evaporating in an instant. I covertly slipped the bracelet off my wrist and into my pocket. "Okay, nice catching up," I said. Then I turned and was barely able to keep myself from running away. Instead, I walked briskly to our RV, opened the door, and shut it behind me. "Dried crickets in my teeth? Really, Norah?"

Great, my partner in awkwardness had turned normal.

I huffed out a breath, then flung my backpack onto the couch.

The door creaked open and my heart caught, hoping it was Skyler coming to explain himself. But Paisley walked in alone.

"Wow, your RV is bigger than ours. This is so cool." She went on a self-guided tour of the kitchenette, the double-decker beds, and the bathroom. "Do you guys take it out a lot?"

"We used to more, but usually only for a long weekend. This will be the longest trip we've ever done."

"I'm excited," she said.

"Yeah, me too." I really was. Even without Skyler, I had been looking forward to the route Mom had shown me and some of the stops we were making—Zion, Yellowstone, Seattle, which housed my future school!—since the beginning. I had never been out of California before and I was more than ready to experience something different.

"Mom said we used to live around here."

"Yes, right around the corner, not even a full block away. You don't remember?"

"Some, I guess. Are there orange trees close? I remember building a fort in them or something with my brothers."

I smiled. "Yeah, behind the neighborhood. A developer bought the orchard, though, so soon there will be more houses."

"Do you remember me?"

"Of course! You were like this tall and followed me and Skyler everywhere." I held my hand up to indicate her height. "Do you not remember me?"

"Did your hair used to be darker?"

I reached up and tugged on the ends of my previously dark brown hair. A trip to the hairdresser just last week had it looking more light brown. "Yes. It's amazing what a bit of bleach and toner can do."

She curled her lip. "I wouldn't know. My mom won't let me touch my hair."

"You should never touch your hair."

She squinted her eyes as if thinking. "Did you used to wear your hair in French braids a lot?"

I laughed. "Ah, yes. The French braid phase. I learned how to do them on myself when I was like ten, so there was a whole year where I wore one every day."

"You'll have to teach me how. I still don't know."

"Are you sure you want a French braid phase in your life?"

"I will use the skill wisely."

Skyler's sister was funny. Maybe she'd be my saving grace on this trip. And maybe she could provide me with a little insight. "So . . . what's up with your brother? Why doesn't he want to be here?"

"Skyler?"

"Yeah."

"I don't know. I heard him say something about some girl around here who had a crush on him. Maybe he's worried about seeing her. He doesn't want to lead her on." When she said *lead her on*, she did air quotes.

My mouth dropped open and I quickly shut it. "That's what *he* said? That's why you air-quoted it?"

"Yeah, that's what I heard him say to Austin."

"To *Austin*?" My eyes were burning.

"What does this button do?" Paisley asked, pointing at the wall over the table.

I heard her question but my brain was frozen on what she'd just said. What I knew it meant. As if I didn't feel stupid enough.

Paisley looked at me and her eyes suddenly went wide. "Wait . . . was Skyler talking about *you*?"

CHAPTER 3

"HE MOST DEFINITELY WAS NOT," I SAID, EVEN though I was certain he was. That explained exactly why he was acting the way he was. "I have never had a crush on Skyler Hutton." And that was the absolute truth.

She shrugged. "It must've been someone else, then." She pushed the button on the wall and the table between the two benches dropped, folding down. "Cool!"

A loud horn sounded from outside and Paisley gasped in surprise.

"That must be the departure bell," I said.

"Oh! Right." She rushed toward the door and, with her hand on the handle, glanced back over her shoulder. "See you at our first stop!"

"Yep," I said, forcing a smile. It wasn't her fault I was mad. She was just the messenger. I pulled out my phone to angrily text Willow the latest development when Ezra, Mom, and Dad filed into the RV.

"Say goodbye to your dad," Mom said.

21

"I already did."

"Well, I'm greedy," Dad said. "I need another goodbye."

I hugged him tight and rested in his arms for a moment, hoping the comfort I felt there would melt away the anger burning in my chest. It worked a little.

"Have fun and good luck on your interview."

My interview. At a school filled with people who had the same passion I had—gaming. My future couldn't come soon enough. "Thanks, Dad. Don't miss us too much."

"I'll try not to."

"Are you sad you aren't coming?" I had never asked him point-blank before.

"No, your mom and Olivia need this."

"What do you mean?"

He glanced at Mom, who was stowing her purse in the compartment by the driver's seat. "I mean, they need some time together."

That's what he said but it didn't feel like the truth. I sighed. Willow was getting in my head, turning me skeptical. "I'll send you loads of pics."

"You better." He squeezed Ezra's arm. "Have fun, son."

I snapped my fingers and pointed at my dad. "Don't even think about it. Equal treatment."

Dad laughed and opened his arms for Ezra. "Come get your hug, son. Blame your sister."

"I always do," Ezra said, letting Dad hug him. Ezra was taller and lankier than my dad and he patted him on the head before pulling away. Then Dad was through the door and standing on the front lawn, ready to wave us on our way.

"Find a seat," Mom said, taking her place behind the big steering wheel of the RV.

Ezra claimed the passenger seat, which was fine with me. I went to the very back, lay on my mom's bed, and twisted the blinds open. *Goodbye, Fresno,* I thought as we drove away. *My future awaits.* Like Willow had pointed out, I would only be gone for three weeks, but this felt like the first step toward discovering my life, toward finding where I really fit in.

After watching the road stretch out behind me for some time, I joined my backpack on the couch, pulled out my phone, and opened my coding app.

I had been entering strings and commands into my phone for a simple game concept the app was teaching me, when something Ezra said pulled me out of my zone.

"It just makes more sense," he was saying. "And I've driven it before."

"Not for this long."

"Yeah, but, Mom, we're literally on this mostly straight freeway for the next five hours. It's not rocket science. Don't you want all this driving time with Olivia too?"

I could tell my mom was considering his request, which I was dreading had something to do with bringing the Hutton children from their very much separate rolling box into ours. This could not happen. "No," I said.

Ezra turned, his brows down. "Miss Positivity back there is voting against me?"

"What's the proposal?"

"You didn't even know what you were voting against? Nice."

"I had an idea."

"I had an idea too," Ezra said. "A very good one."

"I'll think about it," Mom said.

"Think about what?" I asked.

Ezra pointed at the RV on the road in front of us. Across the back windows was written 1-800-IM-4-RENT. "Mom bus." Then he pointed at the floor next to him. "Teen bus."

"No," I said again. "That's a horrible idea. We need some alone time or we'll get sick of each other. We haven't seen them in years—maybe they're all super annoying now."

"Norah!" Mom said, her eyes shooting to mine in the rear-view mirror.

"I mean, I'm sure they're not. I'm just saying."

"I'll think about it," Mom said again.

Great, my argument probably ended up helping Ezra's cause.

* * *

For the record, I wanted to announce after a gas station stop, a sidebar with the moms, and a rearranging of passengers, *I voted against this!* Instead of saying it out loud, I just screamed it in my head as we climbed onto what Ezra had referred to as the teen bus.

"Does anyone else feel like our moms agreed to that way too easily?" Austin asked, which made me realize that he and Ezra had obviously hatched this plan back in our front yard several hours ago and were working the argument from both ends.

"Almost like someone used some cheat codes," I mumbled, and went to the way back again, onto the large bed. I pulled out my flash cards to study.

Ezra and Austin were, of course, up front, Ezra driving, Austin shotgun. Skyler plopped down on the couch and stared at his phone, his familiar look of concentration coming onto his face.

"Don't kill us!" I called out to Ezra as he merged onto the freeway.

"Look at this road, Nor. It would take serious skill to kill you."

The road in front of us was a long black straight line that stretched out endlessly, it seemed, only stopping at the horizon. On either side of the road were miles and miles of flat desert, broken up by dry shrubs and the occasional Joshua tree.

"Is that why you were being so negative about this earlier?" he asked. "You're scared of my driving?"

Skyler's eyes popped up and collided with mine, as though suddenly interested in what I had to say. *Yeah, that's right, Skyler. I didn't want you in our RV. How's that for a crush?*

I was not going to give him the satisfaction of explaining anything. "Yeah, something like that."

Paisley sat next to Skyler and held up her phone. "Let's finish our game."

He smiled at her. "I thought you'd conveniently forget we were playing since I was crushing you so hard."

"When are you going to learn not to gloat before it's over?" she asked.

"I guess when you start winning more."

She shoved his arm and laughed.

I found myself smiling but quickly remembered I was an outsider to the interaction this time. The thought hurt more than I wanted it to. I rolled onto my stomach and looked out the window. The desert landscape wasn't the prettiest—dry, monotonous, and yellow—but there was something about plants and animals being able to survive in such bleak conditions that was intriguing.

* * *

"You're good," Paisley said from over my left shoulder.

I jumped. When I got in a drawing zone, the world around me melted away. "You scared me."

"Sorry," she whispered. "I've been sitting here for like five minutes."

"I didn't hear you." I moved from lying on my stomach to sitting up.

"What is it?" She pointed at my sketch pad.

My drawing featured a girl (me) flinging sharp needles at the retreating form of her enemy (Skyler). I hoped Paisley didn't recognize either figure. I hadn't added too many details yet. "A video game idea inspired by the desert. She's using cactus needles on her enemies."

"I wish I could draw like that," she said.

"Skyler never taught you?" I said it loud enough for Skyler to hear. I wanted to keep reminding him that I actually knew things about him, that we were *friends,* and that *he* was making this awkward, not me.

"Skyler?" she said, confused. "He doesn't draw."

"What?" For the second time that day, Paisley said something that shocked me and I couldn't help myself. "You don't draw?" I directed the question at him. *He* had taught *me.*

"No, not anymore," he answered, obviously having been following our conversation.

"Since when?"

He shrugged. "Since we moved."

He had changed even more than I thought. "Why?"

"I don't know. I got over it, I guess."

I narrowed my eyes. "Got over it?"

"Yeah, I grew up, moved on."

It felt like he was referring to more than just drawing with that statement. "Right," I said, proud at how steady my voice sounded. "You grew out of it." My eyes shot down to my drawing, which *did* feel rather childish at the moment. I gritted my teeth and flipped the page.

"Exactly."

I told myself to just let it go, but then I heard myself say, "You'll have to ask all the artists of the world why they don't just grow up already."

Paisley laughed. "I don't believe you used to draw, Skyler."

"Sometimes," he said.

"Sometimes? All the time," I said. "I think I might even have . . ." I dug through my backpack, searching for the notebook I'd brought before I knew Skyler had turned into a jerk. When we were kids, neither of us had cell phones, so we used to exchange notes back and forth in a notebook and I'd brought it to laugh over with him. Along with notes were silly doodles we'd both drawn, and I turned to one of those now and showed Paisley.

"Skyler drew that?"

I smiled. Holding the notebook made me happy. I glanced over to Skyler and his eyes were locked on the book. Well, frick, if this didn't make him think I was obsessed with him, I didn't know what would. "I, uh . . . found it the other day with some other crap in the back of my closet," I said in the most casual voice I could muster. It was true. I really hadn't looked at the notebook in forever.

"You were pretty good, Skyler," Paisley said. "Apparently you have talent hiding somewhere in you after all."

I sucked in my lips so I didn't laugh.

"Are there more?" she asked.

"Sure, here." I passed her the book because like I'd told Willow and like I'd told Paisley, Skyler and I had just been friends. The book was full of strictly platonic notes that would prove that very thing.

Paisley started flipping pages.

In the front pocket of my backpack, along with all my supplies, sat Skyler's charcoal pencil. It was lined with his bite marks from how he used to hold it between his teeth when he switched between his pencil and his blender. I wasn't going to give it back now. It was mine.

"Does this say Norah Hutton?" Paisley asked, pointing and turning the book toward me. "You practiced signing our last name?"

"What?" My mind raced as I tried to remember signing my name as Norah Hutton. When had I ever done that?

"Flip the page," came Skyler's voice from across the way.

Paisley turned to the next page in the notebook and there

in Skyler's handwriting were the words *Skyler Simons* over and over. "I don't get it," she said.

I didn't remember, either, so now we were both staring at Skyler.

"We did a timed competition. You said your last name was harder to write than mine even though I have two *t*'s to cross and you only have one *i* to dot."

"Your two *t*'s are next to each other, so that's really like only having one *t*."

"Yes, that was your argument."

"Oh . . . it was?" I turned to the notebook. "Who won?"

"Well, my first name is longer."

"So I won?"

His eyes crinkled at the corners. "Not fairly."

I almost threw the pillow next to me at him in a teasing manner. It's what I would've done when we were friends. But I hesitated and hugged it to my chest instead. I was quickly falling into the edited version of me, the personality I put on at school and parties. The personality I didn't think I'd have to use on this trip.

Paisley laughed. "Time *me* writing both of your names." She turned to the very back of the notebook, where there were several blank pages. I felt myself tense. I didn't want her writing in our notebook. Maybe that was stupid of me but I suddenly felt protective of it. It represented a time I'd obviously never get back.

"We already crowned the winner, Paisley," Skyler said. "No need for a retrial."

Did he not want her writing in it either?

"Fine," she said with a huff, then leaned against the wall and continued to browse through the pages.

I tried to catch his eye, but he was looking out the window. I was glad for the first real moment that proved his memory was intact, but it did nothing to ease the tension between us. The tension that existed because he thought I was madly in love with him. Ugh. Had he really gotten *that* arrogant?

"Can I have some of your gummy worms?" Paisley asked, pointing to the open package on the bed between us.

"Yes, have at them."

"Why is this place called Death Valley anyway?" Paisley asked, referring to our first overnight stop on the route. "Is it some sort of burial ground?"

"It's really hot, I hear," I said.

"So people die from the heat?"

"I'm not sure. Don't worry, my mom will make us stop at the park's visitors center. That can be our first question when we get there."

"I'm sure they never get that question," Skyler said.

"Oh, good. I was missing your sarcasm," Paisley returned.

He smirked at her and I wanted to cry. I was surprised by my reaction and quickly looked away.

My phone buzzed by my leg and I picked it up. Willow and I had been exchanging angry texts that included phrases like *How stupid! What a punk! Maybe there are two horns up there after all!* for the last hour or so.

Miss me yet? Willow had texted.

Yes, I do. Why is Death Valley called Death Valley?

You're stopping in Death Valley? Didn't anyone tell you it's hot there? Deathly hot! Not as hot as Skyler, but close.

We agreed he wasn't hot.

Yeah, I'm going back and forth on that.

Negative jerk points are in play here.

Fine. But take a couple sneaky pics so I can remember more clearly. Also, who would win in a fight? That little elf guy from Zelda or that green spinning guy from that fighting game?

Link or Blanka?

Yes, sure. I was going with a green theme. It's an unexpected question for you to practice. Answer it fast.

"What's so funny?" Paisley asked, and I realized I had a huge grin on my face.

"Oh nothing, my friend Willow. She makes me laugh."

"Is she the pretty Black girl who was at your house today?" She set the notebook onto the bed beside her.

"Yes."

"Is she your best friend?"

"She is."

"For how long?"

"Like three years or so. Middle of eighth grade."

She pulled the ponytail holder out of her hair and ran her fingers through it. "I just finished eighth. I'm going to be a freshman."

"Nice," I said.

"Skyler says high school is better than middle school."

The summer before eighth grade was when Skyler had left

and it felt like my entire life left with him. I had no other good friends. I hadn't invested very much energy in extracurricular activities, and I had felt adrift. A scene from PE that year played through my mind, unwelcome.

It had been a rainy day, so the scheduled outdoor activities were canceled, leaving all the classes crammed in the gym.

A teacher had gotten up and asked, "Any suggestions on what we can play?"

I'd yelled out, "The floor is lava!"

A roar of laughter filled the gym. It was one of the first times after Skyler left that I realized I might think differently than a lot of the kids my age. I'd learned to filter myself after that, which helped.

My cheeks warmed with the remembered embarrassment and I shook my head at Paisley. "It's definitely better than junior high."

"I hope so. I failed a class last year." She nodded to a backpack she had brought that was now sitting on the bench alongside the table. "My mom negotiated a special extra-credit assignment to earn a passing grade."

"Oh yeah?"

"Wildlife on the road," she said, and Skyler let out a snorting laugh.

"What does that mean?" I asked.

"It means," she said, "I have to record the flora and fauna of each place we stop."

"Ouch," I said.

"Yeah," she returned. "My kind of vacation."

"The Failed Class vacation," Skyler said.

She pointed her finger at him. "You better stop or I'm going to make you help me."

"He can *draw* the flora or the fauna," I said.

Her eyes lit up. "Actually, that's not a bad idea."

"Or, you could, I don't know, take pictures of them," Skyler said.

"Where's the fun in that?" she huffed. "Maybe *I* can draw them. Or at least some of them. Maybe drawing runs in the family." She looked at the sketch pad in my hands. "Will you teach me?"

"Yes! I'll give you some tips. Here, I brought a few blank pads. You can have one." I passed her one from my bag and she took it reverently.

"Maybe I'll be the next Picasso," she said.

"Well, he was a painter, but yes."

"Oh, right. What do you call someone who draws? A drawer?" She laughed.

"An artist," Skyler said.

"Oh, now he's defending the artists of the world?" Paisley said with an eye-roll. "Mr. *Just Take Pictures*. Mr. *I Grew Out of It*."

This time, even though I sucked in my lips, I couldn't hold back the laugh.

"You two are gonna get along great, aren't you?" Skyler said.

"I think we are," I said.

"Can we use the bathroom in here while we're driving or do we have to wait until we stop?" Paisley asked.

"You can use it."

"Don't crash while I use the bathroom!" Paisley yelled toward the front.

"Crash while you use the bathroom?" Ezra called back. "I mean, okay, if you insist."

"How old are you?" Paisley asked.

"Nineteen," Ezra said.

"And you already tell old man jokes?" she said, then shut herself in the bathroom.

"Wow, harsh critic," Ezra said.

Hello? You're taking way too long to answer the question, Willow texted. *Your interviewer is not going to give you this much time.*

Grown-up Link or Young Link?

Either.

Both versions of Link would win.

If he would win either way, why did you ask me to specify?

I wanted to picture the battle in my head.

So which one did you picture? Grown-up Link or Young Link?

Young Link. It was fun to imagine a kid kicking Blanka's trash.

Please say that to the interviewer if she asks.

I would never say that to the interviewer. She would look at me with that look people sometimes gave me. The one that said *I'm glad I don't live in your head.*

"Please keep talking very loudly while I pee!" came Paisley's muffled voice from inside the bathroom.

Austin laughed, but I understood the request. The bathroom was literally steps away from everyone and the door seemed

34

paper-thin. This was the real argument I should've made when trying to keep the families in their separate spaces.

"There's no talking!" Paisley said again.

"Everyone pees!" Austin yelled.

"Let's just talk," I said. "How is everyone's summer going so far?"

Austin and Ezra had gone back to talking to each other in voices that barely reached beyond the front seats. Skyler's phone dinged and his eyes shot to the screen.

"I guess I'll turn on some music," I said, scrolling through my playlist.

"You don't need to humor her," Skyler said.

"I'm not. I'm going to have the same request when I'm in there." I held up my phone, stared at him pointedly, and pushed play.

He sighed. Seriously, what was his problem? Even if I did have a massive crush on him, like he thought, would that justify his complete indifference toward me? *Unexpected question number twenty-eight, Norah: Why is your childhood best friend acting like your childhood enemy?*

CHAPTER 4

"ONE HUNDRED AND THIRTY-FOUR DEGREES," THE man standing in front of our group at the Furnace Creek Visitor Center said. "The hottest air temperature ever recorded on earth was right here in Death Valley."

"Whoa," Paisley said. "That's hot."

Today it was only one hundred ten degrees, which might've sounded hot if we didn't reach that temperature every summer in Fresno for at least a week, sometimes many weeks. The temperature had been displayed out in front of the center on a digital sign, like a badge of honor. And, of course, our moms made us take a pic next to the unimpressive temperature. I stood on the opposite side of the sign from Skyler. I was determined not to take a picture next to him the whole trip. It sounded childish but it was my small act of rebellion that only I (well, and Willow) would know about. Just the thought of this immature goal made me happy.

"Who would like to know what a hundred and thirty-four degrees feels like?" The man swept his hand to the side, presenting a wood-paneled freestanding room of sorts.

"Is that a sauna?" Mom said under her breath next to me. "They can get way hotter than a hundred and thirty-four."

The man patted the door. "Anybody?"

"Skyler would," Paisley said, shoving her brother forward.

Skyler pulled her around to his side. "Paisley was just telling me this morning how she wished she knew what one hundred and thirty-four degrees felt like. This feels a lot like fate."

Olivia chuckled, obviously thinking her son was amusing. As his mom, she was required to think that.

"I'll try," I said. Again, I sensed I was only saying *yes* because Skyler said *no,* but I was okay with this. Plus, I was determined to experience all the things I could on this trip.

The man's face lit up. "Thank you. Come forward, young lady. This demonstration is much more effective in the winter when it's cold outside, but I think you'll appreciate how different even twenty degrees can feel."

"I'm sure I will."

"Can two people go in?" Paisley asked.

"Yes, would you like to go?" he said.

"No, but my brother really would like to try. He's just embarrassed."

"Paisley, turn off sister mode," Skyler said.

Both Austin and Paisley were now pushing Skyler forward as if this was sibling payback for some previous wrongdoing. Or maybe this was the two of them teasing him about me. Austin was the one Skyler had told about my supposed crush.

This all happened so fast that before I had a chance to change my mind, we were both ushered through the opening and into the small space, the door shutting behind us. My breath immediately left my lungs as the heat radiated off the wood all around me. There was no steam in the air like I had seen in movies. It was just dry. So very dry.

"What was that about?" I asked, sitting on the bench that ran the length of one side, just barely big enough for two people. I really wanted him to refute the internal dialogue I'd had moments before and confirm that it had nothing to do with me.

"What?" Skyler asked, and rather than sit beside me, he remained standing. Still, our knees were millimeters from touching.

"Did you trick Paisley and Austin into doing one of your chores or something? This feels like payback."

"Oh, yeah, they're always ganging up on me. It's their favorite."

"It does seem like a fun pastime."

"Thanks."

"No problem." I tucked my hands beneath my thighs on the bench. I was going to drop my suspicions about Paisley and Austin's motives. I refused to be embarrassed about something that wasn't true. "I think this was really built for one person."

"Me too." A line of sweat trickled from his temple. "How long did he say we were supposed to stay in here?"

"I don't think he did. How long do you think you could stay in here if you had to? An hour?"

"You want to stay in here for an hour?" he asked, eyes widening.

"Don't be stupid. I said if you had to."

"Always turning everything into a game."

38

"Well . . . yeah."

A smile played on his lips and he said, "Ten minutes."

Beads of salty moisture gathered on my upper lip. "Wimp."

"How long do you think you could stay in here . . . if you had to?"

I let the heat settle on my shoulders as I thought about that question. "With or without water?"

"Without."

"By myself?"

"Just like we are now."

"Five minutes," I said back, my smirk matching his.

"Nice."

"But no, I think I could go two hours, no water."

He nodded over his shoulder. "Should I inform the man?"

"This is all hypothetical, of course."

"Why were you so eager to see what hell feels like anyway?"

"You think hell is only a hundred and thirty-four degrees?"

He smiled his real smile at me for the first time since he arrived and nostalgia came pouring into my chest, making it even harder to breathe.

I drew air into my lungs. Hot, dry air. "Remember that plastic playhouse of your sister's in the backyard that we used to sit in?"

"Yes. Why did we ever choose that over air-conditioning?"

"Because we were kids. And we had important secrets we didn't want anyone else to hear."

"Like where to hide the candy stash?"

We'd shared many more real thoughts than that over the

years—fears, successes, worries. I let my hand travel over the smooth wood beneath me. "Isn't it funny that we're in a simulation of Death Valley instead of being, like, actually out in Death Valley?"

He lifted his shoulder to his temple, wiping his sweat on his T-shirt. "So ironic."

Why was he making this so hard? He'd had some fun banter with his sister over the last several hours. He obviously hadn't forgotten how. "Don't humor me, Skyler Hutton. It was a very clever observation."

"It was."

"So it's just me, then?"

"What?" Skyler swayed on his feet and my eyes shot to his knees.

"Are your knees locked?"

"What?" he asked, his voice slow and drawn out.

I jumped up and reached around him for the handle of the door, which I couldn't find with him blocking the way. I took him by the waist and tried to switch places with him, directing him toward the bench to sit. He stumbled, grabbing hold of my shoulders and using me for support, but had only moved an inch, so he still blocked the door.

"Don't faint in here," I mumbled, wrapping my arm around him to keep him upright. With my other hand, I pounded on the door.

A whoosh of cold air rushing around me was my only indication that the door had been opened.

"I'm fine, Norah," Skyler said, unwinding himself from my

hold. And just like that, he was out of the sauna and into the air-conditioned visitors center.

I stood there for several moments, shocked, not exiting, waiting for my cheeks, red from embarrassment, to return to their normal color. Talking and laughing, sounds we hadn't heard with the door shut, swirled around me along with pockets of heat and cold. It took me another few breaths to remind myself that everyone would just think my face was red from the heat, so I stepped down onto the floor.

Cold bit at my arms and neck. I pulled my T-shirt away from my sticky skin and fanned it a few times.

"How was it?" Paisley asked, the only person still standing by the sauna.

"Hot," I said.

"Why did Skyler practically sprint away?"

I rubbed at the back of my neck. "Who knows." I wandered to a rack of postcards along the wall.

Paisley followed me. "I guess there's a place called Artists Palette that your mom thought you might want to go to before we head to the campground."

"Yeah, sounds good." I picked out a couple postcards, thinking it would be fun to send some little letters of my own to Willow over the next few weeks.

Paisley ran her finger over a picture of the sun setting over some dry hills. "The guys want to set up camp and start dinner, so my mom said the girls could take the small RV to the artist place."

"Perfect."

"Okay, I'll go tell her."

"Young lady," the visitors center worker called to me. I turned. In his hands were two bottles of water. He handed one to me. "After one hundred and thirty-four degrees, it's important to hydrate."

"Oh, yeah, thanks."

"I couldn't find your friend," he said, holding out the other bottle.

I took it. "He's not my friend," I muttered as I walked away.

I found my mom in the next room staring at a diorama. The dirt floor looked like a close-up of extremely dry skin. She had a faraway look on her face.

"And I thought I needed some lotion," I said.

"What?" she asked.

I pointed to the display.

"Oh, yeah."

"You okay?"

"Yes, fine. There is so much to do here. I didn't realize I should've scheduled more than one night. We're going to have to narrow it down. I guess we could split up tomorrow if there are strong opinions."

"Are you really anticipating strong opinions about which group of rocks we want to look at?"

"You should've heard the heated debate about starting dinner that we had when you were relaxing in the sauna."

I laughed. *"Relaxing?"*

"It wasn't relaxing?"

Not in the least. "It was hot."

"As most saunas are."

"Well, I'm fine with whatever. It all looks good to me."

She smiled. "I'm so glad you've been as excited about this trip as I've been. Not that I'm surprised. Since you were little, you've always been so eager to experience new things. It's something I admire about you."

"Are you getting sentimental on me?"

"Mothers are allowed to think their kids are the best, most talented, smartest kids in the world."

"Wait, you said all this to Ezra too? I don't feel special anymore."

She hip-checked me. "Come on, I think you're going to love Artists Palette."

"I hear we're taking the rental."

"Yes."

"I need to grab my backpack out of ours. I can't go to a place called Artists Palette without my art supplies."

After paying for my postcards, I headed outside. The RVs were parked in the designated spots across the lot and I weaved through cars and around trucks until I came to our door. I stepped up and inside, surprised when I realized Ezra, Austin, and Skyler were already there.

"Oh," I said. "Hey, guys." I pointed the extra water bottle in my hand at Skyler. "This is for you."

He picked one up from the floor. "Thanks, I already have one."

"Right."

"I'll take it," Austin said, probably for my benefit.

I didn't need anyone's pity but I handed him the water anyway, pretending like everyone couldn't tell Skyler was acting weird toward me. "All informationed out?" I asked Ezra.

"We're hungry," Ezra said. "Mom said the menu is in here somewhere but I can't find it. Maybe you girls should just cook tonight, like normal, and skip the artist place."

"Excuse me?"

He let out a single laugh. "See, didn't I tell you she'd get mad if I said that?"

I'd spent a lot of time in the online gaming community, a network filled with guys, some less welcoming than others. So yes, that experience had made me extra sensitive to subtle and not-so-subtle sexism, but I wasn't going to apologize for making my brother a better person by calling him out on it over the years.

I opened a drawer in the kitchen and pulled out the spreadsheet of all the meals Mom had planned and the coordinating food items they required from the ice chests or fridge. My mom was always extra organized. I rolled it into a tube and hit Ezra on the shoulder with it a few times.

He held up his hands. "I'm sorry, I'm sorry. Girl power! I know you suck at cooking."

I wrapped my arms around his waist and tried to pick him up as if I was going to throw him, but failed, like I always did.

"Weakling," he said.

"One day," I promised, and let him go.

"You wish." He pulled the keys out of his pocket. "You coming with us?"

"I thought you were going with Paisley," Skyler said before I had the chance to answer.

Austin smacked Skyler on the back of the head.

I plucked my backpack with my drawing supplies off the bed. "Don't worry, Skyler, I am." I swung my backpack onto one shoulder and left without another word. I climbed off our RV and onto the other to wait for Mom, Olivia, and Paisley.

I drank half my water before pulling out my phone and texting Willow. *Did you say a throwing ax would be the best weapon against Skyler?*

Uh-oh. What happened?

Nothing new. What are your plans this week?

Reading, and binging that teen fantasy show on Netflix.

Nice. Wait, I thought you were going to the party Kyle is throwing?

Eh. Maybe. It doesn't sound as fun without you.

Whatever. Everyone likes you way better.

True, she replied.

I smiled, feeling a little lighter. *Well, if you go, find Leena and tell her congrats on her brown belt.*

You should text her that yourself.

She won't think it's weird that I remember she took that test, will she?

Why would she think that?

I don't know.

You think too much. People like you, stop overanalyzing it.

Did people like me? This trip was only adding to my ever-growing list of evidence that maybe people only liked the filtered version of me, and sometimes not even that. At least I had Willow. *But that's what I do. Overanalyze.*

Speaking of people who like you, I hear Dylan is going to that party.

Speaking of people who decided they didn't like you, is what she should've said. Dylan was my ex-boyfriend. We'd broken up the summer before because we mutually decided we were better as friends. I hadn't seen much of him since, despite our claim to friendship.

And? I texted back.

And, I don't know. I thought his name might make you feel some kind of way.

What kind of way?

Any kind of way.

I shook my head even though she couldn't see it. *It doesn't. I guess we made the right choice last year.*

You definitely did.

Mom and the others joined me on the RV. *Gotta run. I need to be an artist.*

* * *

I was so happy I'd brought my colored pencils. Micro Line black pens were my favorite medium but as we climbed out of the RV and to a hill not far from the parking lot, I knew this sketch would be in color. The setting sun lit the mountains in the background a fiery reddish orange and in the foreground it looked like someone had dumped chalk dust onto all the rocky terrain.

Turquoise and purple, white and yellow trailed up the sides of rocks, highlighting their shapes and creating a paint-by-number scene. I imagined a sandboarder in a game, gliding down the hills. She'd collect different points for all the different colors she managed to board on.

"Wow," Paisley said in awe. "I don't think this is considered flora or fauna."

Olivia hooked her arm in Paisley's. "Maybe we should make it flora, fauna, and terrain."

"No way," Paisley said. "No adding more work to my work."

"No harm has ever come from doing more than expected."

Paisley huffed out a breath. "I'd be the first to prove that statement wrong."

Olivia gave her a soft laugh.

Mom peeked over my shoulder as I drew. "Are you going to include any of your trip drawings in your portfolio to show the dean of admissions? What was her name again?"

"Dean Collins. Leslie. How should I address her, you think?"

"Dean Collins is good."

"I figured. But, no, I don't think I'll add any new drawings. Two weeks is not nearly enough time to obsess over them. I've done months of obsessing over the others. It wouldn't be fair to the new drawings."

"Or the old drawings for that matter," Mom joked back.

"True," I said. The drawings were just one part of the résumé I'd prepared for my interview, but since animation was what I wanted my focus to be, I felt like they were the most important part.

"Did you end up going with the girl gamer angle you were thinking about for your portfolio?"

"Yes, all the game ideas I included feature girls."

"I hope she's the girl power type."

"She's a woman in gaming," I said. "She is." At least that's what I had bet my entire sketchbook on.

CHAPTER 5

"LET ME SEE IT," EZRA SAID, REACHING FOR MY sketch pad. I moved it to my lap. We had just finished dinner and still sat at the picnic table between the two RVs at our campsite. A soft glowing light shone from the lantern in the center of the table and moths kept bumping into the glass.

I hadn't finished the sketch at Artists Palette, that would've taken too long, but I'd gotten enough down that I could fill in the details later. "No. If you wanted to see it, you should've come and seen it IRL."

"Did you really just say *IRL*?"

Paisley laughed. "She did and it was funny."

"Let me see it," he said again.

"Look up a pic on your phone."

"Mom, Norah is being a brat," Ezra said in a fake tattletale voice.

Because the boys had made dinner, Mom and Olivia were cleaning up—repacking the ice chests, washing the dishes in a soapy water bucket. Mom didn't even look over to humor him.

"I will show it to you," I said, "if you tell Paisley and Skyler and Austin here about that time you ran into the street sign in front of that girl you liked."

"You did not just say that out loud," he said.

"Huge bump on his forehead for like a week," I said, petting Ezra's unruly mop of brown hair. The freckles across his nose stood out in the glow of the light and made him look much younger than nineteen.

Paisley was giggling and Ezra was slapping at my hand with his goofy smile on. It had been a while since I'd seen Ezra so relaxed. It had been a while since I'd spent much time with him at all, actually. He'd just finished his freshman year of college and lately it felt like he was always gone—either at school or work or some other mysterious college function.

"Austin once stepped in a huge puddle of water getting out of his car because some cute guy was across the street," Paisley said. "I swear the whole bottom half of his jeans were wet the rest of the day."

"They were my favorite pair too," Austin said, unfazed.

"Do you really want to start sharing embarrassing stories?" Ezra asked. "Because I have a lot on Norah."

My mind filed through some stories he might have had on me, but it had been a while since I'd made a fool of myself in front of him. Most of my embarrassment stayed in my head, where it belonged.

"Let's hear them," Austin said.

"Um . . ." Ezra looked up, obviously searching his brain. "What about that time you fell in the pool?"

"Like at school or something?" Paisley asked.

"No, in our backyard," Ezra said. "When she was going to go swimming anyway."

I laughed.

"That was a good comeback, bro," Austin said.

"Shut up," he returned.

"What about that time . . ." Skyler spoke up from the other side of the table, where he hadn't said much all night.

My cheeks pricked as the blood drained from my face. Ezra may not have had any stories on me, but there were numerous ways in which Skyler could humiliate me. It hadn't occurred to me until that moment that he would.

"That time we were walking home from the orchard," he continued. "And that big dog chased us."

My mind instantly latched on to the memory. We were eleven. The sky was twilight gray and we were rushing home before we got in trouble for staying out too late. We'd spent the afternoon exploring the orange orchard and our clothes and hands were covered with dust. I'd wiped mine on the back of my shorts.

"Do you think you can beat me in Mario Kart when we get home?" I'd asked.

"Only if you don't pick the stupid rainbow level," he said.

"But it's funny." Skyler was scared of heights and that fear even extended to two-dimensional viewing. His poor characters never stood a chance on a level that took place in the sky with no protective barriers on the edges of the rainbow track. "Do you think you'll be able to drive by cliffs when you can drive for real?"

He'd bumped my shoulder with his. "Do you think you'll be able to shoot turtle shells out of your car?"

"I hope."

"Me too."

As we continued to walk, I'd heard the barking and growling first, coming from behind us. I turned to see a dog that looked as big as a wolf charging at us.

Skyler had taken my hand and pulled me into a sprint. "Keep running," he yelled. "Don't stop."

I didn't know if he had always been guiding us toward the fenced-in front yard ahead or if he'd seen it as we ran, but he didn't slow as we approached and he boosted me over before climbing over himself.

I turned in time to see the dog jump toward the chain-link fence. I thought for sure it was going to clear it, but instead it ran right into it with a loud crashing rattle, its teeth bared and saliva foaming at its snout. And that's when I'd felt the warm liquid trickle down the inside of my leg and puddle in the dirt at my foot.

Skyler didn't laugh even though I knew he saw what I'd done. We just waited until the dog got bored and wandered away. We waited until we were sure it was gone and then he helped me back over and we'd walked home, my shoe emitting a sloshy squeak with each step.

"Are you okay?" he'd asked in front of my house.

"I'm sorry I make fun of you on the rainbow level," I'd whispered, close to tears.

He was facing me and squeezed my arms. "The dog scared me, too, Norah."

"You can't tell anyone."

"I won't." His words had made me feel better that day.

Now, here at the picnic table in Death Valley, his words were digging into my heart. "And then she peed all over" was how he finished the shortened version of the story.

Everyone laughed.

"Is that why you're scared of dogs?" Ezra asked.

I forced a chuckle. "Yeah." I was glad I only said the one word because I could feel the lump in my throat restricting my air. When I finally looked at Skyler, I was sure I wasn't hiding the hurt in my eyes this time. His expression softened a degree and a hint of regret shone in his eyes. Not enough for me to forgive him.

"I forget you probably have tons of good stories on Norah," Ezra said. "We need to keep you around."

Austin looked at me. "I bet you have some good ones on my brother too. Spill."

"She has tons," Skyler said. Now he was ready to walk down memory lane?

"I can't think of any," I said, standing. "That was a whole different lifetime ago."

"Where are you going?" Ezra asked.

"I'm tired. Mom has a full day planned tomorrow."

"She said that?"

I nodded and, trying to bring back my teasing voice so nobody thought I was fleeing because of Skyler's story, whispered, "She said she wishes she hadn't booked us here for only one night."

"Frick," Ezra said. "She's right, we're doing too much tomorrow, people. Mom! We don't need to see everything!"

"Once in a lifetime!" Mom called back from where she and Olivia stood returning several bags to the side storage.

I laughed, or tried to, and left, sketch pad in hand. I had almost reached the door to our RV when I felt a brush at my elbow. I turned and Skyler stood there.

"What?" I asked, taking a step backward.

"I shouldn't have told that story."

"Whatever, Skyler. I get it, we're not friends anymore. You can stop trying to prove that point. Message received."

"No, that's not . . . Well, I mean, we're really not, are we?"

I crossed my arms. "No, we're not."

"I wasn't thinking with the story. I thought enough time had passed that you would think it was funny."

"It wasn't about the story." It really wasn't. It was what him telling that story meant—that he didn't care enough to keep my secrets anymore.

"What is it, then? Why did it bother you?"

"What makes you think it bothered me?"

"I could tell."

"I just . . . I was . . . This was supposed to . . ." I gripped my sketch pad tighter. "No, nothing. It doesn't matter. We were friends in the past and we aren't anymore. Let's just mind our own business and have a fun vacation. Sound good?"

His eyes went back and forth between mine as if he thought I was setting up some sort of trap for him. Finally, he said, "Okay."

"Cool."

I stepped inside the RV, tucked my art supplies in the cubby beneath the beds, then washed my face and brushed my teeth.

I changed into my pajamas and climbed up into the top bunk, pulling the privacy curtain closed, dampening the light. Then I turned toward the wall, hugged a pillow to my chest, and cried. As the tears streamed across my nose and onto my pillowcase, I became even more angry—I hated crying.

I cried for a friendship I once had that was now gone. I cried for the stupid expectations I'd had that this trip would somehow bring back that magical time and make it all real again. I cried that I was the only one who had really wanted that and that maybe this meant my memories were rose-colored, wrong. Maybe things hadn't been as magical and character-shaping as I thought they'd been. Maybe I really wasn't my truest self around Skyler. I cried until I fell asleep. And when I woke up in the morning, I was done crying. I was going to do exactly what I said I was going to do: mind my own business and have a fun vacation. Focus on my art and my coding and my school interview, which was now less than two weeks away. Focus on my future.

CHAPTER 6

I PULLED MY THINNEST T-SHIRT OUT OF MY SUIT-case, knowing today was going to be hot. When I did, a folded piece of paper fell to the floor. I picked it up, confused, before I remembered the notes Willow had left for me. I smiled before I even unfolded it.

There was a picture of a bright, happy sun at the top of the page, and an arrow pointing to it with the word *Norah*. Down below the sun was a stick figure lying on the ground with *X*s for eyes but a big smile on its face. Another arrow pointed at the stick figure and it read *Willow*. I flipped it over, looking for the interpretation, but there were no other words. I took a pic of the drawing and texted it to Willow with the message *WTH??*

I am not an artist was her quick reply.

Well, obviously, but what does it mean?

It means you are my sunshine.

Sunshine that kills you?

But look, I died happy.

I narrowed my eyes at the picture. This didn't seem like a

good thing. Whatever, it was just a picture. Willow would not be happy if I overanalyzed a picture.

I could hear Ezra snoring on the lower bunk, his curtain still closed, but I smelled bacon cooking on the outside grill, so I assumed that's where my mom was. I went to the bathroom and got dressed and ready for the day. But when I stepped outside our RV, only Olivia was at the cooking station.

"Good morning," Olivia said.

"Hi, good morning. Can I help with anything?"

"You want to make a fruit salad?" she asked. "There are blueberries and strawberries in the ice chest over there and here are some bananas." She handed me four bananas from the table beside where she was flipping bacon on the griddle.

I took them and retrieved the other fruit as well, then went back in the RV for the large plastic bowl we kept in the cupboard. I used the indoor sink to wash the berries and cut up the bananas using a knife from the drawer. I grabbed a big spoon, then took the bowl and headed back out. I stepped down from the RV as the sound of heavy footsteps preceded Skyler jogging into view. The neckline of his shirt was wet with sweat, as was his hairline.

"How was your run?" Olivia asked him.

Skyler ran now? With enough regularity to actually call it *a run* and do it while on vacation? I set the bowl on the picnic table we'd eaten at the night before.

"It was good." He kissed his mom's cheek. "What can I do?"

"Will you take over flipping the bacon so I can work on pancakes?"

"Yes."

He gave me a short nod in greeting and I looked away, realizing I had been studying the new athletic version of Skyler.

As Olivia began pouring the premixed batter onto a hot pan next to the griddle, she glanced at me over her shoulder. "How is life, Norah?"

"It's good. We're going to be seniors next year, so lots of things to think about—college and career choices and you know, our entire future."

Olivia laughed. "Is that all?"

I dug through one of the bags by the table, looking for the paper plates and silverware.

"So Seattle?" she asked. "Is that the plan? I hear you have a tour and an interview when we get there in a couple weeks."

"That's the dream." I had this hope that when I finally got to college and was surrounded by other artists and creatives, I'd finally feel like I'd found my place. I'd be with my people. I'd feel the way I used to feel when I was around Skyler, before he'd *grown out of it*, apparently.

"Are you nervous?" she asked.

"A little. I'm not great at thinking under pressure."

Skyler gave me a sideways glance like he was surprised by this admission. He didn't get to pretend to know me now after agreeing we weren't friends the night before.

"I'm sure you'll do just fine," she said.

"I feel prepared."

"Maybe you can get Skyler motivated. He's been talking about going back to California for college for years now but hasn't actually taken any steps to make that happen."

Why would Skyler come to California for college? Had he kept in touch with other people from when he lived here? Maybe he had. Or maybe he simply liked California. It obviously had nothing to do with me.

"Always trying to get rid of me, Mom," Skyler said. There was a smile in his voice but his back was still to me. Good thing because if he had looked, he would've seen my surprised face.

"You know I'd never let you leave my house if it were up to me," she said.

"Wow! You just lie so easily." He laughed. "Like it's nothing."

She swatted him with a dish towel. "I am an angel."

Skyler wrapped one arm around her shoulder. "Yes, you are."

"An angel that likes to nag you about college." Olivia added a pancake to the stack she'd started on a plate and carried it over to the table.

"That would be cool if there really were angels assigned to that," I said. "Maybe I'll request that job in heaven." *Seriously, Norah?*

"You want to nag people for an eternity?" Skyler asked, eyebrows raised.

"Only if it's you."

"Because you're obsessed with me?"

"That's one word for it."

Olivia chuckled like we were teasing each other. We weren't.

"The bacon is done," Skyler said. "I'm going to take a quick shower."

"Super quick," Olivia said. "Breakfast is almost ready."

"Five minutes. Promise."

She flicked him with the towel again as he jogged to their RV.

"You want to tell your family breakfast will be done soon?" Olivia asked me.

"Yes, of course. Is my mom not out here already?"

"I haven't seen her yet."

That was odd. She was usually an early riser. I went inside and pulled back the curtains on Ezra's lower bunk. "Rise and shine, Your Highness," I said when he groaned. "Breakfast."

I knocked on the door at the back, which my mom had slid shut. "Mom, breakfast."

"I'll be right out," she said. Her voice sounded off, thick with emotion. Or maybe just sleep.

"Are you okay?"

"I'm good."

I waited inside while Ezra got ready, my back against the door, staring at my mom's closed slider.

Ezra came out of the bathroom. "What?" he asked.

I nodded toward the back room. "Mom," I mouthed.

"What about her?" he said.

"Did you tell her you were moving out again or something?" I whispered.

"No. Why?"

"I don't know, yesterday she was super sentimental, talking about how awesome I was and today she's . . ." My eyes drifted to the closed door again.

"Tired? She's always tired after the first night sleeping in the RV."

"I know." I really did know that. "But she also seems . . . far away?"

"What does that mean?"

"Like in her head."

"I haven't noticed that. And if you have, it's probably because with Olivia around she's having all these long-lost memories of college life."

"Nostalgia," I said wistfully. He was right. I was the one far away and annoyed. I was projecting. Everyone else was perfectly fine.

"You going to move?" he asked, and I realized I was blocking the door.

"You going to ask nice?"

"Probably not," he said.

I fake punched him in the chest. He pretended it hurt.

"And for the record," he said as he stepped by me, "you're the one moving out. Isn't that one of the reasons for this trip?"

"Oh." He was right. Was that why my mom was getting sentimental? Because she was thinking about me going away to college?

"Austin!" Ezra called the second he saw him across the way. "Ghost town today."

"Yes," Austin said back. "Like that one dude's eighth-grade graduation party."

"Oh, yeah, I'd forgotten about that," he said. "The flamingo in the pool the only guest."

"It obviously wasn't if you two showed up," I said.

"Don't ruin it, Nor," Ezra said.

Olivia shook out a garbage sack and hung it on a hook on the side of the RV. "Miranda and I decided instead of driving these gas guzzlers all around Death Valley that we'll do one of those pink van tours. Then we'll come back here, eat, and hit the ghost town on the way out."

"Norah!" Paisley flew out of the RV. "I'm sitting by you. Did you finish your drawing last night?"

"No, not quite."

"I started a drawing, too, of a lizard, but it's really bad."

"Everyone starts off bad. It's the law."

"I didn't start off bad," Skyler said, stepping down from the RV, his hair wet from his shower.

"Yes, you did and if you need proof, I'll dig it up," I said. If I could just let go of all expectations about what Skyler and I were supposed to be and just accept what we were, I was positive it would help. That was really hard to do, though.

"Good morning," Mom said, joining the group. Her eyes were red with dark circles beneath them and my worry flared up again. "The pink van is going to be here in about forty-five minutes, so plan accordingly."

"I think what she means to say is eat fast," I said.

* * *

Breakfast set the pace for the whole day. After shoveling it down and cleaning up in record time, we'd loaded onto a van that was literally pink and headed out into the desert. Each stop took less than thirty minutes and we got a whirlwind overview— Zabriskie Point, Badwater Basin, Salt Creek, and others I didn't remember but were all uniquely different from each other. Bumpy dirt mounds and a sea of white dust and peaks of rippled sand. This was not the way my artist eyes would've liked to see the area but it was nice for efficiency.

We were pumped full of water in between each location and by the time we were done with our five-hour tour and riding in the cramped van back to camp, I was ready to find a tumble weed on the side of the road to relieve myself behind.

"What's wrong?" Paisley asked, pointing at my knees that were bouncing all around. She'd sat next to me the whole day.

"I have to pee," I said.

"Me too! I think I drank three bottles of water because the guide kept scaring me so much about heatstroke."

"Wait, did you ever find out yesterday at the visitors center why this place is called Death Valley?"

"The pioneers named it," the guide said, obviously a complete eavesdropper. "Someone in their party died traveling through here."

"Of heatstroke?" Paisley asked. "Like we almost died of today?"

"You were nowhere near dying."

"Oh, interesting . . ." Paisley rolled her eyes at me and shook the empty water bottle she held. "I'm going to add this info to my report. Because I like to overachieve."

We pulled up to our campsite and I muscled my way out of the car and took off running.

"Norah!" Mom yelled. "The keys."

I turned and held out my hands. She tossed them to me and I caught them and ran the rest of the way to the RV.

When I came out, feeling much better, the three guys were

cranking down the awnings, disconnecting the water and power and gathering the last of the trash.

"Did you almost have another peeing-your-pants incident, Nor?" Ezra said.

Skyler shot Ezra a dark look that surprised me.

Ezra obviously saw it, too, because he said, "What? That's how brothers work. I will never let her live this down."

"Next time I'll pee in your *bed*," I said.

"Norah," Mom scolded. "Not even a little funny." After her slow start, Mom had seemed fine the rest of the day.

"I thought it was at least a little funny," I said.

"Yeah, Mom," Ezra agreed. "It was Norah funny."

"You two." Mom sighed. "Finish packing up if you want to see this ghost town."

CHAPTER 7

ALL THE TALK OF GHOSTS ON THE WAY OVER HAD me jumpy as we walked through the worn-down buildings in a town that had sprung to life in the gold rush and had probably just as quickly been abandoned. Many were dilapidated at this point but some had obviously been built better than others because they'd at least somewhat withstood the elements.

I had gotten separated from our group and was circling a house made of glass bottles and adobe, amazed it was still standing. "What do you like about this building, Norah?" I asked myself, imitating an interviewer. I sighed. That wasn't an unexpected question or a hard one.

Harder question . . .

"How could you incorporate this building into a video game?" My brain immediately imagined the adobe between the bottles dissolving and the bottles coming loose, causing the characters in the game to roll around the screen, off balance. How would that level be cleared? Fill the bottles with the ghosts haunting this town? No, that was too out there. I needed a more commercial idea. Rebuild the house? Crush all the bottles?

I ran my hand along the wall, which looked like hundreds of multicolored circles, formed from the bottom of the bottles. "Don't worry, I'm not going to destroy you." *Stop talking to yourself, Norah.* Actually, I was talking to a building. That seemed worse.

I started to leave when I heard a scuffing noise around the nearest corner. "Ezra?"

Nobody responded, just more scraping, like footsteps dragging across dry dirt.

"Hello?" I slowly rounded the corner. My eyes shot to the ground, thinking it was a mouse or rabbit or something, but I saw nothing. My heart sped up and I crept toward the next corner.

"No," Ezra's voice rang out. I peered around the building, ready to jump out and scare him but he was on the phone, so I started to back away when I heard him say, "Norah doesn't know."

I paused in my retreat.

"No, I swear," he said. "I told you I wouldn't so I won't."

Footsteps sounded behind me and I whirled around. Skyler was there, his mouth open as if about to speak. I immediately grabbed his arm, pulled him close, and covered his mouth. Then I strained to hear the rest of Ezra's one-sided conversation.

"When, though?" he was saying. "I know, it's just hard. I better go before . . ." He walked in the opposite direction, taking the end of the sentence with him.

That's when I became aware of a very still Skyler, one of

66

his biceps in my grip, his mouth still beneath my other hand. My back was against the wall and his chest was millimeters from mine. I met his confused eyes but before I could pull my hand away, he licked it.

"Ew!" I gasped and wiped my hand on the front of his shirt.

"There was probably a better way to shut me up," he said.

"But not a faster way."

He tilted his head as if he disagreed but I just shoved him away from me and moved to leave when he asked, "What was that about, anyway?" He nodded toward where Ezra had once stood.

"He's . . ." I wasn't sure what Ezra was. My brother and I had always been able to talk to each other. I never expected to hear that he was purposefully keeping something from me. That was new. Was this trip like a litmus test for my relationships? Soon I was going to see that Willow was my only true friend. Maybe I only needed one.

"Something about my mom?" I said to Skyler. That was my best and only guess. And I sensed it was right too. Was she sad? Mad? Was something happening with my parents? Or maybe it was about something else entirely. But what?

"What about your mom?" Skyler asked.

Once upon a time, I would've told him exactly what I thought was going on. All my worries and insecurities. But we were well past that. "Did you need something?"

He must've realized I wasn't going to answer his question because he said, "Have you seen Paisley? Our moms want pictures with the ghost by the bike."

"I haven't seen her." We walked across the hard-packed

barren landscape. It looked exactly like I imagined a ghost town would look—dry brush not more than ankle high, yellow dirt, trees that seemed half dead but had obviously been there for decades.

Our moms were standing by a white plaster sculpture that had been formed into what looked like a robe draped over an invisible shape. It stood, ready to mount an actual bike. It was odd and definitely picture worthy.

Paisley was already there.

Austin and Ezra reached it at the same time I did. I gave Ezra a dirty look.

"What?" he said, tugging on the end of my hair.

He wouldn't tell me now. Not with everyone around. Not after he promised whoever was on the phone—Dad?—that he wouldn't. But maybe if I confronted him in private I could get answers. "Nothing," I said.

"There are twelve of these ghosts just outside of town meant to represent the Last Supper scene. So save some of your good poses for that," Austin said to the group.

"I only have three pose-with-a-ghost looks," I said.

He smiled.

I let the guys fill in around the bike first, then took my place on the opposite side of the group from Skyler, next to Paisley. After our moms took pictures, I made them take a few together and then we took some as separate families. All in all, we took entirely too many pictures with a ghost by a bike. I hadn't saved any of my faux scared faces for a whole other set of ghosts.

Mom gave a loud whistle and pointed toward the RVs. "Let's

go, let's go. It's getting late and we have a five-hour drive ahead of us." She patted Ezra's arm and held out her hand, palm up. "Keys."

"What?" Ezra exclaimed.

"I should drive this leg."

"Why? I'm young, Mom. I'm way more likely to stay awake behind the wheel than you are."

I narrowed my eyes at him. Mom had never had problems staying awake driving.

"Funny," Mom said, her hand still out. Did *she* know that *he* knew whatever it was that *I* didn't know?

"It wasn't a joke," he said with his cheeky smile.

"Please, Miranda," Paisley chimed in. "Norah was going to give me some drawing tips."

Mom looked at Olivia, who shrugged. "Fine," she said. "But if you get sleepy, call me and we'll switch places."

"You too," he said. "If you get tired, we can always pull over for the night."

She hugged me and Ezra; then she and Olivia headed to the other vehicle.

"I can go with you guys," Skyler said, catching up to his mom. "In case you need a spare driver."

"Nice try," Olivia said. "You can't drive the rental." Then she said something under her breath to him. Probably something like *Yes, you have to keep dealing with Norah even though you don't want to.*

Whatever she said, he gave her a half smile, then sauntered over to our RV. Paisley rushed up the steps in front of him.

I stepped forward at the same time as Skyler and then we both stopped, gesturing for the other person to go. Then we both stepped forward again.

"Go ahead," I said.

He gave a short nod and climbed up, then shut the door behind him. I grunted, thinking he was just being thoughtless, but when I reached up to open the door, it was locked. My breath caught in my chest. We used to do this to each other all the time. Was this his call for a truce? Or maybe it was at his mom's suggestion.

I pounded on the door. "Skyler, don't be a punk!"

The latch clicked and the door swung open. Paisley stood there, a confused expression on her face.

I walked in and smacked Skyler on the shoulder as I passed him by, my call for a truce. He chuckled.

The RV rumbled to life and Paisley took her place, cross-legged on the bed with the old notebook. I joined her and decided to sketch the sand dunes I'd seen earlier before they slipped from my memory. But what I ended up sketching was multicolored glass bottles scattered all over the page, their support system dissolved.

"What are all these pics on the bottom corner of the pages?" Paisley asked just as I settled into my zone.

"Which ones?" I asked.

She turned the notebook toward me and pointed.

"Oh," I said. "Animation."

"Bring it here," Skyler said, and she did.

He closed the book. "Watch right here," he told Paisley. She nodded; then he used his thumb to fan through the pages.

"Oh wow, cool," she said. "Did you draw these?"

"Norah did."

She swiped the book from Skyler and rejoined me on the bed. "Is this what you're going to show the school person?"

I smiled. "Not that one, but yes, I brought another book. It's more gaming inspired."

"My dad thinks video games are childish."

I was sad to hear he hadn't changed. "Yes, your dad was always good at discouraging a lot of things."

Skyler avoided my eyes with that statement.

Paisley sat up straight. "What should I tell him so he'll let me play?"

"What?"

"How do you convince haters that video games aren't bad?"

An unexpected question. One I hadn't prepared for. I had prepped myself to talk to video game lovers. I hadn't thought to prepare for that kind of question. Would I be asked that? "I . . . They're . . . relaxing. They can relax people and help with stress." I spit out the same argument three times in a row.

She rolled her eyes. "My dad doesn't care about helping us relax."

"Probably true. But they're way more than that. They're creative outlets. In *Minecraft*, you can build and control your own world. You're right," I said, seeing her face. "Creativity is not high on his list either. He would love a game like *Fortnite*. A survival game that requires strategy and fast thinking. What parent doesn't love that? Or maybe he'd be into *Zelda*. It's high fantasy but there is also puzzle solving and saving a princess. He probably even played it when he was young."

"My dad wasn't born an adult?" Paisley said with a smirk.

"We've never proven otherwise." I pulled out my flash cards and added her question. I needed to think of a less rambling answer. One that didn't sound like me geeking out over video games with a friend. I started flipping through the cards for at least the tenth time that day to review.

"Is that why you want to animate video games?" Skyler asked, his voice thoughtful, curious. "Creativity, strategy, and puzzle solving?"

"Animating and playing are two different things," I said. It was a snarky response. One that didn't answer his question, but I didn't want to answer his question. Not when he hadn't answered any of mine. Maybe I wasn't ready for a truce after all.

"Right," he said, short, curt, cold. He pulled out his phone, probably ready to text his grievances to whoever he had waiting at home, just like I had been doing with Willow.

"Is there a TV in here?" Paisley asked. "Mom wouldn't let me bring my iPad on this trip."

"There is. Do you want to watch it? We don't have streaming or anything, but we do have some DVDs over there in that drawer."

She walked over to the drawer and pulled it open. She flipped through the movies and eventually picked one out, then spun in a full circle. "What now?" she asked.

I stood and slid back the cabinets on the wall across from the couch, revealing the television. "The player is here. The remote is here."

"Thanks, Norah."

"Of course."

I wandered up front and leaned against the half wall between the driver's seat and the bench behind it. "I just started a movie if you want to watch," I said to Austin.

"Nah, I'm good."

"Right." The road was dark in front of us, really dark. The headlights barely cutting through the blackness. It made it feel like we were in the middle of nowhere. Which we pretty much were. "How far until Vegas?" I asked.

"A couple hours," Ezra said.

"Will we be able to see the lights from the freeway?" We weren't stopping in Vegas, but I wanted to at least get a glimpse.

"Have you never been to Vegas?" Austin asked.

"Have you?" I returned.

"When we used to live in Fresno, we did a weekend trip."

I didn't remember them going to Vegas, but I was sure Skyler must've said something at the time.

"Our families actually did things independent of each other?" Ezra asked in fake shock.

I took a pair of sunglasses that were clipped to the visor and put them on. I pushed on the ends behind my ears several times, making them go up and down. Neither of them laughed.

"Whose are these?" I asked.

"Mine," Austin said.

"You wear big sunglasses."

"Let me try them on." Ezra reached out and waved his arm in my direction.

I batted his hand away and put the sunglasses back. "No, you'll crash us."

"Why do you keep insisting I'm going to crash?"

"I'm not letting you wear sunglasses at night."

"Did you mean to quote a song?"

"That's not a song."

"Austin, I wear my sunglasses at night. Is that a song lyric?"

"Yes," he said.

"You two are like an old married couple," I said, even more annoyed. I'd said they'd hung out as much as me and Skyler had when the Huttons lived in Fresno, but they really hadn't. Skyler and I had been the superior friendship. Austin and Ezra were default friends. Friends because our families got together a lot and they were the same age. But now they only served as proof of how far apart Skyler and I had drifted. And with Austin here in our RV, when was I ever going to be able to talk to Ezra alone and find out what he was keeping from me?

CHAPTER 8

ZION NATIONAL PARK IN SOUTHERN UTAH FELT just as hot as Death Valley had. But it was gorgeous. Where Death Valley had seemed mostly flat and dry, Zion's rocks rose like skyscrapers striped red and orange.

"Water time!" Ezra shouted, climbing off the bus that had taken us to the entry point along the river. A girl by a trailer was handing out blue and yellow tubes, and we got in line behind another group of tourists to collect ours.

"Is my life jacket tight enough?" Paisley tugged on the straps.

"You're good," Skyler said. "Don't be scared."

She rolled her eyes at him. "I'm not scared, stupid. The guide said this was like a lazy river. Why would I be scared of that?"

"Stupid? You calling me stupid?" He took her in a headlock and she screamed and smacked his back. He let her go with a laugh.

"You put sunblock on, right?" Mom asked.

"Yes," I said. "Lots."

"You too, Ezra?"

"Yes, Mommy," Ezra said, like he always did when he felt he was being treated like a child.

"Hey," she said. "When I don't ask, you get fried. What about you, Austin, Skyler, Paisley?"

I laughed. "She's your mom, too, now," I said.

Olivia hadn't joined us for the tubing. She wanted to do some shopping and said she would meet up with us for lunch after.

"Yes, we did," Austin said. "Thank you for the concern, Mrs. Simons."

"See, kids, that's how you respond to that question."

"Kiss-up," Ezra said, punching Austin in the arm.

We got to the front of the line, and Ezra said, "I got your tubes, Mom and Norah." He looked ridiculous trying to carry three big tubes that he could hardly walk with.

"I can carry my own tube," I said. "So can Mom." As I handed it to her, I had the sudden thought that maybe she couldn't. Did the secret everyone was keeping from me have to do with her health? She wouldn't be floating down a river if she couldn't carry her own tube. Right?

She took it without argument, easing my temporary bout of anxiety.

"I was just trying to be nice," Ezra said. "Am I not allowed to be nice?"

I patted his arm. "My abilities do not detract from yours, Ezra."

The guide raised his hand in the air for everyone's attention. "Remember about an hour and half downriver you'll come to the takeout site. Keep an eye out for our signs. But most importantly, have fun!"

The water was colder than I thought it would be as we stepped in to launch ourselves. But after a few minutes, I became accustomed to it. Right away, I realized that no matter how lazy the guide said the river was, it had a mind of its own. We should've linked hands or something because we were quickly becoming separated.

"Ezra, wait up," I said, paddling on the sides of my tube. This would be a perfect opportunity to talk to him. I reached out for him as I got close. "Ezra!"

He looked back and put his hand up to his ear, pretending not to hear me. "What?"

He was just out of my grasp, so I stretched out my leg. "Grab my foot!"

"My ability to float the river does not detract from your ability to float the river. I believe in you!" He gave me his annoying smile and paddled forward.

"You are such a punk!" I kicked, splashing him.

He laughed and paddled toward a current off to the left that swept him farther ahead.

As our tubes spread across the river, they reminded me of the game Frogger. A classic. I tried to think of variations of that game that hadn't been done. But after a while, I gave up and relaxed back into my tube, trying to let go of my irritation with Ezra.

The journey was scenic as we were carried through canyons and by trees that seemed like they wanted to be in the river, too, with the way their roots crawled down the banks, dipping their branchy toes into the water.

The sun beat down on my shoulders and I laid my head

back, letting my hair drape over the edge and into the water. I must've closed my eyes because after a while they snapped open as a jolt jerked me upright. I had collided into a stranger's tube.

"Sorry," I said.

"No problem," the guy said, flashing me a smile. He looked around my age with dark hair and friendly eyes.

I waited for the water to send us apart again, but instead it was like our tubes had been glued together in the collision. I tried to paddle away but made no progress.

"This isn't awkward at all," I said.

He laughed. "You here alone?"

I nodded behind us. "No. I got separated from my group."

"Welcome to the Oliveras family," a woman on the other end said.

I smiled her way. "Wow, you take new members so easily."

"The river forces us all to make friends."

"We can't disappoint the river," I said, even as I was begging the river to send me on my way. Up ahead were some small rapids, where we would probably pick up speed.

"Here," I said. "Maybe if I shove off your tube."

"Maybe if we both kick off each other's?" he suggested.

"Yeah, let's try that." We each placed our feet on the side of the other's tube. "One, two, three." I gave a hard push, but his shove must've been twice as hard because my tube toppled over backward, flipping me.

The cold water shocked me as I went under with a scream and then popped back up again right as we hit the rapids. My tube was launched ahead, and I knew it was pointless to chase after it because in seconds it had traveled halfway to the bend ahead.

"Here." The guy reached out and I grabbed hold of his hand. He dragged me closer and I clung to the side of his tube. "Are you okay?"

"Yes, I'm fine. I needed to pee anyway."

"Um . . ."

"I'm totally kidding." *This is why you don't have a boyfriend, Norah.* As my tube rounded the corner ahead, I sighed.

"What's your name?" he asked, obviously realizing he was stuck with me.

"I'm Norah."

"I'm Ty."

I did not want to spend the next hour and fifteen minutes clinging to the side of some stranger's tube, even if I did know his name. And even if now that I was much closer to him, I saw just how cute he was—golden brown skin, thick lashes, toned abs. Willow would love this; she knew how to talk to strangers. "Where are you guys from?"

"Arizona," he said. "You?"

"California," I answered.

"Oh, nice. Beaches."

"Not really. We're right in the middle of the state. So more like farmland."

"Oh."

I glanced over my shoulder and with a rush of relief, I saw Skyler gaining on us. "There's someone from my group," I said. "Skyler!"

Skyler didn't see me at first, so I lifted my hand and waved.

He looked at me and it took him a moment to register the situation. When he did, he seemed even more confused.

"Just get over here!" I called out.

He flipped onto his stomach on the tube and used his hands to paddle on either side like a surfboard. I should've thought of that.

"Making friends?" he said when he reached us.

"The river chooses our friends, Skyler," I said, transferring myself from Ty's tube to Skyler's. My knees scraped along rocks as I did. This was not a very deep river. It was perfect for tubing, not for being dragged by a tube.

"Bye, Norah," Ty said as we finally went our separate ways. I waved and smiled, then grumbled, "Thanks a lot, water."

"What's that?" Skyler asked with a smirk.

"Now you have another embarrassing story to share over dinner," I said.

His smile slipped off his face. It had been a joke, but I realized my voice sounded more irritated than I meant for it to.

He twisted back to a sitting position and, like me, analyzed the one-person tube. "Why don't you get in the tube and I'll hang off the side?"

"I think we can both fit," I said as my knees scraped over some rocks again. I sucked air between my teeth.

"I won't get cold," he said.

"No, it's not that." Although it *was* getting cold. "It's just too shallow."

"Oh, yeah. Okay, well, get up here."

"Easier said than done."

"Here." He grabbed me by the armpits and as he pulled, I tugged until eventually I was over his lap in the tube.

"Okay, okay, just steady it while I . . ." I twisted and sat the opposite way of him, knowing that was probably the only way we'd really fit. And we did, just barely. We faced one another, my legs hanging off the tube to his left and his legs hanging off the tube to my left. We both had our hands in our laps but after a few minutes of shifting and balancing and adjusting, we ended up draping our left arms over each other's knees.

"You good?" he asked.

"I'm good. You?"

"Yeah."

We sat in silence for several minutes. It was weird being this close to Skyler after all these years. He wore a tank top, maybe for warmth, because it didn't seem like he had anything to hide. His arms were massive, but then again, I was used to his gangly thirteen-year-old arms. Also new were his scruffy sideburns and leg hair.

"What happened?" he finally asked. "Where is your tube?"

I looked away, realizing I was probably staring. "I got flipped and it got ahead of me. We can keep an eye out for it."

"Okay."

We hit another pocket of rapids and water splashed up and onto my back. I let out a small squeal.

Skyler seemed to find humor in this.

"It's cold," I said, reaching over the side and sending a splash his way.

He grabbed hold of my wrist with a laugh. "Don't, brat."

I squeezed his knee with my free hand, knowing his ticklish spot, and he laughed and released me. His eyes shot to my side, my ticklish spot, and I squealed again before he'd even made a move. He averted his gaze and kept his hands to himself.

The water settled again and we slowed, silence taking over once more.

"You should've told a story on me at dinner," he said after a few minutes. "You have a million."

I hadn't wanted to. He'd trusted me not to embarrass him for years. I didn't want to destroy that trust now, even though he didn't feel the same. "Yeah, I should've."

We floated by some large rocks sticking up from the middle of the river. Once safely around them, Skyler asked, "What's Ezra doing these days?"

We were trapped in a tube together, no way out for at least another hour, and that's the question he wanted to ask me? "You want to make small talk?"

"It was just a question."

"So your answer to my question is, yes, you want to make small talk." I folded my arms across my chest.

"I don't know, Norah, I just want to get through this, I guess."

"I didn't realize this vacation was a torture session for you."

"It's not."

"So you meant talking to me? You just want to get through talking to me."

"Now you're putting words in my mouth."

"Well, you sure aren't putting any there."

"And you are?" he said, obviously irritated. "You're avoiding every question I ask."

"I don't trust you anymore," I spit out, not even sure if that was true.

"Same."

My mouth fell open in shock. "*You* don't trust *me*? I'm not the one sharing your secrets with everyone."

"Everyone? You mean our siblings? Is that everyone now?"

"It felt like it."

He let out a scoffing huff. I folded my arms tighter against my chest and looked up at the red rock canyons that surrounded us now. Vines dripped down the walls and I let my tight shoulders loosen. I didn't want to feel this way. I was tired of it. Skyler's jaw was as hard as the rocks that surrounded us.

"He's going to school," I said. "He wants to be an electrician or something."

"What?" Skyler asked.

"Ezra. That's what he's doing these days."

His lips twitched with a smile. "Nice."

"What about Austin?"

"He's going to community college."

"For what?"

"He doesn't know yet. That's why he's just getting his generals out of the way."

"Smart." We passed a family picnicking on the shore, the kids ankle-deep in water, sifting through the rocks just below the surface. My eyes flitted back to Skyler's. "And you? Why college in California? You still have friends there or what?" I had no idea if he kept in touch with anyone from Fresno.

He tilted his head and narrowed his eyes a bit, focused on the cloudless blue sky above.

"What?" I asked.

"Like who?"

I laughed. "You had other friends."

He let his palm skim over the clear water next to him. "I probably had more enemies than friends."

In school, Skyler always had a sketch pad and weird facts at the ready. It drew the attention of people who weren't as sure of themselves as he was. But *enemy* was an aggressive description. "Like who?"

He stared at me for a long moment, contemplating whether to say something. But in the end all he said was "Oh, you know, that online bully in *Minecraft*."

"I only bullied you occasionally," I joked. I wasn't going to force him to tell me something real. We'd literally just confessed we didn't trust each other.

"And Willow?" he said. "I don't remember her."

"She moved to town in seventh grade but I didn't meet her until eighth. You probably never met her before you left."

"I didn't." He drummed the side of the tube with his fingers. "And how is it?"

"How is what?"

"Being in with the popular crowd?"

I wanted to say that I wasn't, but he was right. Willow had somehow dragged me kicking and screaming into the more well-known group at school over the last couple years. Probably the main reason I never felt like I could be myself—I didn't belong there. "How do you know my friends?"

"I've seen some of your posts."

Right. We may not have communicated much lately, but we did still follow each other on social media. I just thought he hadn't been paying attention. "It can be fun," I said. And that was true.

He nodded slowly.

I didn't understand that reaction. I really didn't know him at all anymore and that killed me. He'd given up art and he stared at his phone and was judging me for who I hung out with even though he lived thousands of miles away. And he ran. On purpose. "What do you . . . Why did . . ."

"What?" he asked.

"You're different." I didn't mean to sound sad when I said it, but I knew I did.

"So are you."

My mouth opened, then closed. I couldn't argue with that. I was. At least on the outside.

His eyes lit up as he looked at something over my shoulder, downstream. "It's your tube."

My tube was turning circles in some sort of dead zone. He hopped out of our tube, nearly flipping me for the second time that day. And by the time I'd centered myself and paddled to face the front, the river had separated us again.

CHAPTER 9

"MAYBE EZRA IS RIGHT. MAYBE I *AM* A MAN HATER because there is not one guy on this trip that I like right now," I whined to Willow as I lay in my bunk after lunch.

Willow laughed. "Ezra called you a man hater?"

"Not in so many words."

"You are not."

"Also, you were right. This trip is about more than my college interview."

"Really? Why do you say that?" she asked.

"Ezra is keeping a secret from me," I said.

"What secret?" she asked.

"I haven't figured it out yet but I'm going to. Something about my mom or my parents. I'm so mad that he knows and I don't. Do they think I can't handle it? That's so annoying that they think Ezra can handle something that I can't. He can't handle anything!"

She laughed again. "Okay, maybe you are a man hater."

I let my head flop off the side of the bed, taking in the now upside-down view of the empty RV. Everyone else had gone to the clubhouse to play pool or arcade games or whatever they had there. I'd locked myself inside to vent to Willow.

"Call your dad," she said. "He'll restore your faith in men."

"He's obviously keeping the secret too!"

"Do you want to talk to my dad?"

I hummed. "Your dad is pretty great."

"And Skyler? He hasn't redeemed himself at *all* from day one?"

"No, he's even worse than before. He said he doesn't trust me when I am completely trustworthy."

"So trustworthy." She said it with such a serious tone that I couldn't help but laugh. I knew talking to Willow was the right call. I was already starting to feel better.

"Will you do some snooping for me?" I asked.

"Snooping?"

"Go by my house and take pictures of the medicine cabinets in my parents' bathroom while my dad is at work. And look through the stack of mail in the brown basket in the kitchen while you're there too."

"Norah!"

"What? I'm serious."

"I know you're serious and that makes it worse. I just called you trustworthy!"

"It's not my fault everyone has no faith in me."

She laughed.

"So you won't snoop for me?"

"No, I will. I just had to act appalled first."

"You're the best."

"I know. And what are you going to do about Skyler? Should I fly to Ohio and break into his house as well? Find the secrets to breaking down the wall he's put up?"

"Will you?" I sighed. "No, nothing. I'm going to do nothing." He was my past. Sure, a huge part of my past. But sometimes that's where the past belonged. "He's leaving in two and half weeks. It's not like we were going to suddenly be long-distance best friends."

"See, not a man hater. You are an independent woman. Like you've told me before, those things aren't synonyms."

"If I'm so independent, then why was I complaining about the fact that I don't have a boyfriend today?"

"Are you telling me that love and independence can't co-exist?"

"Yes," I said.

"You really feel that way?"

"No, they can coexist. But not for us. We are loveless independent women. Together in our aloneness forever!"

"Forever?"

I laughed. "For now."

I could almost hear her eye-roll. "I'll text you if I find anything during my break-in."

"Love you," I said.

"You better."

We hung up and I rolled onto my stomach and looked out the window. The day was bright and my mom had declared free time for the remainder of it. I slid my arms under my pillow to push myself to sitting when my hands hit something hard. I pulled out what I thought was going to be my sketchbook but what ended up being mine and Skyler's notebook. I turned back the cover.

In the handwriting of two ten-year-olds, the names Norah Simons and Skyler Hutton were written across the top of the first page. I remembered when we decided to start this book. Our parents had denied our petitions for cell phones, a request made after Ezra and Austin had gotten their first phones. Sure they were two years older, but we needed them just as much, we'd told our parents. They hadn't agreed. So we started passing this notebook back and forth every time we saw each other.

I ran my hand over our names and flipped the page. Mine was the first entry:

I hate homework. Don't we do enough work at school? If teachers can't teach us everything they need to at school, maybe they should try harder. Also, do you have the voice recorder? I need it.

The voice recorder. My mind drifted back to the day Skyler had first shown it to me. We were in the orange orchard behind our neighborhood.

"These sticks are all too small. They're not going to make a good fort," I'd said.

"This one's okay." He picked up the biggest in the pile we'd made. "We need to find ten more just like this."

I drew shapes in the sand by my feet. "If you had to be a stick or a rock, which would you want to be?"

"Those are my choices? A stick or a rock?"

"Yes."

Like always, he didn't just dismiss my odd question, like other people did, or laugh at it; he really thought about it. "A rock."

"Why?"

He broke the stick he'd been holding over his knee and held up the two parts as his answer.

I raised my eyebrows at him. "Oh really? You think you're Superman now or something?"

"Shut up. My point was to show how weak it is, not how strong I am." Then he smirked. "But I am strong."

"Keep telling yourself that."

He took one of the stick halves and pretended it was too hard to break again. "What about you? Rock or stick?"

I swiped the stick from him and pointed at the tree with it. "This used to be up there, flying in the sky."

Skyler's eyes lit up and he rushed to his backpack. "I can't believe I forgot."

"What?"

He pulled a long, thin electronic thing out of his backpack.

"What is it?"

"A recording device." When I didn't process what that meant, he held it up to his mouth and pushed a button. Then he cawed like a bird. He pushed another button and the same caw echoed through the orchard. "A recording device. So we can collect sounds you can put in your video games."

"Is that how it works?"

He shrugged one shoulder. "I think."

Later I'd found out that sort of *was* how it worked, but on much higher-quality equipment. Our thousands of staticky sound bites we would collect over the years would be useless. But at the time I'd thought it was the best thing in the world. He'd tossed me the recorder.

I studied the buttons along the side, then pushed the middle one with the red circle. "I am a robot who steals brains in my quest to become a real person," I said into the microphone in my best robot voice.

Skyler laughed. "And I was just a boring bird."

A rattling of the door handle brought me out of my memory. Then there was a knock. "Norah!" It was Ezra. "Did you seriously lock the door?"

I opened it for him. "Yes, I lock the door when we're at an RV park and I take a shower," I said, smoothing my hair. "Do you know how many creeps stay at these places?"

"I've never counted them."

I pointed to him. "One . . ."

"Funny." From behind his back he pulled out a cookie. "I'm sorry for ditching you on the river earlier."

I took the cookie. "Apology not accepted."

He let out a grunt. "Then give me back the cookie."

I turned around and took a big bite. "Never."

"You're really still mad at me?"

"Yes." I stood on my tiptoes to see if he was alone. When I saw he was, I pulled him inside and shut the door. "Because you have a secret."

"What?" A look of surprise took over his face for a split second before it was gone and he said in a perfectly convincing voice, "No, I don't."

"Seriously? You're not going to tell me?"

"I don't know what you're talking about."

"I know it's about the parents."

He shook his head. "The parents?"

I shoved the half-eaten cookie back into his hands. "I don't want your secret-keeping bribes."

"Norah, just eat the cookie. And if you think something is going on with Mom and Dad, then talk to them."

"Ezra, do you swear to me that you're not keeping a secret about Mom or Dad?"

He held up his hand like he was taking an oath. "I swear."

"So it's a secret about something else, then. What?"

"What are you talking about?"

"I heard you on the phone. You said you wouldn't tell me something."

He looked up as though thinking, then shrugged. "You must've misheard me."

I tried to remember exactly what he'd said, but I couldn't. I knew I'd heard my name. Or at least I thought I had. I *had* been a little jumpy that day. "Fine, whatever." I'd let him win for now. Maybe Willow would find something that would force him to tell me.

He looked from my wet hair and my tank top down to my cutoff shorts and bare feet. "Get ready and come play Ping-Pong with everyone."

I slid my feet into flip-flops. That's about as ready as I was going to get for a game of Ping-Pong. "Give me my cookie back."

Ezra ate the rest in one bite.

"You're the worst."

CHAPTER 10

THE RV PARK CLUBHOUSE WAS ONE BIG ROOM WITH
several groupings of couches surrounding several different multi-
player games—foosball and pool and Ping-Pong. There was even
a big table with board games. The room itself was well-worn but
cozy. And like at the river, there were several other visitors taking
advantage of the space. Our group had taken over the Ping-Pong
table, and the current matchup was Skyler versus Olivia.

As we headed that way, I heard a voice call out, "Norah." I
looked to my left. By the foosball table was Ty and the rest of the
Oliveras family. He lifted his hand in a wave.

"You know that guy?" Ezra asked.

"Sort of. I'll meet up with you in a sec." I changed direction
and walked toward Ty, who met me halfway.

"Twice in one day?" Ty said.

"The river has a wider influence than we realized."

His brows shot down in confusion.

"Just a joke. Earlier, your mom said that the river forces
everyone to make friends."

"Oh, right. Yeah." He pointed back over his shoulder. "Want to play some foosball with us?"

I scrunched my nose. "Sorry, I promised my brother I'd beat him at Ping-Pong."

"Okay, I'll come your way." He walked toward the Ping-Pong table as if I had made the invitation. I followed after him.

When we reached the loud corner of the room where Skyler and Olivia's game was still going strong, Ty and I paused behind the couch to watch a couple volleys. Apparently Skyler wasn't taking it easy on Olivia. He was finishing his hits with dramatic grunts like he was some famous tennis star or something and everyone found this incredibly funny. Olivia would laugh and yell out, "Crap!" every time she missed the ball, which was nearly every time.

I narrowed my eyes at Skyler as if he could see me. I wanted to say, *Maybe you're not so different after all. Maybe you're only different with me now,* but instead my mind just filled with other instances when he'd acted like a goof around me over the years—solo caroling at my bedroom door one Christmas, sticking all the bows from my birthday presents on his head, Hulk-smashing a spider on the living room floor.

Paisley noticed me first and she called out, "Hi, Norah! Can I play you next?"

"I get her next," Ezra said.

"Are you good at Ping-Pong or something?" Ty asked from beside me.

"Not really. I'm better at virtual games."

"Like video games?"

I nodded.

"Wow, a girl who's good at video games?"

"A girl can't be good at video games?" I asked.

"No, I just don't know a whole lot who are."

I bit my tongue. I'd gotten in many debates with gamers over the years. I wasn't going to get in another one right now.

Skyler looked in my direction and as he did, the ball whizzed by him and landed on the floor.

"Yes!" Olivia cheered. "I win!"

"I was ahead by twenty," Skyler said.

"I said *next point wins*."

He smiled that genuine Skyler smile of his. "You're right. You win."

She winked at him. "Yes, I do." She turned toward the group and held up the paddle. "Who's next?"

"Me and Norah," Ezra said.

As I reached for the paddle Ezra was holding out, I said, "Oh, by the way, everyone, this is Ty. He basically saved me on the river today."

"I thought *I* saved you on the river today," Skyler said.

"You didn't," I assured him as I swiped the paddle and took my place at the Ping-Pong table.

My mom stood and turned toward Ty. "Hi! Welcome. You saved my daughter? What does that even mean?"

"She lost her tube."

"Really?" Mom looked at me like I should've told her this story earlier. I hadn't thought I needed to.

"Technically, you flipped me and then I lost my tube."

Ty looked down as though embarrassed and smiled. "That's true. I'm sorry again."

"Is that how you pick up on people?" Austin asked. "I need to take notes."

"Not sure it worked," Ty said.

Then suddenly all eyes were on me like I needed to verify right then if Ty's flirting (which I knew had not actually been flirting at the time) worked. Instead, I hit the Ping-Pong ball over the net and Ezra missed the return shot. "One to zero."

"I wasn't ready!"

"Are you ready now?"

I ended up beating Ezra pretty handily. But the noise level in our corner of the room had dropped considerably since Skyler stopped playing. It didn't stop me from turning toward the group and bowing at my win.

Mom clapped and Ezra pointed his paddle at me like a sword. "I demand a rematch."

"Too bad. I'm going out on top."

I rejoined Ty by the couch and he said, "Are you some sort of Ping-Pong hustler? Pretend you're no good and then crush the unsuspecting competition?"

"You caught me. I should have made you bet money on the game."

"Yes, you need to work on your skills." He nodded toward the door. "Do you want to go for a walk?"

I hesitated, not sure if I did. Ty was cute and seemed nice (though his opinions about girls and video games needed to come into this decade), but it also sounded exhausting. Small talk was not my specialty.

I didn't know if Paisley sensed something in my body language or she was just incredibly perceptive but she said, "Norah, you promised to help me draw some of the local plants."

I cringed in Ty's direction. "I'm sorry, I totally did."

"Can we exchange info or something? Maybe we can meet up tomorrow."

"Sure, my Snap is NoWaySims."

"That sounds like a fake account," Ty said.

"It's not."

Someone from Ty's group called out his name and he gave me a head nod. "I'll catch up with you tomorrow."

"Okay."

He left and I hooked my arm in Paisley's. "Thank you," I said.

"You don't have to give someone your info if you don't want to," she said.

"I know, but it's not hard to say hi to someone occasionally on social media. It's not like I'll ever see him again."

Paisley raised her eyebrows at me.

"I mean, after tomorrow."

She laughed.

"You ready to go find some flora?" I asked.

"Yes, I am."

Skyler walked by, giving us a sideways glance as he left the clubhouse. I wondered for a moment if he'd heard that whole exchange. Seeing him reminded me that yes, sometimes it was hard to keep in touch with someone long distance—even if that person was your best friend.

CHAPTER 11

I STARED AT TY'S FRIEND REQUEST ON MY PHONE. Paisley was right—I didn't have to accept it just to be nice. I wasn't sure why I needed this reminder; I'd often given the same advice to Willow. I yawned and tucked my phone into my pocket. I'd decide in the morning. I slid off my bunk and to the floor, then went to the bathroom door and knocked.

"Ezra, hurry up already. I want to get ready for bed."

"Don't be a bathroom bully."

"Don't use the word *bully* so casually."

"My bathroom routine is serious business." A distinct buzzing sounded through the door.

"Are you texting in there? You're seriously making me wait so you can text?" I could've used the RV park's public bathrooms, but I'd gotten a whiff of them on our walk back earlier and decided they hadn't been cleaned enough today.

"I'm washing my face, Norah."

I growled, then eyed my mom's closed door. She and Olivia had gone on a walk after dinner and then she'd gone to bed. Ezra had sworn that his secret had nothing to do with the parents. Mom had said she was fine. And even if they both were lying, Willow was investigating for me. There was nothing more I could do right now except stop letting it distract me from what I should've been focusing on.

I grabbed my hoodie and flash cards off the couch and stepped outside. I'd forgotten my shoes, but it didn't matter; I wasn't going far. I rounded the back of the RV and climbed the ladder to the roof. Someone had once told me desert stars were amazing and they were right. I lay back and took in the vastness of the sky.

It reminded me of Skyler's childhood room. He'd painted it a navy blue with bright white stars. Then he'd littered the walls with pages and pages of drawings. The thought of it took me back there. Maybe I was remembering one specific day or maybe it was a combination of several but in my mind I was running to his house, my hair flying behind me as I circled the block.

I'd run through the side gate, like I often did, and through the back door that was always unlocked. I heard the television on in the living room but snuck by it and to the hall, where I opened his bedroom door quietly and stepped inside. I was breathless as I closed the door behind me. Some papers pinned to the wall fluttered with the motion.

Skyler was sketching on his bed and he looked up with my entry, his face brightening with a smile.

"Hey," he said. "I didn't hear the doorbell."

"I didn't ring the doorbell." I ran and jumped onto his bed, landing on my knees next to him. "What are you drawing?" I peeked around to look at the pad he held. It was a sketch of his little sister. He was always good at making people look like the actual people. I struggled with that. "That's awesome."

"Not yet." He rubbed at one of the lines, the sides of his hand smudged with pencil. There was even some on his cheek.

I twisted around and pressed my back against the headboard next to him, our shoulders touching. "How do you always shade your drawings so perfectly?"

"It's not about the shade. It's about knowing where the light is." His eyes twinkled as they met mine.

I sat up and shook off the memory, hugging my knees to my chest.

Below me, a figure, a blur of white, streaked through the darkness, running. The dim light of a phone flashlight barely lit a few feet in front of the person. My heart gave a leap, startled at first, but as the figure got closer, I realized it was Skyler. Was he on a night run? Part of his new Skyler ritual, apparently. Just as I was thinking my unfair thoughts, he pointed his phone over his shoulder, lighting up a creature of some sort. He let out a whisper-curse. So did I. What was that?

He made a sharp turn toward the back of our RV and I heard him ascending the ladder with lots of clanking and cursing. When his head didn't appear over the top of the roofline, I was confused. I crawled across the roof, toward him.

I got to the edge of the RV and peered over. Skyler was frozen, halfway up the ladder, clinging to a rung, his knees almost to his chin. At the bottom of the ladder, staring up at him, was a . . . goat? It had the fattest horns I'd ever seen and they curled out of its head, their ends pointing back toward the front.

"What are you doing?" I asked quietly, trying not to scare him or the goat.

I thought Skyler would yelp or jump in surprise, but he just tilted his head up and looked at me. Had he seen me climb up here earlier? "Isn't it obvious? I'm studying the fauna of the area. This is a bighorn sheep."

"A sheep? Huh. I thought it was a goat."

As if insulted by my words, the sheep rammed its head forward, hitting one of its horns against the metal. Skyler scrambled up one more rung.

"Right. Yes, I see that now," I said.

"What are *you* doing?" he asked like we were in the middle of a perfectly normal conversation.

"Looking at the stars."

At my words, he adjusted his gaze to the sky. "Wow."

"Yeah." I bit my lip, trying to contain the smile that was attempting to take over. "Are you more scared of heights or getting rammed by that goat?"

"Sheep," he said. "And I'm trying to decide."

I laughed. "Get up here, dork."

"Fine. Fine. Scoot back."

I inched backward to make room for him.

"Just don't pull me or anything," he said as he slowly climbed up another rung.

"Why would I pull you?"

"It's just something you would do."

"Don't worry, I've been told I'm different now," I said.

He didn't say anything to that, but his jaw tensed. I wasn't sure if it was a reaction to my words or the fact that he had reached the top of the ladder. He brought his knee onto the roof and then ever so cautiously crawled, inch by painfully slow inch forward.

When he sat down next to me, out of breath, he smiled. "I did it."

I rolled my eyes and pushed his arm.

He swatted at my hand. "Don't push me up here."

"You are such a baby."

"It is a legitimate fear, Norah. Lots of people have it."

"I'm teasing you, Skyler."

"I know. My heart just feels like it's about to leave my chest. Apparently that makes me defensive."

I nodded toward the sheep that seemed to be pacing at the bottom of the ladder now. "I hope you got some good pictures for Paisley."

"I did." He turned his phone toward me and started scrolling through several shots. "I wasn't that close. These are zoomed in."

"Bighorns must've thought otherwise," I said.

"You've named him already?"

"Of course."

As he continued to scroll, I had the perfect view as a text came in. At ten o'clock at night. From someone named Riley.

Good night.

That's all it said. No hearts or kissy faces or anything to give me context to who Riley was. He tucked his phone away and we both pretended like the text never happened.

And then we went quiet. I could hear voices in the distance from another campsite, and occasionally the sheep would tap its horns against some part of the RV, but mostly the night was still. "Ask me an unexpected question?" I said.

"For the interview?"

"Yeah."

"Um . . ." Skyler fiddled with a button on the sleeve of his flannel. "What's the earliest memory you have of a piece of art that moved you?"

I retrieved the flash cards out of the pocket of my hoodie and flipped through them until I found the card I was looking for. I turned it toward him. The question he'd just asked me was written there almost word for word.

"Not so unexpected," he said. "I'm a disappointment."

"I agree." As the words came out of my mouth, I immediately wanted to take them back. "No, I mean, not in general. I don't even know what you do, so I have no . . . It was a joke," I finally spit out.

"Wow," he said. "And I was about to take it as a joke too."

I moved to put the flash cards back in my pocket, obviously flustered, because I completely missed and the cards scattered all over the top of the RV. I gasped and scrambled to gather them up.

"Be careful," Skyler said, picking up several himself.

As my hand grabbed a small stack, it bumped into several others and they slid toward the edge. I dove forward to save them and was jerked to a stop by my ankle. Two cards fluttered over the side and landed on the ground where, no joke, the sheep began munching on them.

I looked over my shoulder to where Skyler was gripping my ankle, his eyes wide.

"I wasn't going to fall," I said.

His shoulders rose and lowered several times before he released me. "Don't . . . just don't ever do that again."

My heart fluttered in my chest at his intense tone. I wasn't sure how to react to his reaction, so, with our eyes locked, I ended up saying, "Bighorns is eating my questions."

There was the squeak of a door opening below. Then Ezra's voice called up, "Is that a pack of racoons on top of our RV or some other pests trying to keep the people inside from actually sleeping?"

"Watch out for the sheep," I called down.

"Is that supposed to be some sort of sleep joke?" Ezra must've scared it away because the sheep was gone.

"I guess this means you're done with the bathroom."

"I've been done forever," he said.

I shook my head. "Sure."

Skyler headed down the ladder first. When I got to the bottom, I found a half-chewed card, but the other one had obviously been completely devoured. I wondered which question had been on the card. The one Skyler had asked? The first piece of art that moved me? That answer was easy. It was a charcoal sketch of a mom watching a sleeping baby. Her face had expressed love or happiness or peace or something my nine-year-old mind couldn't quite tap into but it made me feel something in my chest I'd never felt before while looking at a picture. Skyler had drawn it. And that had made me feel something too—pride.

I turned to say good night to Skyler but he was already in his RV, the door shutting behind him.

CHAPTER 12

THE NEXT DAY WE HIT THE NARROWS, A TRAIL THAT cut a path through the canyons in Zion National Park. The water was green and knee-deep in some places, and the canyons were red and stretched up to the sky above us as we walked. The rocky walls were smooth, as if someone had taken sandpaper to them, creating rounded edges and hollowed shapes.

"This is cool!" Paisley said, her water shoes sending an arc of water out in front of her as she stepped over a boulder.

"So cool," Skyler said.

Olivia narrowed her eyes at him as though he was being sarcastic, but I could tell he wasn't. She must've come to the same conclusion because she just said, "It really is."

Mom and Ezra were walking ahead of the group arm in arm and I wondered what they were talking about. My suspicions were still on high alert. They stopped in front of a circular cutout in the wall and snapped a selfie.

My phone buzzed in my pocket. It was a text from Willow: *"Wish You Were Here" should not be written on any postcard from a place called Death Valley.*

She'd gotten the postcard I'd dropped in the mailbox at the Death Valley RV park. I typed back, *This coming from the girl who left a note in my suitcase of me, in sunshine form, killing her.*

True true.

Mom laughed and I glanced up to see Ezra saying something else that had her smiling.

I turned my attention back to my phone. *Have you broken into my house yet?*

Not yet. In the meantime, take this quiz. I took it. It's official, we're the best best friends.

Below her text was a link to a *Teen Vogue* article: THE ULTIMATE BEST FRIENDS QUIZ

I replied: *I don't believe you needed a quiz to tell you that.*

I went to click on the link when I tripped on a rock, nearly face-planting in the water. Someone caught me by the elbow and I looked over to see Skyler.

"You should probably watch where you're going," he said.

"Yeah, thanks."

He was right. We were hiking in a rocky canyon through water. I was lucky I hadn't dropped my phone. Willow would have to wait and so would that quiz.

Next to me, Olivia stumbled on a rock as well. Several other people on the trail had walking sticks. We should've brought walking sticks.

"You trying to make me feel better?" I asked.

She hooked her elbow in mine. "We can steady each other."

"Good call. How did your shopping go yesterday, by the way?"

"I found some beautiful wind chimes. I'll have to show them to you back at camp. Are you a wind chime girl, Norah?"

"Possibly. I have no idea what that means."

"Some people get annoyed by their sound. The music isn't a pleasant background noise to them but a distracting nuisance."

"Oh . . . I'm not sure. We've never owned one." The sides of the canyon were closing in up ahead, forming a narrow passage of the towering walls, proving how this trail got its name. It was gorgeous. "I think I'd like them."

"Miranda, you've never had wind chimes?" Olivia called to my mom.

"They're too loud!" she called back over her shoulder.

I laughed.

"You see," Olivia said. "Your mom is not a wind chime girl."

"Are you a wind chime girl, Skyler?" I asked.

He smiled. "You know it."

"How is your project going, Paisley?" Olivia asked.

She took out her phone and snapped a picture of a scraggly plant growing out of the rocks. "It's practically writing itself."

"I hope that's not how much effort you've put into it. This is so you don't have to retake a class next year," Olivia said. "This shouldn't be a hard assignment. Look at this place." She smiled up at the strip of sky above us. Her smile was contagious and I found myself drinking in our surroundings as well.

"Look at this place!" Paisley said in a playful mocking tone. "It's like Mother Nature was trying to show off!"

Olivia's eyebrows popped up. "Later, I want to look over what you've been working on."

"Ugh, Mom, please, don't helicopter me. I'm getting it done."

Skyler smirked at her and Paisley shot him a look that said, *Don't you dare contradict me.*

And that's how Skyler, Paisley, and I ended up sitting at the table that night in the RV, huddled over her project as Ezra pulled onto the road out of Zion.

"This is all you have?" Skyler asked, scrolling through the pics on her phone. "Mom will hover the rest of the trip if this is all you show her."

"I also have this," she said, holding up a badly drawn lizard. She pointed at Skyler. "Unless you want to draw it for me, shut up."

"I said nothing." He put her phone down. "Fine, it's terrible. Hand it over."

She slid the book across the table to him, along with a pencil.

"Have you written anything for the pictures you took?" I asked. "That would help."

"I figured I'd google some facts about them later."

"You're such a procrastinator," Skyler said.

"That's how creatives work best," she said. "By waiting until the adrenaline sets in."

His pencil moved over the lines she had already drawn as if just his bit of added graphite would magically fix it. And it was working. His smooth strokes and steady hand were making it look like an actual lizard. And seeing Skyler drawing again was doing something to my chest, making it tight or expanding it or something. His eyes flicked to mine for a moment as if he knew I was staring. I looked away.

Paisley put the back of her hand to her forehead. "Who knew saving a damsel in distress is what would reignite your drawing flame. When's the last time you held a pencil, dearest brother?"

"This is why you ace drama and fail science," he said.

"*This* is why? Wow, another mystery in my life solved."

I laughed.

"Are you going to help or just laugh?" Skyler asked.

I bumped his elbow, sending a line across the middle of his drawing. "Oops," I said.

"You did not," he said.

Paisley found this hilarious.

"I took a few pics you can use," I said to her. "And of course I'll draw you a few as well."

"You've both given up on my drawing skills so fast."

"No, it's not—" I started.

"I'm kidding, Norah," Paisley said. "I suck. Let me see your pics."

I handed her my phone and while she was looking, a text buzzed through. *Did you take the quiz yet?*

"What quiz?" Paisley asked.

"Oh, it's a best friends' quiz Willow sent me."

"Ooh, I'll give it to you. Can I?" Her finger hovered over the link.

"Go ahead."

"You're really not going to do your project?" Skyler said.

"Shhh, be still, Dad. I'll get to it."

Skyler's jaw clenched with those words, which let me know his relationship with his dad still wasn't his favorite. He didn't say anything, though, just continued to clean up her drawing. He wasn't making it in his own style, the one I remembered; he was just taking what she had and making it a better version of itself.

110

"Okay, question one." She paused before reading it. "You two used to be best friends, right?"

"That's the question?" I asked.

"No." She looked up. "You and Skyler. I'm giving you two this quiz."

"What?" Skyler said, sliding the finished lizard back to her. "Pass."

"No, come on, it will be fun." She turned her attention back to my phone. "First question: Do you know their phone number by heart?"

Of course I knew Willow's phone number by heart. But was I taking this quiz about Willow or Skyler?

"We didn't have phones at the time," Skyler said, obviously deciding to participate after all.

"And you didn't give each other your numbers when you got them?" she asked.

"She's in my phone," he said.

"Same," I returned. We had mostly communicated through DMs on social media, though.

"But not memorized?" Paisley said, clucking her tongue. "First question failed." She scrolled on. "Question number two: Do you know the name of the first person they had a crush on?"

"Cynthia Fields," I answered quickly. "You had a thing for her, right?"

"In like the third grade," Skyler said, giving me a sideways glance.

"It said the first."

111

"True." He studied me for a moment before he said, "Leo Morales."

I gasped. "I did not!" I scrunched my nose. "Fine, I did."

"I knew it!" he said.

"Good job. That's a star for both of you," Paisley said. "What about first pets?"

"Too easy," I said. "Goldie Goldfish."

"Aw, poor Goldie," Skyler said; then he tapped his fingers on the table. "Your dad's allergic, but I do remember you had an outdoor cat once. You named it Velma because you were such a nerd."

"It was a good name," I said. We rounded a curve on the road and an empty water bottle someone had left on the counter fell to the floor, rolling until it hit the wall. I stood and swiped it up, depositing it into our recycle container.

"Next," Paisley said when I sat back down again. "Do you know how to tell when they're mad?"

I clenched my jaw and pointed at it.

"That's true," Paisley said. "You're such a jaw clencher, Skyler. That can't be good for your teeth."

"It's better than the silent treatment," he said, nodding toward me.

"The silent treatment doesn't bother my teeth at all," I said.

"Ha!" Paisley said. "She has you there."

"But," he said, "when you're beyond mad, you cry."

I swallowed. He was right and he probably also remembered that I hated to cry, especially in front of other people. It was one of my least favorite things. So I pretended like he didn't say it and asked Paisley, "Are there more?"

"A few. Who's the last person they made out with?"

My cheeks immediately went hot. I definitely didn't know the answer to that. I could probably look at his Instagram and figure it out. Or maybe I could ask who'd texted him on the roof the night before. Riley? That would be a safe bet. "I don't know," I said before things got more awkward.

"No clue," Skyler said.

"Makes sense," Paisley said. "You haven't seen each other in four years. I guess you aren't giving each other make-out reports. I'm not going to lie, it would've been awesome if you were."

"Next," I said, ready to move past the question.

"Next one is, Do you know how to make them feel better in any situation?"

Of course I knew that answer. When Skyler was sad, I would badly sing a song he loved while changing the lyrics to fit whatever sad thing he was dealing with.

"Don't do it," Skyler said with a smile, as if I was about to belt out a bad tune.

"Don't worry, haven't done it in forever." I had retired that particular quirk of mine long ago. "Why would I start again now? You're perfectly happy."

"Yes, I am," he said.

"Good."

"What is it?" Paisley asked. "What did you used to do?"

"Make a fool of myself for your brother," I said.

"And what about you, Skyler?" Paisley said. "What did you do for her?"

He would hug me. Just give me a huge, lanky-armed hug

and tell me that whatever I was feeling was exactly the right way to feel. His eyes met mine. "What is it your mom calls you? A ray of sunshine? Whoever needs to make a ray of sunshine feel better?"

I blinked in surprise before controlling my expression and saying, "So true. How did you ever find light without me?"

Paisley's gaze went back and forth between us a couple times before saying, "Last question: Have you ever kept a secret from each other?"

"This is stupid," Skyler said. "I'm sure we have tons of things we haven't told each other."

"But back when you were besties," Paisley said.

"No," I said. "I told him everything back then."

"Yes," Skyler said. Was he agreeing with me or answering the question?

Paisley must've assumed the first because she said, "Oh my goodness. You two were so cute." She clicked a button on the screen. "But you still got two wrong so you only get Bronze Level Besties. Better luck next time."

Skyler sighed. "That was a colossal waste of time."

"Was it, though?" Paisley asked. "Was it?"

"Yes," both Skyler and I said at the same time.

CHAPTER 13

"PARK CITY, UTAH," OLIVIA SAID AS WE GOT OFF THE shuttle bus. "Isn't this cool?"

"Isn't Park City where celebrities come to ski?" Austin asked. "Maybe we'll see someone famous."

"It's June." I looked up at the ski runs that in the winter were obviously blanketed in white but were now yellow and green with brush and trees.

"Wow, now I have two annoying little sisters?" Austin said.

"She's not as annoying as me," Paisley assured him.

"Yes," Mom said. "There is lots of skiing here in the winter. But the 2002 Olympics were in Utah and some of those events happened here at Olympic Park."

"So now we get to pretend we're Olympians from twenty years ago?" Paisley asked.

"No, now they've turned it into a park. There's extreme tubing and rock climbing and zip lining."

"You had me at extreme tubing, Miranda," Austin said.

"Do we have to stay together?" Ezra asked.

"You have your passes," Mom said. "Run free."

115

Ezra and Austin looked at each other and then walked out ahead.

"Be careful!" Olivia called after them.

Skyler hesitated, glancing once at the retreating forms of our brothers and then to Paisley and me.

"You can go," Paisley said.

"We don't want you here," I added.

He smiled, rubbed Paisley's head, and then said, "Wait up!" as he ran after Ezra and Austin. Old Skyler would've never chosen . . . well, *anyone* . . . over me.

"We're going to sit in the café," Mom said when we came to a fork in the walkway between the surrounding buildings.

"Okay." I watched them walk away.

"What?" Paisley said. "Why are you giving our moms a dirty look?"

I smoothed out my features that I could feel were scrunched in suspicion. "I'm surprised my mom is going to sit in a café. They didn't even buy themselves passes."

"That *is* weird," Paisley said. "My mom usually loves the thrill rides."

"My mom too."

"What are you thinking?" she asked.

I hesitated, not sure if I wanted to voice my fears out loud. That always made them more real. I'd already told Willow and she didn't seem as convinced as I had been that something was going on. And she's the one who had been skeptical about this whole trip to begin with. "Do you think it's weird that our moms wanted to do this trip now, after all these years?"

Paisley shrugged. "Not really."

"Yeah . . ."

"You obviously think it is. Why?"

"I don't know. I overheard Ezra talking about some secret on the phone, but he's denying it now. Or at least denying it has anything to do with our parents."

"What secret?"

"That's the point, I have no idea. It just makes me feel like something is going to be sprung on me."

"Like what?"

"I don't know." And I really didn't. "I'm trying to figure it out."

"I'm really good at snooping," Paisley said. "I'll help you."

"Deal."

* * *

The blisters on my heels that night proved we had walked way too much at Olympic Park that day. We were staying in Park City for two days, which meant no driving that night. Which meant the Huttons were in their own RV.

I sat on the couch, putting Band-Aids on my heels, when my phone buzzed beside me. It was from Willow and my heart seemed to leap to my throat when I saw it was a picture. Was I about to see what medicine my mom had in her cabinet? Or what suspicious mail had been delivered recently?

But when I pulled up the pic, it was of a girl I didn't recognize standing by a lake and laughing at the camera. She was beautiful. The sun was going down and she had the ethereal glow that only the last drops of sunlight could create.

Who's that?

Riley? Willow texted. *Or maybe this is Riley.*

The next picture she sent was one of a guy wearing a hat and eating a massive M&M's cookie.

Are you stalking Skyler's social media??

Who? Me?

Stop!

Oh, please. Don't tell me you haven't done it.

It had actually been a while since I'd looked through his social media. *I haven't!*

How is the hot demon anyway?

Back and forth.

Between?

Indifferent and punkish.

Hmm. Maybe he's still trying to decide if you're in love with him or not.

He better not be. Pretty sure I've proven that I'm not. The quiz we'd taken the night before and my reactions to some of the questions made me cringe now. Maybe I *had* dug that hole deeper. Maybe that's why Skyler hadn't wanted to answer the question about how he used to make me feel better. Was he worried I would think him hugging me meant something more than it had?

Have you really proven you're not in love with him though? Another picture came through.

This one was a candid shot of me and Skyler. We were in my

118

backyard by the pool staring at something on the towel between us. Our foreheads were touching and this didn't seem to faze us at all.

I racked my brain trying to remember what was on that towel. A bug? A frog? It could've been anything. That was kind of the point. This picture could've been taken almost any day of any summer we knew each other, that's how often a scene like this occurred.

Pretty sure little Norah adored little Skyler, Willow texted.

Where did you find that? Was it on his social media? Why would he be posting childhood pics of us?

In that scrapbook in your living room.

You were in my house?! Why didn't you lead with that?!! Did you find anything??

Nope. That's why I didn't lead with that. But I was thinking . . .

What?

If your mom was taking meds for some mysterious health issue, wouldn't they be there? Wouldn't she take them with her?

My eyes shot to her closed bedroom door. Of course she would bring them.

You're right.

Always am.

The bathroom door opened and Ezra peeked his head out, steam billowing out with him. "Ten more minutes?"

"It's fine," I said.

I dug under my pillow to grab my flash cards, to get my mind off the fact that I couldn't immediately search through all my mom's possessions, when I came up with the notebook instead.

I petted the cover several times, then sat down on the couch and turned back the cover, looking for where I had left off.

I'm sorry your dad embarrassed you today was written in my handwriting. *You're right, he's harder on you than on Austin. But maybe you'll get closer when you're older.*

I tried to remember what I had been talking about in this entry. Skyler's dad was prickly, especially to Skyler. My mom often said it was because they were too much alike. But I never saw Skyler in Mr. Hutton. Skyler was sweet and funny and empathetic. Mr. Hutton was hard and closed off and critical.

I kept reading. *And maybe next time, just say you were the one who left the gate open.*

Just like that, I remembered the exact incident. He and I had run into his house after swimming at mine to grab his sketch stuff. His dad called out, "Skyler Hutton!"

Skyler skidded to a halt in the hallway and gave me his worried face. "What do you think that's about?"

"Who knows," I said. "He's always grumpy."

Skyler agreed. "Come on." He led the way to the kitchen, where Austin sat at the counter eating a bowl of cereal even though it was past lunchtime. One of his best friends, Lydia, sat next to him.

Mr. Hutton glanced our way from where he stood by the fridge. "Skyler, the dog got out earlier. I had to chase him down."

"Oh."

"Don't *oh* me. You left the side gate open. Get your head out of your sketchbook and grow up."

"I didn't leave the gate open."

"Don't backtalk, Skyler. Just apologize."

"You want me to apologize for something I didn't do?"

"You were the only one back there today."

"It wasn't me," Skyler insisted.

"I might've been back there," Austin said.

His dad pounded his fist on the counter and Skyler's cheeks went bright red. "Next time pay attention!"

Skyler put his chin in the air and stormed down the hall.

Lydia and I exchanged a wide-eyed look. Austin just kept munching away at his cereal.

I joined Skyler in his room a few minutes later.

"Austin could let a thousand dogs out of the backyard and my dad would probably praise him for it."

"Where would he get a thousand dogs?" I asked.

"You know what I mean."

"I do." He obviously wasn't in the mood for my jokes and I understood why. His shoulders were tense and his jaw was clenched. "I'm sorry."

He gave me a quick hug and said, "I'll meet you at your house later."

"Or you could come now. You'll feel better. I will sing you a song about mean dads."

He smiled a little. "Fine, but no to the song."

"He's a loser, Skyler, and he never listens." I sang to the tune of "Loser" by Beck.

He put his hands over his ears. "Seriously, Norah, stop ruining good songs."

"You know you love it."

He laughed, that carefree, comfortable laugh.

"Norah!"

My head snapped up and my brother stood there, hair wet from a shower.

"Hi, what?" My heart was pounding with the memory. The memory of how close we used to be, of how he would share everything with me.

"Jeez, where does your brain travel to?"

"Sorry."

"Bathroom is free."

"Thanks." I got up, tucked the notebook away, and grabbed my toiletries.

"Hey, Nor?" Ezra asked before I made it into the bathroom.

"Yeah?"

"Did you have fun today? We kind of ditched you and I know Paisley didn't want to do a lot of the rides."

"I had fun," I said.

"Is Skyler still being a punk to you?"

"You noticed he's being a punk?"

"Well, yeah. You two used to spend every waking moment together. And now . . ."

"And now what?" I asked, curious if Skyler had said something about me when they were hanging out.

"And now it's like he goes out of his way to avoid you. Did something happen?"

"Time, I guess. I don't know." I didn't want to admit to my brother that Skyler probably thought I was crushing on him.

"And you tried to tell me a couple days ago that the time apart wouldn't make anything awkward."

"Apparently I underestimated my ability to make everything awkward."

"Awkward? You?" He gave me this weird, sad smile and then said, "We'll all stick together tomorrow."

Great. He felt sorry for me. I pulled the bathroom door shut behind me and leaned against the counter. The mirror was still steamy from Ezra's shower. I reached up and pushed on the bottom right corner, releasing the latch and revealing shelves. There was only a bottle of aspirin, sitting alone on the middle shelf.

CHAPTER 14

PARK CITY DAY TWO HAD BEEN DECENT SO FAR. WE shopped and ate at a restaurant, which was nice after all the camp food we'd been eating. And we'd stayed together, like Ezra had promised. Now we were browsing in some overly priced clothing shop. I had an armful of items and took them to one of the curtain-lined dressing rooms at the back of the store. I stepped out of my shoes and shorts and pulled on a pair of distressed jeans first.

As I was looking at myself from all angles in the mirror, Skyler walked into the dressing room beside mine. I could tell it was him because there was literally only a curtain between us and I could see his gray Vans in the one-foot gap at the bottom. He kicked them off his feet and soon his shorts were in a puddle on the ground and my eyes shot to the mirror in front of me as if I'd been caught doing something wrong.

I shucked my shirt, which felt even weirder with only the thin piece of cloth between us. Is this always how people used dressing rooms? How come I had never felt so aware of it until now? I pulled on a green T-shirt that said PARK CITY across the front, the outline of trees behind the words. It was too tight. If I liked it, I would've gotten the next size up, but I didn't.

"I like your socks," Skyler said.

I used one of my feet to slide my shorts closer to the middle of the stall. He didn't need to see them discarded there. "Thanks."

"What are you trying on?" he asked.

"Nothing exciting. Just some T-shirts and jeans. What about you?"

"Shorts and a sweatshirt. I don't like them enough to justify the price tag."

"Same."

"Do you pay for your own stuff?" he asked, that curious voice of his back.

"Yes, I have a job."

"Really? Where do you work?"

"Michaels. Mainly for the discount on art supplies." I took off the jeans I wouldn't be buying and put my own shorts back on. "So my paychecks are next to nothing."

He chuckled.

"What about you? Job?"

"I'm a server at this diner near our house."

"I bet you get lots of tips."

"Why would you bet that?"

"Because you're adorable."

"Adorable," he said, a smile in his voice. "Exactly the word a guy likes to be described as."

"Like a cute kid brother," I added, because I was worried

that I hadn't convinced him I wasn't in love with him and telling him he was adorable was not going to help in that goal.

"Even better," he said.

I flipped through the other shirts I'd brought in. They were all the same size as the one I had on, which probably meant they'd all be too small.

"Did you draw that?"

"What?" I asked.

"Your socks."

I had forgotten which socks I was wearing. "Oh . . . yes. My mom put one of my drawings on a pair of socks and gave them to me for Christmas one year. Moms are overly proud like that."

"They are." His feet turned to face me. "Pull them up."

"My socks?"

"Yes, so I can see them better."

My original drawing was a strawberry and it had been replicated multiple times on the sock. My feet warped all the versions, but I pulled up my sock anyway. "I know, forward-thinking art right there. I was going through a Beatles phase. Don't ask." Why was I getting so defensive about my art? Probably because he was the one who had introduced me to it and I still felt an immense amount of pressure to make him proud.

"It's really good," he said.

I kicked at his foot with mine, his words making my stomach a little fluttery. "Don't get carried away. It's a strawberry. On a sock."

"I like strawberries. And the socks display them so well."

I laughed.

"You can't see through this curtain, can you?" he asked.

"What? No! Wait. Can you?"

"No, it's just so thin. You sound like you're standing right next to me."

"I am."

"You know what I mean." He pressed his hand against the curtain and I saw its perfect outline. "See."

I reached up but stopped short of pressing my hand against his. Instead, I leaned my shoulder against the one real wall. "Can I ask you a question?"

"Um . . ."

"I'm not going to propose marriage or anything. It's just a question. You don't have to answer if you don't want to."

"I thought the marriage was already taken care of," he dead-panned. "Didn't our parents arrange it at our birth?"

I chuckled. "Knowing our moms, they probably did."

"Right? What's your question?"

I took a slow breath and stared at the gray curtain separating us. "Did you stop drawing because of your dad? Because he always acted like it was some kid hobby, not something adults did?"

He sighed. "I don't know. Maybe that got in my head."

"If not that, why?"

"I guess I stopped enjoying it."

I nodded slowly even though he couldn't see me. "That's a good answer." The only acceptable one, really.

"I have your permission to stop?"

"That's not what I meant," I said.

"What did you mean?" he asked.

"I meant what I said. If you don't enjoy it, you shouldn't do it."

"Exactly."

"I guess I'm just sad you don't enjoy it anymore. And I hope you're not letting your dad dictate your joy." I placed my foot slightly under the curtain as if my warped feet-strawberries would remind him of what he was missing.

"You haven't talked to me, like really talked to me, in over two years, Norah. You don't get to do this."

"Do what?"

"Go back to acting like you're the expert on my life."

I pulled my foot back into my own space. "And there it is."

"There what is?" he asked.

"Were you worried you were saying too much? Being too nice? Worried I would get the wrong idea?"

"No, I was worried you'd give advice without knowing anything."

"Yeah, because that's me. Sticking my nose in everyone's business." I pulled my slip-on Vans back on. "For the record, you haven't talked to me for over two years either."

"I know."

"Also," I said with a huff, "I used to be the expert on your life."

He released a choked laugh.

"And you used to be the expert on mine." My voice cracked with emotion, surprising me.

He gave a heavy sigh. "I didn't mean to hurt your feelings."

"You didn't." That wasn't true.

The curtain rippled as he obviously shifted or knocked it or something. "I'm a loser, baby," he sang in a soft voice. "So why are you trying?"

"No," I said, taking a single step back. "That's my thing. You don't get to use my thing on me as if you don't remember your thing."

"I remember my thing."

I blinked once, twice, wondering if he was going to let himself through one of the many openings in this curtain and give me a hug. The thought of that scared me—thrilled me?—but I didn't wait around to find out which of those emotions would win. I hastily pulled my sweatshirt back on and left the dressing room.

Our families were nowhere to be seen. They had probably moved on to the next store. I beelined it for the door, and just as I was about to push on the handle, an alarm went off on either side of me, accompanied by flashing yellow lights. The employee behind the counter practically vaulted the desk and was at my side before I even registered what was happening.

"Oh." I suddenly realized. "I'm sorry, I forgot to change back into my shirt." It was probably still sitting on the floor in the dressing room. I started to move back toward the curtained rooms but he stepped in front of me.

"I need to call security."

"Are you serious? I just told you I forgot to change back into my shirt. I'll do it now."

"Take off your sweatshirt please."

"Excuse me? I'm not taking off my sweatshirt."

He took a walkie-talkie off his belt and spoke into it. "I have a code seven up front."

"You don't have a code seven." I didn't know what that meant but I knew he definitely didn't have it. "You have zero codes. I'll just pay for it. Will that work?"

"Take off your sweatshirt."

"Fine!" I pulled off my sweatshirt, revealing the too-small Park City T-shirt underneath. "There. You see. If I was going to steal a shirt, don't you think I'd steal one that fit?"

Skyler came walking up at that moment. "She didn't steal it," he said. "She got distracted. I distracted her."

"I don't need a hero, Skyler," I spit out. "I'm handling it."

He held up his hands.

"If you pay for it," the worker said, "I'll let you off with a warning."

"Great," I said, walking toward the register. That's when I re-membered I'd given my purse, with my money and cell phone, to Paisley to hold while I tried on clothes. I closed my eyes and exhaled in frustration. What would be worse? Mall jail or asking Skyler for help? It was a tough choice.

I turned toward him. "Paisley has my purse."

"What's that?" Skyler asked, hovering by the front doors.

"Paisley. She's holding my purse."

"So are you saying, Norah, that you *do* need a hero?"

The store worker had the audacity to laugh.

"I'll pay you back," I said.

He walked to my side and retrieved his wallet out of his pocket.

"Can I at least get the right size?" I asked the worker.

He leveled me with a stare.

Skyler handed over some cash. "It looks like the right size to me."

"You did not just say that," I said.

He smiled. I elbowed him in the ribs and this time he laughed. The guy behind the counter came at me with the sensor-removing device.

"Don't even think about it," I said, holding out my hand. He placed it in my palm and I removed the security sensor and handed it back. "I'm going to get my actual shirt." As I walked back to the dressing room, I saw that half a dozen people were milling about the store, all staring at me. I waved, swiped up my shirt, and left.

Skyler was waiting outside, a stupid teasing smile in his eyes.

"I'll pay you back," I said again.

"You're welcome," he returned.

I saw Ezra up ahead, exiting a candy shop. "There's Ezra, let's go," I said, instead of "thank you." Those words seemed too hard to say to him right now.

CHAPTER 15

MY PHONE RANG IN MY HANDS, MAKING ME JUMP and lighting up the dark row where we sat that night watching an outdoor movie. We were supposed to be on the road, but the moms decided they didn't want another night-driving session, so we were now leaving first thing the next morning.

FaceTime from Willow scrolled across my screen.

"Shoot," I whispered. She hardly ever FaceTimed me, so I looked both ways down the aisle trying to see which exit was easiest to navigate to. As the call continued to vibrate in my hand, I got up and shuffled past Paisley and Ezra on my right. When I reached Skyler, he gave me a questioning look and I shook my phone at him and kept walking. By the time I got to the exit, the call had stopped. I stepped out anyway and kept walking, trying to put some distance between me and the amphitheater. The phone started ringing again. I swiped to accept the call.

"Hey," I answered in a soft voice. "What's up?"

"Guess who's here?" Willow yelled, her mouth taking up

the whole screen. Music and voices came through the speaker as well.

"Where are you?" I asked, finally far enough away to talk normally.

"At the party!" She obviously decided to go after all.

"Willow, you don't need to yell. I can hear you." I sat on a picnic table in a grassy area by a tree.

"What?" she yelled back, her ear suddenly taking up the whole screen.

"Are you drunk?"

"How can I be drunk? I only had one drink!" Her phone pointed out at a group of people now but it was so shaky that it was making my eyes hurt. "Do you see him?"

"Who?"

"My soul mate!"

"What?"

"Remember that guy from my dream you drew?"

Last year Willow told me she dreamt of the most beautiful boy in the world but didn't know him in real life so it must've been her soul mate. She forced me to draw a picture of him while describing him in detail. Then she'd pinned the picture to the wall in her bedroom. We both laughed every time we saw it so I figured it was just a running joke at this point, but right now, she was dead serious.

"Yes, I remember."

"He's here!" Her phone was still pointing at a group of people too far away for me to make out. "He's beautiful!"

"I can't see him."

"Beautiful boys are the best. Speaking of, how is your demon ex–best friend doing?"

My eyes shot back toward the theater. All I could see was the big screen, the movie playing like a silent one, since I couldn't hear the sound anymore. "Shhh."

"Is he still a huge jerk?" She said it so loud that I was glad we weren't in the RV at the moment. "If not, make him yours. You need a man. A maaaaannnnn."

"Willow, seriously, you're drunk."

"One drink, Nor. I think."

"Who did you go there with?" And how was she getting home?

"I'm going to meet my soul mate." Her lips were back on the screen. "Go get your soul mate toooooo."

"No, wait, just—"

The phone went dark as she hung up. I hated being hundreds of miles away because now I had no idea what to do. I stared at the black screen of my phone for several long moments before I attempted to call Willow back. It spit me into her voice mail.

"No."

My mind was spinning. Had she really only had one drink? It wasn't like her to drink at all, but something wasn't adding up.

I went down my list of contacts and pressed on Leena's name. The phone rang.

"Come on, come on, pick up, Leena." Again, I was dumped into voice mail. "Hey, Leena," I said, deciding to leave a message. "It's Norah. Are you at Kyle's party? Will you call me if you get this?"

I hung up and shot her off a text, too, in case she didn't listen to voice mail. Then I tried to think of who else would be there.

Dylan! Willow said he was going to the party. It had been a while since I'd talked to my ex-boyfriend, but he was still in my contacts. I pressed call and waited, gnawing at my lip, when I saw a dark shadow just beyond the picnic table. I gasped.

"It's just me," Skyler said.

"You scared me."

"Sorry. Is everything okay?"

I was expecting to have to leave another voice mail when I heard a wary, "Hello?"

"Dylan?"

"Norah, hey."

Skyler paused at the edge of the table, then turned as if he was about to leave.

"Wait," I said to him, and he stopped. Back in the phone, I said, "Are you at Kyle's party?"

"Are you?"

"No, I'm on vacation." I could hear lots of commotion and music in the background, so I knew he was there. "Can you find Willow for me?"

"You called me to find Willow?"

"Yes, it's important."

"Why don't you just call her?"

"I did. She's not answering. Please, I'm worried about her."

Skyler sat on the table beside me, his brows drawing down. He put his hand on my arm and it was like his steadiness instantly grounded me. Without much thought, as if instinct took over, my shoulder leaned against his.

"I see her," Dylan said. "She's fine. Looks like she's having fun."

"What does that mean?"

"It means, stop being so dramatic. You're such a buzzkill, always ruining the vibe."

I flinched. "Can I just talk to her?"

"Hey, Willow," Dylan said.

"Dylan!" I heard Willow's voice in the background exclaim. "You're here! I gotta tell Norah and her feelings."

"You want to dance with me, beautiful?" he said.

"Dylan, stop. Just put her on," I said.

"Let's dance," Willow said.

"Don't worry, Nor. I'll take care of her." And then for the second time that night, I was hung up on.

I set my phone on the table and squeezed my eyes shut.

"Dylan?" Skyler said.

I nodded.

"What's going on?"

"I don't know. I just have this horrible feeling right here." I pressed my fingers against my diaphragm. "What if someone slipped something into her drink? Or what if she drives like that? Or . . ." I shook out my hands.

"Norah." Skyler's voice was calm and I stilled and looked at him. "Do you think either of those things is true or are you worrying because you're not there?"

"Both."

"Okay, then who else can you call?"

My brain was so busy worrying that it couldn't think.

Skyler picked up my phone, held it out for me to unlock, then pushed some buttons. Soon it was ringing over speaker.

"Hello?" It was Dylan again.

"Hey, Dylan," Skyler said. "Put Willow on."

"Who is this?"

"Her father." He shrugged at me when I gave him wide eyes.

"Okay, yes, um, hold on," Dylan stammered.

There were some muffled words and sounds on the other end and finally Willow's voice came on the line. "Dad?"

"Hey, Willow, it's me," I said, because I knew she wouldn't believe Skyler was her dad.

"Norah! You scared me. It's just Norah!" she announced to the party. "She's not here because she has to visit this tiny college in Seattle where she has to beg to be let in!"

"Hello, hey, Willow."

"Have you had your big boss battle yet?" She laughed hard. "Remember when you told me your interview was like battling the big boss in a video game?" *Is she making fun of me?*

"Yes, I remember."

"Did you defeat the boss?" she yelled into the phone.

"I haven't had the interview yet," I said. "But listen . . ."

"Good, because your answers are sooooo boring. Think of better answers, Norah, or you'll never beat the level."

I swallowed a breath of air in surprise, but reminded

myself she was not acting like herself right now. "Willow, is Leena there?"

"Who was that guy on your phone?"

"Skyler."

"Skyler? Hi, Demon Skyler, Norah's soul mate!"

I should've taken the phone off speaker right then but I didn't and in the background we both heard Dylan say, "The Nut Hut? Norah still talks to that loser?"

"Tell Dylan to shut up," I said, then shook my head at Skyler to reassure him that I'd never called him any of those things. I hadn't even realized that Dylan knew Skyler. I hadn't met him until high school.

"Norah said shut up," Willow said.

"Give me my phone back," Dylan said.

"Willow, find Leena, okay?" I said.

"I took a picture of the boy you drew. I'm sending it to you." The phone beeped in my ear several times. "This isn't my phone." She laughed and then she was gone again.

I gnawed on my lip and stared at my dark screen, my own hazy reflection staring back at me.

"There's nothing you can do," Skyler said.

"Should I call her parents? I can call her parents for real."

"You'd do that?" he asked. "You're not worried about what the group would think about you for that?"

"I'm worried about *her*, Skyler. That's all I care about."

"Then yeah, call her parents."

I opened my phone again when it rang in my hands. I answered it, seeing the name scroll the screen. "Leena?"

"Hi. What's going on?" She sounded perfectly sober.

"Are you at Kyle's party?"

"Yes."

"I think someone might have slipped Willow something. Or she had too much without realizing it."

"Oh no," Leena said.

"Can you get her home?"

"Of course I can. I'll take her back to my place first and feed her. I'll text you when we get there."

"You don't have to leave now."

"It's boring anyway."

"Thank you."

We hung up and the tension poured off my shoulders.

"Feel better?" Skyler asked.

"Yes. Apparently I needed a hero twice today." I nodded to my phone on the table. "Thank you."

He raised his eyebrows. "You *do* know those words."

I lifted one corner of my mouth. "Sometimes."

Skyler shifted to slide off the table.

"Hey." I lightly brushed my hand on his arm and he stopped and met my eyes. "I'm sorry for what Dylan said . . . and Willow. I've never called you my soul mate; she was drunk. Although, to be honest, we've been calling you demon since my house when you didn't come in right away."

"Fair enough."

As my tension eased, the last several minutes sank in. "You really think I care more about my reputation than my friend's safety?"

"I don't have much to go on. Instagram isn't a very good judge of character."

"Fair enough," I said, even though, like earlier today, it hurt.

"Should we get back to the movie?" he asked.

"Yes." Was it too late to take back my *thank you*?

CHAPTER 16

I WASN'T SURE IF THE HUTTONS WANTED TO SLEEP longer, or needed a break from us, but the next morning, my mom declared she was driving and that we were eating breakfast on the road to save time.

"Save time for what?" Ezra asked as Mom started the engine.

"We were supposed to leave last night," she said. "If we don't stick to the schedule, we'll run out of time to see all the things we planned to see before Norah's school interview."

"It's okay if we don't do everything on the schedule," Ezra said.

"No, it's not," Mom snapped.

"I'll get breakfast started," I said, giving Ezra the *Are you sure you don't need to tell me anything?* look.

"There's oatmeal packets in the cupboard," she said, a little softer, possibly realizing how she sounded.

Ezra joined me, pulling some bowls down from the cupboard as I peeled open the box of cinnamon and spice instant oatmeal.

"Talk," I said.

"Honestly, Nor, I told you before, I have no idea."

"Then I'm calling Dad and asking him."

"Okay."

That was too easy. *Is he calling my bluff?* "After we eat." I dumped two packets into each bowl and Ezra covered them all with water and plopped them one at a time in the microwave.

My phone buzzed and I pulled it out of my pocket. It was a selfie of Willow with her hand over her eyes.

I'm glad you're alive, I responded.

Barely. And I only remember pieces of last night. My phone shows I facetimed you a couple times. Tell me who this is:

A blurry picture of a cute Black guy came on my screen.

I studied him. He didn't look familiar. Then I remembered something she'd said. *Your soul mate?*

OH! That's right! But he looks nothing like that picture you drew.

I laughed. *Yes, you were out of it.*

I may have had more than I intended to.

So you weren't drugged?

You thought I was drugged?!

You don't drink, Willow.

I know, I was feeling anxious without you there.

Since when?

Since I normally go everywhere with you.

It's my job to feel anxious.

Ezra set a bowl of oatmeal on the table, where I had wandered while texting. "I thought you were making this," he said.

"Yeah, well, I had to check on my best friend."

"Willow?" He tilted his head toward my phone.

"Excuse you." I turned my phone facedown but then it buzzed again. *Thank you for looking after me last night.*

"What happened last night?" Ezra asked.

"Are you seriously reading my texts?"

"Yes, I'm standing right here."

I shoved him. "Nothing. Willow"—I glanced toward the front of the RV, then lowered my voice—"got drunk."

"Really? Why?"

"Probably because she was too nervous to talk to her soul mate."

"Her soul mate?" he asked.

I flashed him the pic she sent.

"Who's that?" he asked.

"I just told you."

"And?"

"And what?" I asked.

"Did she talk to him?"

"I don't know. We didn't get that far. You interrupted, nosy."

He took a bite of oatmeal, then picked up one of the other bowls and pointed toward Mom with it.

Back to Willow I texted: *Did you talk to your soul mate, btw?*

I don't remember.

I'll let Ezra know.

Why would you let Ezra know?

He's being his typical nosy self. Speaking of soul mates, Skyler heard you call him my soul mate demon last night. I'm questioning whether or not to forgive you.

He heard me call him that?! I'm sorry!

You are not.

She sent a GIF of a girl laughing. I smiled but the thought of something else she'd said the night before turned my smile into a grimace. *Are the answers to my interview questions really boring?*

No, why? she answered a little too fast.

You said they were last night.

Don't listen to drunk Willow. She obviously lies her face off.

Okay, I won't listen to her.

There was a long pause this time before she answered: *Is it possible you're just saying what you think the interviewer wants to hear? Your answers don't exactly sound like you.*

Good. I didn't want to sound like me. I wanted to sound professional and poised, not like an immature fangirl. *I'm saying things they'll want to know I know. I'm expressing my passion and experience.*

Okay. I'm sure you're right. You know way more about gaming than I do.

Yes, I did, I told myself. I was prepared, more than prepared, for this interview. To her I typed, *Gotta run and make sure my mom and Ezra aren't talking about things they don't want me to hear.*

What do you mean?

I'll explain later.

K

I took a bite of oatmeal, then picked up the bowl and carried it toward the front of the RV. Just as I was about there, with my spoon halfway to my mouth again, Ezra looked back from where he sat in the passenger seat and gave me a quick, stern shake of his head. I paused. Then he flicked his hand in a shooing manner. My brows shot down, but his pleading look was on his face.

Really? I was being left out of the loop again? *I* was the one who suspected something was wrong. No, I wasn't going to be selfish. If he was about to discover something important, I'd let him.

I did an about-face and climbed up into my bunk with my bowl of oatmeal. I sat cross-legged, opened the blinds on the small window, and shut the privacy curtain. Outside, cars on the busy Utah freeway buzzed by. Mom stayed steady in the slow lane.

Texting with Willow reminded me of what Skyler had said about me the night before. I pulled up my Instagram. Post after post was just pics of me with Willow or groups of friends or scenery or food. Did Skyler have a problem with me posting food pics? Did that make me shallow? Sure, I had posted the occasional selfie but that didn't mean I cared more about my reputation than my friends like he had implied. Was my *Instagram* what had him acting cold toward me from day one?

I huffed out a breath. "Way to forget our entire history over a few social media posts."

I started to close out Instagram and then hesitated. Before I thought too much about it, I typed Skyler's name into the search bar and went to his profile. I couldn't find the pics Willow had sent me. Where had she found them? I scrolled back as far as I could on his page. It didn't take me all the way back to when he'd left, but close. Most were pics of the scenery or candid shots of older people who I could tell were just random strangers, captured in an interesting angle or light. "Always an artist," I whispered. I looked in the comments to see they were mostly from me or Austin. It took me a dozen or more posts, representing months of time, until I found another name pop up in the comments section. Was it a stranger or a friend?

Ezra's head appeared at the edge of the curtain. "Are you talking to yourself in here?"

I hit him on the forehead. "So? What did you find out?"

"A whole lot of nothing."

"But I thought you were about to learn something and that's why you shooed me away."

"I thought so, too, but she kept insisting everything is fine."

I stirred around my oatmeal, which was getting harder by the second. "Ezra, I overheard you in Death Valley talking on the phone. You said you wouldn't tell me something. You're really going to keep pretending you don't know something?"

"Let's call Dad," he said.

"Okay." We'd been gone a week and I felt guilty that I'd only sent him a couple texts and a pic of one of my drawings.

"FaceTime him," Ezra said, crawling up into my bed and pulling the curtain closed behind him.

"It's not really a sound barrier," I said, nodding at the curtain.

"Just do it."

I clicked on Dad's name and the phone started ringing.

"Yellow," Dad said, his very dad version of hello. His face filled up the screen.

"Hi, Dad." I waved.

"Oh, look at that, I get both my kids for the price of one. I guess you two aren't killing each other yet?"

Ezra's chin was on my shoulder so we'd both fit in the view. "Hey, Pops. How's it going?"

"Missing you guys. Are you sad you signed up for a three-week trip yet?"

"It's been fun," I said, which was only half true.

"Mom is letting me drive a lot," Ezra said.

"So I've heard."

"Speaking of Mom," Ezra started, and I pinched his side. "Ouch. What?"

I pushed mute. "You're really going to come right out and ask him?"

"Why not?"

"What are you going to ask him?"

"If she's okay."

"I thought you were going to ask him if they were getting a divorce," I whispered.

"Why would I ask him that?"

"Okay, fine. The okay question is good." I unmuted the phone. "Sorry, we're back."

"What was that about?" Dad asked. "You needed a sidebar?"

"Is Mom okay?" Ezra blurted out.

Dad's eyes darted to the ceiling before they were on us again. "Mom is . . . fine. Just give her extra love, okay?"

"Why?" I asked.

"She could use it right now. Look, I have to run, but I promise Mom is going to be fine." He hung up the phone.

"Well that was cryptic," Ezra said.

"And he totally hung up on us."

"So wait, do you think they're getting a divorce?" he asked.

"I don't know, that was just one of my top theories."

"And your other theories?"

"I don't want to think about them." As far as I knew, my mom and dad had a great marriage and Mom was perfectly healthy. "We need more clues."

CHAPTER 17

A BISON WELCOMED US TO YELLOWSTONE NA-
tional Park (thirty-five hundred miles of wilderness sitting on
top of a volcanic hot spot, at least that was what the brochure
we were handed on arrival read). It didn't wave or even glance
our way, but the huge creature sauntered into the road in front
of our RV and stopped, forcing us to come to a halt. I had been
in the passenger seat for the last several hours, giving Mom extra
love but figuring out no extra facts.

Ezra appeared between us, curious why we had stopped.
"Whoa. It's huge."

"It's cool," I said. "But I thought they wandered in packs."

"Packs?" Ezra said.

"Herds?" I asked.

"I think they do," Mom said. "Maybe he's looking for his
friends."

"In the middle of the road?"

"Honk at it," Ezra suggested.

"We were told not to harass the wildlife. This is their home,"
Mom said. "We'll just wait."

"But what about our schedule?" Ezra asked in faux distress.

"You're such a smart aleck."

"I think you meant a different word but I appreciate you censoring your language for Norah's underage ears."

I backhanded Ezra across the stomach as my gentle reminder that we were supposed be giving Mom more love.

Ezra sat on me.

"Get off. You're crushing me." I tried to push his back but it was useless, so I changed up my tactic and hugged him around the waist instead.

He slapped at my hands on his stomach and stood up.

"I win," I said.

He leaned on the dashboard. "How long do you think it's going to stay there?"

"As long as it wants to," Mom said.

I laughed and pulled out my camera, snapping a few pics for Paisley. "Ezra, go out there and try to scare it away. I'll record you."

He moved toward the door as if he thought I was serious.

Mom grabbed hold of his arm. "That is a wild animal. You will not leave this vehicle."

"Mom, it was a joke. We were joking. That thing would eat me for breakfast."

"Okay, good. I thought I'd raised smarter kids than that."

"You didn't," I said.

"Yeah, you did a pretty poor job," Ezra said.

Mom laughed, which felt like a victory.

Somebody in a car in the opposite lane laid on their horn. The bison shifted, facing that car.

"Oh, shiz," Ezra said. "Are we about to see some property damage?" But instead of ramming the tiny Corolla, the bison walked onto the grass on the other side.

"I fear we just had our peak Yellowstone experience too early," I said. "We might as well exit Wyoming and go on to Spokane at this point."

"You do know Yellowstone is the place where geysers spew boiling water four hundred feet in the air, right?" Mom asked.

"I thought we established you didn't raise smart kids," I said.

She smiled. "I've missed your road trip banter."

"Well, don't get used to it," Ezra said. "This is the teen bus and it's been a while since you were one of those."

This time Mom smacked his stomach. He grunted, then laughed.

* * *

"This is the most beautiful place in the world," Paisley said as we set up camp. She threw her arms out and spun in a circle as if the tall pines and blue skies that surrounded us were her doing. Ezra was attaching the water and power, Mom was rechecking ice chests, and I was pulling suitcases out from the side storage. "What took you guys so long?" she asked after her spin.

"A bison crossing," I said.

"What? We missed it!"

"I took some pictures for you," I said.

Skyler emerged from their RV and smiled my way. My stomach fluttered a little. Why did it do that? He did have a really

151

nice smile, despite his punkish comments about my Instagram. "Hey, we thought you guys got lost."

"Nope," I said. "We're here."

"I'm going to go see if this camp has any common spaces."

"Okay."

"Do you want to come?" he asked.

"Do you want me to come?" *Me and my selfish Instagram?*

He seemed surprised by my question. "Yeah."

"I just need to put these suitcases inside," I said.

He walked the space between the RVs and helped me carry them. Once we were done and about to leave our campsite, Paisley came running up between us.

"I'm coming too."

Skyler draped his arm around her neck. "Sure thing."

"Did you draw anything from Park City?" Paisley asked.

"I didn't," I said. I'd been distracted. "It was more a tourist stop."

"I bet you can find a million things to draw here."

"Norah?" The voice came from a campsite we were passing by and I was equal parts surprised and terrified as I turned to see who I could possibly know this far from home.

"Oh no," Paisley said, seeing him a split second before me.

"Ty?"

He walked over to meet us. "We must be on the same RV loop."

"Wow, what a coincidence."

"You never added me back," he said, patting his pocket, where I could see the outline of his phone.

"Sorry, we've been busy. I haven't been on social media much."

"Really? We've had such long stretches on the road, I figure everyone else has too."

"Yeah . . . ," I said, out of excuses.

"We're going to check out the main building," Skyler said, maybe rescuing me from my awkward exchange, maybe not realizing what was going on at all. "Want to join us?"

"Sure, I'll come. They don't have a game room like Zion did but they have a gift shop and stuff."

The main building was a big brown cabin-like structure that housed the laundry, guest services, a conference room, and the gift shop, where we were now. I hadn't gotten Willow any souvenirs yet, so I searched the aisles. I never understood buying souvenirs for a person who didn't go on the trip. It seemed like a smug reminder that they didn't get to go. But whatever, I told her I would, so now I would try to find her something she might actually like or use.

"Do you collect anything on your travels?" Ty asked from beside me. He'd followed me down each row.

"No. You?"

"I used to collect rocks. You know, the ones you can buy in a little stamped velvet bag for like five dollars."

"Yeah, I know what you're talking about. But you stopped?"

"I guess I grew out of it."

"That's a weird saying, isn't it? That we grew out of something? Like we're embarrassed to like something we liked as a child because that means we're immature or something. I don't think we have to grow out of things. Maybe we were our truest selves as children, before we let the expectations of everyone else dictate who we should be."

"Um . . . yeah," Ty said, and I realized I had totally gone off.

"That speech was meant for me," Skyler said from the next row over. "So don't be too offended. You're allowed to stop collecting rocks."

"Stop eavesdropping," I said.

"I think the whole store heard you," he returned.

"Yep," Paisley said from several rows over.

"Well, it's true!" I said.

"How are you two related again?" Ty asked.

"We're not," I said, then picked up a Yellowstone candle. "Do you think this says, *I wish you were able to come to Yellowstone with me. I missed you*?"

"As good as anything else does."

"Do you know what this store really needs?" I said. "A candle that shoots hot wax in the air after you light it. That would really bring the spirit of Yellowstone home." I really said that out loud.

Skyler, obviously still eavesdropping in the next row over, laughed.

"You should suggest that to the candle makers," Ty said with a grin.

"I should. That's a million-dollar idea right there." I carried the candle to the register.

Paisley joined me, holding a pair of bison socks. "More like a million-dollar lawsuit."

"Where did you get those?" I asked.

She pointed to the far wall.

"That's a better gift. I will tell the bison story and Willow actually likes socks."

Skyler was at the register now, too, holding a magnet. Who was he buying a magnet for? Riley? Did Riley have a magnet board with pictures of her and Skyler all over it? Ticket stubs of places they'd gone together?

Stop, I told myself. *Why do I care?*

I went to the sock wall and found a pair of green and brown bison socks. As I was about to turn back, I noticed a rack of beaded friendship bracelets. They didn't look exactly like the one that Skyler had given me, but they had the same feel. They were sold in pairs, of course, like all friendship jewelry was. I found myself taking a blue and silver pair off the hook and carrying it to the register with the socks.

"Are you guys still here tomorrow night?" Ty was asking as I rejoined them.

"I'm not sure," I started to say when Skyler said, "Yes, we are."

"Well, this is random," Ty said, "but we're having this dance thing at our campsite. We came with my aunt's family and we invited a few other people we've met and you all should come."

"A dance thing?" Paisley asked as the woman rang up my purchases. I added a couple Yellowstone postcards that were in a small stand by the register—one had some dramatic canyons surrounded by dark green trees. And another had the famous gushing geyser.

"Yes, I know it sounds lame, but we did it last summer, too, and it's pretty fun. We string up lights and we dress up, or at least as dressed up as we packed, and we turn on some music."

"That's cool," Skyler said. "We'll be there."

"Awesome," Ty said. "Invite the rest of your family too."

"Will do."

* * *

"Will do?" I asked Skyler as we headed back after separating from Ty.

"What?" he said.

"Seriously?" Paisley said. "You're either clueless or doing this on purpose."

I pointed at Paisley. "What she said."

"What? It sounded fun. Something different."

"Okay, clueless," I said.

"That guy likes Norah."

"He doesn't know me," I said. "He just hasn't seen a girl he isn't related to in weeks."

Paisley rolled her eyes. "Whatever the case, he thinks he likes you."

"And?" Skyler said.

"And she doesn't like him back."

"I'm pretty sure Norah is used to that dynamic."

"What?" I asked, more than shocked by his statement. Was he kidding? "No, I'm not."

"Huh. Well, he's throwing a party in the middle of a national park. That seemed like the kind of thing you'd be into."

I narrowed my eyes at him. "What is that supposed to mean?"

He shrugged. "Just a hunch."

Was this the same hunch he'd been using while looking at my Instagram? "Yeah, well, your hunches suck."

* * *

"Do you know why she's called Old Faithful?" Paisley asked the next day as we stood behind wooden barriers ready to see what drew people from all over the world here.

I had my pad out and was sketching the surrounding area of dark green pines and sandy hills, waiting for the main show. "Because she erupts like clockwork or something?"

"She erupts every thirty-five minutes to two hours. I personally don't think something with an hour-and-a-half window should be considered faithful. I mean, if I were an hour and a half late to something, nobody would call me good old faithful."

"Maybe if you were *always* between thirty minutes to an hour and a half late, they would."

Paisley smiled. "True."

Steam had been seeping from the geyser since we got there, like a warning.

Some kid from another group near us said, "Why do we have to be so far away?"

"Because the water is two hundred degrees," an older guy next to him said.

"So," the kid returned.

"So it would boil your skin right off."

"Nice," Paisley said.

"I only like fried skin," Skyler said. "With a little flour and seasoning."

I didn't reward his comment with a laugh this time. I was still irritated with him about the little digs he'd been making at my social life. Wasn't he the one who said we weren't experts on each other's lives anymore?

"Ew," Paisley said.

"Are you vegetarian now?" he asked.

"After that thought, maybe I am."

"Bacon," Austin said. "The only thing keeping me from becoming full-on vegetarian."

"Really?" I said. "The only thing?"

"That and steak."

A low murmur from the crowd drew my attention to the geyser, where steamy water was slowly bubbling up. A foot at first, then five, building and building until it shot in the air at least a hundred feet. At this, the crowd let out a cheer.

"That's pretty awesome," Ezra said.

"See." Mom patted his cheek. "I can still show you new things once in a while."

"Are you taking credit for Yellowstone?" I asked.

"I'm taking credit for *bringing* you to Yellowstone," she said.

Me and Ezra exchanged a look. One that said, *Were we just imagining it?* Because Mom seemed perfectly fine now.

"What's this I hear about a dance tonight?" Olivia asked.

"Blame Skyler for that," I said.

CHAPTER 18

I SAT ON THE FLOOR NEXT TO MY SUITCASE, STUDY-ing each outfit I'd brought. I had not packed for a dance in the middle of an RV park in the middle of Wyoming. Actually, not the *middle* of Wyoming. Kind of on the edge of Wyoming, if I remembered the map right, but whatever part of Wyoming we were in, I did not think there was going to be dancing.

Ezra was ready and waiting outside but my mom was in her bed reading a book.

"What do you think about this one?" I asked Mom.

She laid her open book on her chest. "Might be kind of cold for a sundress once the sun goes down."

"The only other thing I brought is T-shirts, jeans, and shorts. And my interview outfit, but Willow says it looks like some-thing a librarian would wear, so I don't think it would work for a dance."

"The librarian I know wears T-shirts and jeans. Her T-shirts say the funniest things on them too. *Book this. My schedule is booked up. The book was better.*" Mom, who'd been looking up while trying to recall the snarky T-shirts, returned her attention to me. I was still holding up the dress. "I'm sorry, yes, wear the sundress. It's cute. Or wear a paper bag if you want, you'd be cute in whatever."

"Why do parents say stuff like that? Nobody would be cute in a paper bag. So now I question whether or not your sundress opinion is valid."

She smiled and threw something at me that hit my arm and landed in my open suitcase. It was a hair tie.

I picked it up and twisted it and untwisted it around my finger a few times. "You tired? It's only seven."

"No, just reading." She showed me her book.

"What are you and Olivia going to do while we're gone?"

"Maybe we'll walk around or turn in early. I'm not sure."

"Are you fighting with her?" I didn't know why I asked that. I hadn't seen signs of it. But maybe she and Olivia were having the same issues as me and Skyler—time away had put a strain on things—and that's what was bothering her.

"With Olivia?" She laughed. "No, of course not."

Now I felt stupid for asking. *Of course not.* That was only my problem. "Okay, good." I held my sundress up to my body and my eyes caught on something in the corner of my suitcase. Another note. I unfolded it. This was a picture of mountains and two stick figures climbing one of the peaks together. *It's the climb.* We used to say that whenever something silly happened: like they were out of the taco we wanted at the food truck on campus or the size shirt we wanted when we were shopping.

I smiled and tucked it back into my suitcase. That's when I saw something else. The friendship bracelet from Skyler. Maybe its best friend juju could work some magic. Trying not to think about it too hard, I slipped it on my wrist, then went to the bathroom to change.

* * *

I didn't know how everyone else felt, but I felt awkward walking through camp, hair done, makeup on, in a dress. I should've just worn jeans and a tee. Too bad I didn't have a snarky tee. One that said *I'd rather be reading* or *I almost wore a sundress. How stupid would that have been?*

"Should we have a code word for if we want to leave?" Ezra asked. He was in a polo shirt, dark jeans, and Converse, which was similar to what both Austin and Skyler were wearing.

"That is the main reason cell phones were invented," Paisley said. She must've known to pack for a just-in-case party because she looked adorable in a skirt and long-sleeved striped sweater. "Someone wanted to leave a party early."

"In case one of the party throwers is too close to covertly text about our boredom," Ezra said.

"Ezra likes to read people's texts," I said from where Paisley and I were walking arm in arm in front of the guys. "But, yes, let's make a secret word."

"It needs to be something that can be said naturally in a sentence," Paisley said.

"Bighorns?" Skyler said.

161

I twisted the bracelet on my wrist. He'd said that for me, I was sure. He probably sensed my irritation.

"What's that supposed to mean?" Austin said. "Is that dirty?"

"No!" Skyler said.

"How would that be dirty?" I asked.

"More importantly," Paisley said, "how are we supposed to use that naturally in a sentence?"

"Be creative," Skyler returned.

We saw the lights up ahead and as we walked closer, the music drifted through the air. We arrived at the outskirts of the dance and fell silent. There were more people than I anticipated. Ty and his family, who I recognized from my tube-crashing incident on the river. Then there were at least a dozen other people I didn't recognize at all.

Ty saw us and a smile took over his face. He sidestepped around a few people and walked over to greet us. "I thought you might stand me up again," he said to me.

"No . . ." I didn't remember standing him up a first time, so I wasn't sure what else to say.

"Well, come in." And by *in*, he meant the circle of grass and dirt bordered by three RVs. "There are drinks in that big metal bin over there and snacks on the table across the way."

"Nice," Paisley said, making a beeline for the drinks.

"Come on. Let's dance," Ty said to me.

"Oh." Right, this was an actual dance, even though nobody was really dancing; they were all just standing around talking.

Ty must've noticed my gaze because he said, "Someone has to be the first."

I nodded. "Sure, let's go."

The song was a fast one, which I was happy about. As Ty led the way to the middle of the grass area, I glanced over my shoulder. "Guys! Dancing is happening now."

Ezra just smiled and pretended not to understand me. I pretended to flip him off by holding my fist in the air. Austin laughed. Was it too early to yell, *Hey, is that Bighorns?*

"You look nice," Ty said.

"Thank you. I was trying to decide between this and a paper bag. I was told I'd look the same in either."

"What?"

I shook my head. "Nothing."

"Where are you all headed next?" Ty asked as we started dancing.

"Spokane."

"We really are on the same route."

"Oh yeah? That's where you're going too?"

"Yes. Portland after that?"

"No, Seattle. I have a school tour."

"Oh, cool. Which school?"

"I'm sure you've never heard of it. It's a small video game and graphic design school." When I was only met with a blank stare, I added, "They don't have the capacity for tons of admissions every year, so I requested an in-person meeting. I figured it could only help." Unless my answers ended up being super boring and I dressed like a librarian (not the cool librarians with the funny T-shirts but the movie librarians who were always shushing people).

"You want to make video games?"

"I do." Then, remembering how he had implied girls weren't good at video games, I said, "Even though I'm full of lady parts."

"No, I . . . It's . . . ," he stuttered. "I'm sure you'll do great."

I laughed. "I'm just joking with you. I often don't think before I speak. I'm getting worse on this trip, it seems." My eyes shot to the food table, where the rest of our group was filling up plates and talking. Skyler appeared to be biting a cracker into different shapes and holding up the results for Paisley, who was not humoring him at all. I turned my attention back to Ty. "What about you? What do you want to do with your life? Rock collecting?"

"No, I grew out of that, remember?"

"That's right."

"I think I want to be a nurse or a doctor."

"Cool." As we stepped back and forth to the beat, I looked up at the lights they had strung between the RVs. This really was pretty awesome. "It's fun that your family does this."

"Yes, they are fun."

"What's your favorite thing from your route so far?" I asked.

"This is top three for sure."

I smiled. "Okay, kiss-up. What are the other two?"

"Old Faithful was amazing. And I liked Arches National Park a little better than Zion. Did you stop there?"

"No, we did Park City in between Zion and here."

"How was Park City?"

"Nice."

"Obviously not in your top three so far."

"We saw a bison yesterday. It's going to be hard to top that. It almost charged a Corolla."

"It did?"

"Not really, but it definitely gave it a dirty look."

He laughed.

"*Frogger*!" I blurted out. "Bison and tiny cars."

"What?" Ty asked, understandably confused.

"Sorry, I've been trying to think of a good spin-off of *Frogger* for days now. Would you rather be a bison who has to destroy cars to cross a highway? Or would you rather play the tiny car that has to avoid bison while crossing a highway?"

The song ended and a slow one took its place. Ty took a hesitant step forward.

"A bison for sure," Skyler said, suddenly at my side. "Is that even a debate?"

I imagined the design. "The visual of a lot of bison and only one car on the road might be a better visual than the opposite, though," I said.

"Cars are colorful—they'd make the better moving backdrop. The bison would make the better main character."

"Are you going into video game design too?" Ty asked Skyler.

"No, but do you know how many games this girl has forced me to play over my lifetime?"

"You've known each other for a lifetime?"

"Most of it." Then to me he asked, "Do you want to dance?"

"I . . ." I looked around and saw that others were dancing now, the slow song still playing. Even Paisley was dancing with a guy who looked like a kid. He was at least a head shorter than her. She mouthed "Bighorns" to me several times but I could tell she was kidding.

Skyler raised an eyebrow at Ty. "I'm just going to . . ." He stepped closer to me.

"Yeah, of course," Ty said, backing away and then joining a group by some camping chairs.

"I figured since I was the one who didn't pick up on obvious signs earlier that I would save you from a slow dance."

Right. He was only doing it because he felt guilty. "It would've been fine. Ty is nice."

"So you like him now?"

"I don't really know him."

We seemed to both realize we were just standing there talking and not dancing at the same exact moment. He put his arms out to the sides and I stepped forward.

"Where do . . ."

I directed his hands to my waist and put mine on his shoulders. "Have you never slow-danced before?"

"No, actually. I haven't been to a dance."

"Really? You're just over there in Ohio breaking girls' hearts, then." I looked at his light brown eyes, which were soft and friendly.

"You know me."

"I think you've told me at least twice now that I don't anymore."

"Bronze level has to count for something," he said, and a smile forced its way onto my face despite me trying to stay annoyed.

Even though he claimed to have never danced before, he

knew the basics. He swayed back and forth to the beat, turning me slowly in the process. He smelled good, like musky soap and cherry ChapStick, and my insides flip-flopped. Why did they keep doing that? My cheek brushed his shoulder and I realized how close we'd gotten.

My chest felt hot and my feet felt heavy.

"Who's Riley?" I heard myself spit out.

"Have you been looking at my phone?"

"You were showing me pics. So yes." Had he forgotten that was when I'd seen the text?

He smiled. "Just a friend."

"Does she like the lake?"

"*He* plays on a community rugby team with me."

Why was I so relieved by that? It didn't matter if he had a girlfriend or not. "Excuse me? Rugby? Since when?"

"Just started this year."

I reached up and playfully put a hand on each of his temples. "Are you trying to bash your beautiful skull in?"

"You sound like my mother."

"Well, your mother is smart." My hands returned to his shoulders by taking a roundabout path down the back of his neck. A shiver went through him. Goose bumps formed on my arms at his reaction and my cheeks heated. What was wrong with me? I cleared my throat. "Is that why you run now?" I'd seen him run a few more times at our various stops.

"To bash my skull in?"

"To get in shape for rugby."

"No, running was first. Rugby was second."

"You couldn't pay me to run," I said.

167

"It's a good head clearer."

A head clearer? Why does he need to clear his head?

We circled a couple more times in silence. "I didn't force you to play video games," I said.

He let out a single laugh. "Yes, you did."

"You didn't like them?"

"I liked them."

"Then you need to rethink your definition of *force*."

"Fine, I knew that if I wanted to hang out with you, I had to play video games."

"*Had* to? That's just as bad as force."

He smiled. "The bison game? Was that his unexpected question?"

"What?"

"Was that the answer to a question you *forced* Ty to ask you?"

I gasped and shoved his chest. He laughed and his grip shifted on my waist, sending a tingle up my spine.

I swallowed. "No. That wasn't the answer to a question. You think I'd say that in my interview? Do you want to be a bison or a car, Dean Collins?"

"Why not?" he asked. "It's funny. More you."

"More me than what? My other answers?"

"No . . . sort of. You should sound prepared, but you can probably relax a little more, say how you're feeling, not what you think she wants to hear."

"That's how most things in life work, Skyler. We say what we think people want to hear."

"Like your Instagram."

And here it was. Good. We needed to hash this out. "What do you mean, like my Instagram?"

"Nothing. Never mind, just forget I said that."

"I can't forget you said it. Explain it to me."

"It just doesn't feel real."

"You're saying I'm fake? My answers are fake, my Instagram is fake. My friends are fake."

"I'm saying you're *not* fake, but looking at your page makes it seem like you are."

"Why? Because I post a few selfies?"

"I'm just surprised at who you're hanging out with these days."

"You know my friends?"

"Some of them. I did grow up there, Norah. I know that crowd." His voice was full of judgment.

"They're nice, Skyler. We take care of each other. You saw how Leena rescued Willow the other night."

"From being drunk . . ."

Why was he making me feel like I had become the worst kind of person? "I don't get drunk if that's what you're saying. And neither does Willow. It was an accident."

"She accidently got drunk?"

"Why are you being such a judgmental jerk?"

"Because those people aren't you. Those captions you write with each post that say nothing at all, they aren't you."

"Maybe they are me now."

"That's what I'm worried about."

I took a step back, but he matched my step, holding on to me.

"Don't be mad," he said.

"What am I supposed to be? Happy? Maybe you're the one who's fake. You stopped drawing, Skyler. And you say I don't know you anymore but you refuse to share anything real with me."

"Maybe I have trust issues."

"You're the one who left," I snapped. "You packed up and took away my whole life, my entire heart. Those first few months felt like drowning. Meeting Willow was the first time I could breathe again. So I'm sorry if you just wanted me to sit there and drown without you and I didn't. I'm sorry if you don't approve of my life rafts. They're my friends. And being popular isn't a character flaw, last I checked."

I twisted out of his grip and left the way we'd come. I made my way past people sitting in front of their RVs eating meals, and people walking the path to the main building and the big brick bathhouse in the middle of the property, until I got to our campsite.

CHAPTER 19

AS I PASSED ONE RV, MY EYES FOCUSED ON THE other, I heard the moms talking inside the rental. I slowed, then paused at the door, pressing my ear against the glass.

"We can tell the kids that we need to ride in our separate RVs again," Mom said.

"They seem to be enjoying themselves," Olivia responded.

Why did the moms want to separate us? Had something happened? Had I been right about my mom and Olivia fighting? What were they fighting about?

"And besides," Olivia continued, "Skyler and Norah are finally getting along."

No, we really aren't.

There was a long pause. "It's nice to see the kids together again, isn't it?" Mom said.

"This won't be the last time," Olivia said.

"No, of course not. I didn't mean to make it sound that way."

"I know. Sometimes it feels that way, though."

"Don't think like that."

"You'll come my way next?" Olivia said.

"Yes, as soon as I can." There was some shuffling inside and it seemed like one or both of them were moving, possibly about to discover me.

I stumbled back and away from the door. I wasn't sure what I just overheard, but it did nothing to ease my worry. Why were they talking like the world was ending?

The distance between the two RVs wasn't more than thirty feet, but it seemed to take forever to cross it, as I was trying to be both fast and quiet. I reached the door, let myself in, and pressed my back against the wall. I stood very still and listened for my mom. Everything was quiet. My eyes drifted to the back room that was open. After several more long moments, I glanced once over my shoulder, then tiptoed toward it. I flipped on the main room light switch but when I got to her room, I left the light off. I didn't want her seeing it through the windows.

Her suitcase sat on the bed. I bit my lip. I really wasn't a snooper, but this felt really important and she refused to tell us anything. I opened the lid before I talked myself out of it. Her clothes were all folded neatly and tucked beneath the elastic strap. In the top, behind the zippered mesh section, was her toiletries bag. The zipper sounded like it was opening through a megaphone as I pulled it along its track. Once open, I retrieved the bag and plopped it on top of the clothes. I stared at it forever before opening it. And then I stared at the contents before I blew out a breath and went digging. Past the shampoo bottles and razor, cotton balls, face wash, night cream, lip balm, my fingers hit the plastic bottom. I felt all around, shifting everything multiple times, but only found a bottle of melatonin. Nothing incriminating about that.

I put my hands on my hips and stared at the rest of the unassuming suitcase. I felt around in the corners, opened zippered pouches, and— The outside handle on the door rattled. I gasped, shut the suitcase without zippering up all the zippers, and flew out of her room. I climbed up into my bed and yanked the curtain shut just as the door opened.

"Hello," Mom called out. "Is someone in here?"

I sat, my heart beating in my ears, trying to decide which response might make her leave: me being in here or me not being in here.

"I know someone is in here," she said, making my decision for me. "I didn't leave the lights on."

"It's just me, Mom. Sorry, I had my earbuds in." I peeked my head out of the curtain.

"Oh, hi. How was the dance? Are you already back?"

"It was fine. You were right, I was cold."

"I have a cardigan that would look nice with your sundress if you want to—"

"No," I interrupted as she walked toward her room. "I'm fine. I was done anyway."

She stopped. "Okay." She changed her route and went to the fridge instead, where she pulled out a bottle of wine. She held it up, pointed to the door with it, then said, "You good?"

"Yes, of course. Go drink the whole thing with your friend." I sucked in my cheeks. *Stop acting weird, Norah.*

"You make it sound so irresponsible," she said.

"No, sorry. I'm not sure how to wish someone well when they are going to drink in an RV."

She laughed and shook her head. "You're such a character."

"Thank you?"

"Believe me, it's a compliment."

Was it, though? I nodded and she left. I waited several minutes before I slid off my bunk and put her suitcase back together, having discovered nothing from my sleuthing.

Back in my bunk, I hugged my pillow against my chest, exposing the notebook. I wanted to chuck it out the window but instead I picked it up and opened it.

I read through several entries until I came to one that triggered a memory I couldn't quite fully form. It was a Skyler entry. First he'd drawn an angry eye at the top of the page. I ran my finger around it, then read the words he'd written.

Remember the guy I've been telling you about in PE? The horrible one? He made up a stupid nickname for me today. I don't even care what he thinks about me but I still let it get to me. I finally said something back. It was dumb. Now I'm sure he'll never leave me alone. I wish I could learn to keep things inside sometimes.

"You seemed to have learned that really well lately," I said to the notebook. "Keeping everything inside." I kept reading.

If you had to choose no friends at all or friends that were horrible people, what would you choose?

And then it came to me: the memory. It must've happened after this notebook entry, although I wasn't sure how much time had passed. We were in the seventh grade sitting outside by the bleachers at lunch.

"Did you pack extra chips for me?" I had asked. My mom always packed healthy snacks like granola with raisins or rice cakes in my lunch. His mom gave him the good snacks.

"Of course." He handed me a bag of Doritos.

"You're the best!"

"Yes, I am."

As I pulled open the bag, a group of guys walked by us. I didn't recognize any of them, so I assumed they were older kids. One of them chucked an apple core our way and it hit Skyler on the leg. They all laughed.

"Nice catch, Nut Hut!" someone from the group yelled, and they kept walking.

"Jerks!" I picked up the apple and threw it back but it fell short of hitting anyone. I let out a huff and turned back to Skyler. "Who are they?"

"Some eighth graders from my PE class."

"Well, they're stupid."

"I thought if I was nice first they'd be nice back."

"Yeah, right. They're probably mad that you do your own thing and don't fall at their feet." I put my hand on his arm. "Always do your own thing."

He gave me a half smile. "What thing is that?"

"You know, art and reading and being a total goof. Who cares what they think."

"You need to work on your apple-throwing skills," he said.

I laughed. "I will. Then next time that punk comes around, I'll be ready."

The nickname *that punk* had yelled out weighed heavy on my mind as I clutched the notebook in my hands. I had never put two and two together until this moment. Maybe I was wrong . . . but if I was right . . .

"Frick." I picked up my phone and clicked on Willow's name. It rang several times before she answered.

"I thought you were at some redneck dance tonight."

"I think Dylan was one of Skyler's bullies" was how I responded.

"What?"

"My ex-boyfriend used to pick on my ex–best friend and I didn't remember it until tonight."

"You *forgot* that?"

"I remembered that kids used to pick on Skyler. He was a loner and used to just sit and draw a lot and give certain people dirty looks when they'd try to talk to him."

"You're saying he deserved it?"

"No! Not at all. I really thought it was a few kids who said a few mean things. Skyler never mentioned anyone by name and always acted so tough about it. I didn't think it bothered him that much. I didn't know one of those kids was Dylan! I didn't even know Dylan then."

"You dated your best friend's enemy. No wonder Skyler hates you. And you thought it was because he suspected you were in love with him. How cute."

"Not funny!"

"Did Skyler stop talking to you around the time you started dating Dylan?"

"I don't know. We'd been drifting apart for a while, but maybe . . ."

"Who sent the last message?" she asked.

"I don't remember. Hold on." I took my phone away from my ear and pulled up my DMs, the main way we had communicated. I scrolled and scrolled until I found Skyler, then clicked on his name. My eyes scanned the last message, which was from two years ago. From him.

"Oh no . . . ," I said.

"What?" Willow's voice rang out from the speaker.

"He said, 'Hey, Norah, I miss you. You think your mom would ever let you come visit?'"

"Okay," Willow said. "And your response was?"

"Nothing. My response was nothing, Willow. I read it and didn't respond. I remember thinking that I'd ask my mom first and see what she thought. I remember being super disappointed when she said no. But I didn't tell him that! Instead I forgot to respond at all!"

"Wow."

I groaned and put my hand to my forehead. "And I had just started dating Dylan at that time. That has to be why Skyler thought I didn't answer. I'm an awful person. Of course he has trust issues."

"Well good, that mystery is solved. You're the demon. Do you have one horn or two?"

I groaned again and took the phone off speaker, pressing it to my ear.

"Listen, babe," she said in a sincere voice. "This is all just a big misunderstanding. Talk to him about it. Clear it up. It will be fine."

"I would but I just got through calling him a judgmental jerk, so there's that."

"Why did you do that?"

"Because he was acting like one, but I didn't realize the history of his opinion. It makes sense now. Of course he hates my friends. Of course he thinks I've turned into a mean girl. I dated one of his tormenters and then started ignoring him!"

"He hates me?"

"He would love you if he knew you."

"Good answer. But seriously, just explain it to him. And it sounds like you were already drifting apart before the whole Dylan thing."

"We were."

"So hopefully he'll understand."

"I hope."

"Good luck."

"Thanks, I'll probably need it."

We hung up. As I stared at the closed blinds next to my bed, my phone buzzed in my hands. A picture came onto my screen. It was another picture of Skyler and me, a little older, that Willow must've taken from the scrapbook. It was from right before he left. We were sitting on the couch in my living room. He was looking at the camera and I was looking at him. My eyes were happy and something about looking at the picture now made my chest ache.

The picture was followed by a message from Willow: *I know I'd forgive anyone who looked at me like that.*

I smiled. She was right. We had too much history to let this misunderstanding come between us. *You're the best.*

True. Also, study that pic. You can no longer deny that your thirteen-year-old self wanted to kiss his face off.

My heart seemed to take up residence in my ears as it thumped three times as loud as normal. I zoomed in on the picture, my dreamy eyes, my smile. No, she was wrong. I may have loved Skyler with all my best friend heart back then, but I hadn't wanted to kiss him.

No, I didn't, I texted back.

My heart kept thumping in my ears as I slid my finger across the screen until Skyler's magnified face came into view. His light brown eyes crinkled at the corners, his expression happy. No, I hadn't wanted to kiss him back then.

But maybe I do now.

I knew it!! Go get your mannnn!

I dropped my phone on the mattress and covered my eyes with my hands. Why did I have to make this complicated?

One thing at a time. First, I needed to clear things up, get our friendship back on track; then I'd sort out those other things. I was not going to ruin my childhood friendship over messy feelings.

CHAPTER 20

BEFORE I FACED SKYLER, I NEEDED TO WALK, WORK off some of the nervous energy now coursing through me, make sure my newly discovered feelings weren't written all over my face. Because despite what I'd discovered about Dylan, I hadn't forgotten what Paisley had implied at the beginning of our trip. That Skyler was horrified at the thought of me liking him.

I stepped down into the cold air and headed aimlessly into the night, twisting and twisting the bracelet on my wrist. Skyler had been my best friend. He had to forgive me for hurting him.

I had hurt him.

That thought made my insides clench and my stomach ache.

I wasn't sure how long I walked or where I walked or even what I thought about. But as our RV came into view again down the path, I realized I was shivering from the cold.

"There you are." Skyler was walking toward me. He'd pulled a sweatshirt on, which meant he'd been back to the RV.

"Hi," I whispered through my chattering teeth.

"I'm sorry I was a jerk." He was using his phone as a flash-light and it created a perfect circle of light around our shoes when he stopped in front of me.

"No," I said.

"Have you been out here this whole time?"

"Yes."

"I'm sorry," he said again. "I didn't know it was so hard for you when I left."

"It was Dylan, wasn't it?"

"What?"

I rubbed my arms and looked over at the lantern of a neigh-boring campsite. Insects zipped in and out of its glow. "He was one of those guys in middle school who picked on you all the time."

"You're freezing, Norah. Let's go inside."

"I can't right now. You need to tell me. Was Dylan one of those guys?"

He nodded. "Yes, now come on."

"No, wait. I need to say I'm sorry."

"You said it." He pulled off his sweatshirt and handed it to me.

"No, I haven't yet."

He smiled. "Okay, say it, then."

"I'm so sorry. I didn't know him back then, so I didn't re-member."

"It's okay."

"No, it's not. I should've been more observant at the time and I definitely should've at least remembered. Even if I didn't remember, I should've seen the kind of person he was. Love is blind, I guess."

"You *loved* him?"

"No, I didn't. Not at all. But I was caught up in liking him enough to overlook his flaws."

He studied my face. "I understand."

"No, you can't understand yet. There's more."

His eyebrows popped up in amusement.

"I didn't answer your DM about coming to visit. I thought I had. I meant to. My mom said I couldn't and I was sad about that. And I thought I answered it."

"Can I say I understand now?"

I nodded.

"Because I do," he said.

"I don't want to fight anymore. I want to be friends again."

He took the sweatshirt I was still gripping in my hand and pulled it over my head. I snaked my arms into the still-warm sleeves.

"It was hard for me when I left too," he said. "You are like sunshine Norah." He brushed a piece of hair off my temple. "You radiate positive energy, and when that was out of my life, I was in a dark place. It took me a long time to come out of that. And the thought of coming back here, of remembering what it felt like to have you in my life every day only to have to leave again was a hard thought."

His speech made me realize even more that I couldn't tell him how I felt. Why would I throw that out there when we only had two more weeks together? When we were leaving each other again. "That's why you didn't want to be here?"

He nodded.

"Not because of Dylan?"

"Well, the Dylan thing and you not responding to my message is what made me think you wouldn't care if I was distant."

I swallowed down the lump in my throat. "So you weren't distant because you thought I was in love with you?"

"No, I . . . Wait, what?"

"Your sister told me. She told me that she heard you tell Austin that I had a crush on you."

He let out a half laugh, half sigh. "No, Austin was being stupid. *He* said that you had a crush on me. *He* said I shouldn't lead you on. She must not have stuck around for the part where I told him he was wrong."

"I never had a crush on you."

He raised one hand like he was taking an oath. "I know."

"You were my best friend," I said. "And I just want to be friends again."

"Norah, we are friends," he said. "We've been friends our whole lives."

"I know."

"Why are you crying, then?"

I wiped at my eyes, which were now leaking unwanted tears. "Because I'm glad we're okay."

"These are happy tears? Not mad tears?"

I nodded and his brow went down like he didn't believe me. And he shouldn't believe me. Even though I was happy we were okay, I knew how devastated I'd be in a couple weeks when he left again.

I reached out and took his hands in mine.

"Your fingers are like icicles." He brought my hands up to his warm neck and placed them there, covering them with his.

My breathing slowed, my stomach fluttered, and my eyes shot to his lips. My brain screamed, *No!*

"How did you remember about Dylan, anyway?" he asked.

"The notebook," I said. "Tonight I read the entry where you mentioned someone making up a nickname for you."

"I mentioned that in the notebook? I'm disappointed in my past self for giving him page time."

"No, I'm glad you did. I just wished I'd reread the thing a couple years ago."

"Would it have changed things?"

"Yes."

"I want to read the notebook too. I'm sure there are a ton of things I forgot."

"Okay."

"We'll read it together?"

"Yes, let's."

"Hey, Norah?" His hands, which were still covering mine on his neck, moved to circle my wrists.

"What?"

His grip on my left wrist tightened; then his brows went down in confusion. He brought my arm in front of him and pulled up the sleeve of the sweatshirt, revealing the friendship bracelet. His mouth opened slightly in surprise. "You still have this?"

I nodded. "Of course."

He smiled and my stomach did that weird flippy thing again.

Skyler had an amazing smile. He let go of my hand and I lowered the other one from his neck. They were warm now, and being this close to him was not helping.

"Thanks for talking," I said. "We should probably . . ." I looked toward the RVs.

"We're good?" he asked.

"Yes, we're fine, Skyler. Everything is going to be fine."

He surprised me by pulling me into a hug. His neck was warm and his arms applied just the right amount of pressure on my back. I had forgotten what a good hugger he was.

"I've missed you," he said.

I willed myself not to cry again as I sunk into him. "I've missed you too." I held on tight.

"You feel better?" he asked.

I nodded against him.

"See," he said. "I remember my thing."

CHAPTER 21

"WHY DON'T WE DRIVE IN OUR OWN RVS AGAIN this leg," Mom said casually at breakfast the next morning, reminding me of the conversation she'd had with Olivia the night before. The syrup I'd been pouring on my pancakes slowed to a drip as my hand dropped slightly.

"What?" Ezra said. "Why would we do that?"

"No!" Paisley exclaimed, shaking her fork in Mom's direction.

Skyler didn't say anything, just exchanged a curious look with me. I'd slept in his sweatshirt the night before, not really a good step toward stomping out any unwanted feelings. The opposite, in fact, it smelled so much like him that he made an appearance in every dream I'd had.

"It's not a bad idea," Olivia said.

"Booooo!" Austin chimed in.

"It was just a thought," Olivia said. "We won't ruin all the fun. Plus, it's kind of nice being in control of the radio for the first time in years."

Despite their efforts, after breakfast, cleanup, and a bit more sightseeing we separated into mom and teen RVs once again. And once again, my suspicions were on high alert.

"What do you think all the talk at breakfast about driving in separate RVs was about?" Skyler said, sitting next to me on the couch as we left Yellowstone.

I looked up from my sketch pad. "I was wondering the same."

He playfully squeezed my knee.

I yelped and pulled my leg out of his reach.

"Is this what you were talking about the other day?" Paisley asked from where she sat at the table.

"What were you talking about the other day?" Skyler asked.

"Her mom is acting strange. Something is up."

"Strange how?" Skyler asked.

"I overheard our moms talking last night. They made it seem like they weren't going to see each other for a while after this trip."

He bit his bottom lip. "Is that weird, though? They hadn't seen each other in four years before this."

"Yeah, you're right . . ."

"But?"

"But that's just one thing that has felt off." I summarized the other things that had happened on the trip so far. And finished with their conversation from the night before.

I couldn't shake the suspicion about our parents that I'd told Ezra, and the thought of divorce scared me. Could two people who seemed perfectly happy with each other drop a surprise bomb like that?

As if Skyler could read my mind, he said, "Don't worry about specifics until you have to."

"Yeah, you're right."

"I didn't find anything on our end, by the way," Paisley said. "I looked everywhere."

"Paisley!" Skyler scolded. "You've been going through Mom's stuff?"

"Well, yeah. Why wouldn't I?"

He shook his head in disappointment.

I raised my hand. "I went through my mom's stuff too."

Paisley laughed.

"Not cool," Skyler said.

"Well, maybe people shouldn't keep important secrets," I said.

"Exactly," Paisley agreed.

"Not a good enough excuse," Skyler said, standing up and stretching his arms in the air. "Speaking of uncovering secrets. Where is our notebook?" He started walking toward my bunk.

"I'll get it," I said, remembering his sweatshirt on my pillow.

"I got it," he said, a smirk on his face letting me know he suspected I didn't want him to.

I sprang off the couch after him but he had already been halfway there so he beat me. He threw back the curtain and his eyes scanned my bed, but he obviously found nothing suspicious about his sweatshirt sitting there because he turned and said, "I don't see it."

I sidled up next to him, stood on the lower bunk to boost myself higher, and reached under my pillow and to the far back corner. "You'll be very disappointed to see that we didn't write down tons of secrets in here. Although, I've only read a handful of entries. Maybe I haven't gotten to all your secrets."

He raised his eyebrows and took the book back to the couch. I joined him there, sitting close so I could read over his shoulder.

He turned back the cover and quietly read through the first entry.

* * *

It was way more fun reading the book with Skyler. We'd been laughing and talking about every entry for the last several hours.

"We were so obnoxious," he said after reading several entries about how we kept moving Ezra's phone charger to different places around the house. We would write in detail about how Ezra had reacted.

"He swore he was going to set up video cameras to prove he wasn't the one losing it," I read out loud, and laughed.

"Don't get any ideas, Paisley," Skyler said, but then put his finger to his lips. I turned and saw that Paisley had fallen asleep on my mom's bed. He closed the notebook and set it aside. "We'll read more later."

I was sitting sideways on the couch, my elbow on the back, practically resting on Skyler's shoulder. Now, without the notebook as an excuse, it felt intimate. As if that thought was written all over my face, Skyler met my eyes. My breath caught in my throat and I averted my gaze to the window. Yellow hills dotted with bright green pines greeted me as we drove through the mountains of Montana. A creek ran along the highway. "We had some good times."

"We did."

I shifted the bracelet on my wrist and then remembered

something. I stood and went to my bunk again and to the little shelf where I had stored the new set of friendship bracelets. I untwisted the tie that was holding them in place, then carried one back over to the couch. "I bought something for you in Yellowstone."

"You bought me a *wish you were here* gift? Is it because you were pretending I wasn't there?"

"Pretty much," I said. I held up the bracelet.

"I thought you bought those for Willow."

"No, I bought it because it looks like the one you gave me and a friendship bracelet isn't a friendship bracelet without a match."

He lifted his arm and I sat next to him again and slid the bracelet on. I let my fingers glide along the beads, unable to avoid brushing his skin in the process.

He smiled. "I was going to steal the other half of yours from my grandma's old best friend, but I guess this works."

"You were not."

"I was not," he agreed, and put his bracelet next to mine. They really didn't match, but they had a similar feel. "So you're saying we now have official best friend powers?"

I tapped my bracelet against his several times. "Yes."

"What do they consist of?"

"The power of inside jokes and being able to read each other's minds and, of course, backup power."

"Backup power?" he asked.

"You know, the thing where you have to back up your best friend in public even if they're doing something you disagree with."

190

"And then later in private you tell them how stupid they were being?"

"Yes, exactly."

He turned his hand, which was still next to mine, palm up. "I can agree to this contract."

I placed my hand on top of his. "Good, then it's official."

He wrapped his fingers around mine and our eyes collided again. My cheeks prickled and I took my hand back just as my phone buzzed on my lap.

Did you tell him? How did it go??

The text was from Willow. I quickly turned my phone face-down.

"Willow?" Skyler asked. I wasn't sure if he'd seen the text or was just guessing.

"Um, yeah." My gaze went back to him. "Is Riley your Willow?"

His eyes lit up. "Is he your replacement, you mean? He's a good friend, yes."

I pushed the button on the side of my phone a couple times. "She wasn't a replacement you."

"What?"

"Willow. She's my best friend but she didn't replace you. Nobody could've done that."

His eyes were intense and seemed to look right into me.

Did I really just say that? "I mean, we've known each other our whole lives. There's something about a childhood friend that feels different. Maybe it's because we knew everything about each other. Maybe it's because when we were together we didn't worry about image or acceptance or saying the perfect

thing in the perfect way. I don't know, it just feels different . . .
felt different . . ."

He bit his lip. "Norah, I—"

The RV jerked, cutting him off mid-sentence.

"What was that!" I called out to Ezra.

"I don't know. I didn't do anything."

The engine sounded weird. Like it was struggling up a hill.

"Who let the moms plan a leg from Yellowstone to Spokane without an overnight stop in the middle anyway?" Ezra said.

"If you're tired of driving, I'm sure Mom would switch with you!"

"Stop being such a traitor!" he yelled.

In all the noise, Paisley sat up and groaned. She walked over to the window to investigate. "What's going on?"

"Nothing," I started to say when the RV jerked again, sending Skyler into my side and Paisley stumbling forward until she caught herself on the captain's chair. This time Ezra slowed and steered onto the shoulder of the road just in time for the engine to start smoking. He turned the key, powering it off.

"Sorry," Skyler said, and I quickly released him, realizing I had grabbed hold of his shoulders when he flew into me. "Did I hurt you?"

"No. I'm okay." If I didn't count the embarrassment I felt at the confessional I'd given moments before. *Did I really tell him nobody could replace him?*

"Is it on fire?" Paisley asked. "Do we need to evacuate?"

"There aren't any flames," I said.

Austin and Ezra rushed out the door as if they would somehow know what a smoking engine meant. I went to find the fire extinguisher, just in case.

Out the front window, there was no sign of the rental RV. "Where did the moms go?" I asked, twisting the knob on the glove box. It fell open with a heavy clunking sound.

"I'm calling them," Skyler said. He already had his phone to his ear. After a moment he pulled it away and looked at it. "There's no service."

"Of course there isn't, because this is the first time we actually need it," I said. I lifted a stack of papers and pulled the extinguisher out of the bottom of the deep compartment. "This is your fault, Ezra!" I said as he came back inside the RV, obviously not having magically fixed it.

"Mine? Why?"

"Because you were complaining that we didn't have an overnight stop in between Yellowstone and Spokane. You put that in the universe. It granted your wish."

"If the universe is going to start granting my wishes, I want a million dollars and a girlfriend."

"In that order?" Austin asked.

"You could ask for anything in the world and you only asked for a million dollars?" Paisley said. "That's why you don't have a girlfriend."

Ezra chased Paisley around the RV while she laughed and screamed. He caught her and he and Skyler smooshed her into a hug.

"Stop it! You both stink!" she yelled.

They laughed and let her go.

"So do we need this?" I held up the fire extinguisher.

"No, it was just smoke," Austin said.

I replaced the compact-sized extinguisher back in the glove box, and as I went to shut the door, the paper on top caught my eye. It was a reservation receipt for one of the RV parks we stayed at. The whole stack was, I realized, as I flipped through the papers. That wouldn't have surprised me at all if I didn't see that on every single page, representing every single place we'd stayed or would stay, the booking date was three weeks ago, not six months ago, which was when my mom had claimed this trip was planned and paid for.

CHAPTER 22

"I'M GOING TO WALK TO THE NEAREST GAS STATION for a phone," I overhead Skyler say as I was flipping through the glove box papers a second time to make sure I was reading them right. "So the moms don't get too far ahead of us."

I shoved the stack of pages back in the glove box. "I'm coming with!"

"We're in the middle of nowhere," Paisley said. She was sitting at the table looking through her flora and fauna pics.

"You don't think they'll eventually notice and double back?" Ezra asked, opening the fridge and finding some leftover hot dogs from the night before.

"Just in case," Skyler said, pulling on his shoes.

I retrieved my shoes from under the table and put them on. "How far back was the last town we passed?"

Ezra, a cold hot dog in his mouth, shrugged. "Ten miles?"

"Maybe closer to five," Austin said.

"Super helpful. Both of you."

We stepped outside. It was still light out and cars buzzed by on the freeway. I turned one way and then the other.

"What do you think?" he asked. "Do we go with our un-observant brothers or face the unknown?"

"Let's face the unknown," I said, and then started walking before I turned that into a double meaning with some doe-eyed look at him.

Cars whizzed by on our left, the wind they produced blowing my hair. Skyler ushered us farther off the road.

"When did your mom tell you about this trip?" I asked.

"Two weeks before we left."

"How did she explain that?"

"She said she and your mom had been planning it for months as a surprise for us."

"Yeah . . . my mom too."

"Why?" he asked.

I explained what I found in the glove box.

"Maybe she just paid three weeks ago?" he asked, trying to come up with a logical explanation.

"No, because there was a booking date where she paid a deposit and another date where she paid in full."

"That's weird."

"It is, right? Why would they pretend like they'd been planning this for months?"

"So we wouldn't be suspicious?"

"Exactly," I said. "Something is wrong."

"We'll talk to them," he assured me. "Together."

"Thank you." Mom would have to tell us once I spelled out the things I had discovered. I pulled at a tall yellow wildflower growing along the shoulder as we walked. It tore free and I proceeded to tear off each petal, letting them fly away in the wind of the passing cars.

"Would you rather," Skyler said, starting a game we often played while walking from his house to mine or vice versa. He was obviously trying to distract my worried mind. "Travel forward in time or back in time?"

"Would I be able to talk to myself in either choice?"

"Sure," he said. "If you want to be limited to the span of your life."

"Oh, I can go beyond my life?"

"Yes," he said.

"Probably forward," I said. "Messing with the past can get complicated."

He chuckled. "It sure can."

I elbowed him playfully. "Would you rather," I said, "stand on the top of a hundred-story building and look at the ground or show your favorite artist in the world your most recent sketch?"

He moved his head from side to side. "Probably the hundred-story building."

"Really?" I asked, surprised. "But your last sketch was years ago, right? Why does it matter anymore?"

"I guess the hundred-story building thing is less humiliating."

"Who is your favorite artist these days anyway?"

"You," he said with a wink.

I rolled my eyes. "Okay, sure. Based on what? My strawberry socks?"

"Well, that and from what I remember when we were younger. But if you want me to . . . I mean, if you'd let me . . ."

"What? Spit it out, Hutton."

"Can I look at your sketchbook?"

"Oh." Why had I not expected that question? And why did everything in me want to say no? Maybe because his opinion of my art mattered to me more than anybody's. "After my interview? I need to keep up my confidence until then."

"I would somehow take away your confidence? What kind of best friend would do that?"

"The kind that wouldn't mean to. It's me, not you. I promise."

He laughed. "Wow, I get the breakup speech over a sketchbook?"

"You understand, right?"

"Yes, I really do. I always found this extreme amount of pressure associated with drawing. Like it had to be perfect and I had to be creative and original and everyone expected so much."

Who had expected so much? I wondered. His mom? Because it wasn't his dad. His dad thought it was childish. Would much rather have had him into sports, like Austin was.

"I didn't know you felt a lot of pressure," I said.

"Yeah."

"Well, maybe that's just part of being an artist, then, because I feel it all the time. This little voice telling me I'm not good enough, that other people are way better. That I'm fooling myself to think I could be one of the few to animate a popular video game . . . or any video game at that."

"And how do you talk yourself out of that feeling so you're not paralyzed?"

"I don't know that I have," I said. "Sometimes I'm able to ignore it."

"Smother your inner voice? Sounds like a plan."

I crinkled my nose in his direction, then pulled out my phone to check the bars.

"Anything?" he asked.

"No." I swiped over to my camera. "Take a selfie with me."

"A freeway selfie?"

"Yes, memories and all that."

"You actually want to stand next to me in a picture?"

A laugh burst out of me. "I didn't think you noticed."

"Oh, I noticed."

"It was my passive-aggressive payback for . . ."

"For me ruining our reunion?"

"Yes, but that was before realizing my past self totally ruined it."

He smirked. "Come here." He situated himself slightly behind me and put his face next to my cheek. His hands went to my hips and logically I knew it was to stabilize himself, but a shiver went through me.

"Look how cute we are," I said to cover up my reaction. I snapped several pics and then tucked my phone away.

"There's a sign," he said, pointing ahead.

"Five miles?" I said. "I was hoping this way would produce a closer town."

"Maybe we'll get service before then?"

"We better. I don't remember the last time I walked five miles."

He laughed.

"You and your new running rugby body think I'm kidding."

"Running rugby body?"

I waved my hand up and down, indicating the whole of him. "Wait . . . is that why you do rugby now?"

"Because of my body?"

"No," I said, and laughed when I realized he hadn't heard the thought process I'd had in my head so of course that's what he would think I meant. "Your dad. Do you do it for your dad?"

His brows furrowed together in irritation. "Why do you think I'm doing everything for my dad?"

"I don't know. Rugby is just so . . . new."

"I have grown up a little, Nor."

"I know." I *definitely* knew. I kept my eyes straight ahead so I wouldn't check him out with the statement.

"Tell me something new about your life that would surprise me," he said.

"You don't like all the new stuff in my life. I'm a mean girl now."

"Stop."

I smiled at him to show I was mostly kidding. "New . . ." *Well, apparently, I want to kiss you. Is that new enough?*

A blue truck honked and the guy in the passenger seat stuck his head out the window and yelled, "A ride for a ride!"

I flipped them off.

"Well, that's new," Skyler said.

"What? Being catcalled or me flipping them off?"

"Both," he said. "It's weird."

"Weird how?"

"You've grown up too," he said, and I could've sworn his cheeks went a little pink.

"Yes, I have." I shoved my hands into the pockets of my jeans because I wanted so very badly to grab his hand, and we continued walking. I could have self-control. We were in the best place we'd been since the start of this trip and I was happy about that.

CHAPTER 23

AN HOUR AND TWENTY MINUTES. THAT'S HOW long it took us to walk five miles. But our phones were still showing no service, so we really did end up at a seedy gas station just off the highway.

"Do you have a phone we can borrow?" I asked the guy behind the counter. "Like the kind that plugs into the wall?" I pulled at the neck of my shirt to fan myself, still feeling hot from the walk. "You know, the kind with a cord."

"The kind with a cord?" Skyler teased from next to me. "I think it has square buttons, too, that you push."

"Shut it," I said, my smile growing.

"No," the guy said, not thinking we were funny at all.

"Is there a place close where cell phones work?" Skyler asked.

"I can give you the Wi-Fi info."

"Yes, that would be great," I said. "Thank you."

I entered it into my phone and we went out and sat on the curb to FaceTime my mom.

She picked up after a few rings. Her smile stretched across the screen. "Hello, daughter of mine."

"It's both of us," I said, scooting closer to Skyler.

"Hi, Mrs. Simons," Skyler said.

She squinted. "Where are you guys? Is that a building behind you?"

"So you're not on your way back," I said.

"What?" Mom asked.

"We haven't been behind you for at least an hour and a half," I said.

Her gaze went to what I assumed was the side mirror. "The kids aren't behind us," Mom said out loud.

"They aren't?" Olivia said.

"We're two hours from Spokane," Mom said.

"We are not. The RV broke down."

"Broke down?"

"Made funny noises, spewed smoke, and is now sitting on the side of the freeway."

"Why didn't you call us a couple hours ago?" she asked, voice slightly panicked. But I saw the familiar look of concentration come onto her face as she switched into planning mode.

"We had no cell reception. Skyler and I walked to a gas station."

"On the freeway? That's super dangerous," she said.

"But obviously super necessary, thanks to our oblivious mothers," I said lightly.

She cringed. "Yes, sorry."

"We talk too much," Olivia called out.

"What do you want us to do now?" I asked.

Mom's head turned toward Olivia; then she pulled on her bottom lip. "It's almost eight. I need to call roadside assistance."

"We'll come back your way," I heard Olivia say in the background.

"No," Mom quickly argued. "That's too much driving for . . . That's unnecessary."

"You're not going to come back?" Skyler asked.

"If we need to come back, we'll do it in the morning. Otherwise, we'll meet you guys in Spokane. Call us when you know what's going on."

"Um . . . okay," I said. "Can I call an Uber so I don't have to walk back?" I had the app on my phone but it was linked to her credit card because we'd only set it up for emergencies.

"Yes, of course."

"Thanks. And I'll text you the location of the RV for Triple A."

"Sounds good."

I hung up the phone, texted her the info, and then tucked my phone away.

"We are definitely talking to them," Skyler said, obviously thinking that was as strange of a development as I thought it was.

"Agreed."

"Come on, let's go pick out some snacks and then call an Uber."

I stood first and reached out my hands to help him up. "Do you think they have Coke freezes?"

His eyes lit up with that thought. "I haven't had one of those since Fresno." Before I could turn to walk away, he grabbed hold of my shoulders and looked straight into my soul.

"What?" The word came out like a whisper.

"What you said earlier about me in the RV . . . about our friendship being irreplaceable . . ."

"Yeah, right, sorry, that was pretty intense. I just—"

"I feel the same way," he said, cutting me off.

"Oh."

He dropped his hands and moved toward the door first. My heart, which seemed to have stopped during that exchange, began beating again. I shook out my hands and followed Skyler.

* * *

By the time AAA came, refilled the coolant, replaced the battery, and sent us on our way, it was nearly 1:00 a.m. So Ezra drove to the closest Walmart parking lot, texted our moms, and parked for the night.

"Where are we all supposed to sleep?" Paisley asked, hands on hips, turning a circle in the middle of the RV.

"Two people can have my mom's bed," I said. "And the couch converts into a bed too."

Austin did a running jump onto the big bed in the back. "I get the real bed since I'm the oldest."

"I'll share if we put up a pillow wall and you swear not to fart in your sleep," Paisley said.

"I can agree to one of those two things," Austin said.

"I guess I get the couch, then," Skyler said.

* * *

I lay in my bunk, staring at the ceiling, listening to the heavy breathing of sleep echoing through the RV all around me but unable to sleep myself. All sorts of theories about my mom, each worse than the last, were circling in my mind. It was making my head feel heavy. Plus, my throat was dry; all that walking today had left me dehydrated. It didn't help that Ezra's phone had buzzed three times in the last five minutes.

I slid down from my bunk and my bare feet landed on the laminate flooring. I gently pulled back Ezra's curtain. "Silence your phone, idiot," I whispered. He didn't answer, apparently asleep while his phone was being a menace.

I reached over him and patted the mattress by his head until my hand hit the cold glass. I picked up his phone and it immediately pulled back, tethered to the wall by a charging cord. The screen lit up with the movement, though, and I saw the preview of the three messages I'd heard from my bunk. They were all from a contact he'd labeled *Bunny*. Two of the messages were just emojis that, out of context, made no sense. But the third was half a sentence: *If you hate it so much, then when you get home . . .*

"Couldn't sleep?" a soft voice said from my right.

I jumped, nearly dropping the phone.

"You scared me," I whispered in Skyler's direction.

"Sorry."

I returned Ezra's phone, then walked the ten steps past the foldout couch where Skyler lay, hands behind his head, to the fridge. Three night-lights—one on the wall, one shining from the open door of the bathroom, and one above the sink—lit my way. I found a cold bottle of water. I opened the bottle and downed half of it.

"Did I wake you up?" I said softly.

"No, I can't sleep either. Ezra's phone keeps buzzing."

"I know. I tried to turn it to sleep mode but it was locked." I heard Ezra shift in his bed before his breaths became even again so I lowered my voice even more and said, "Hopefully Bunny is done texting."

"What?" he said.

I sat on the edge of his bed and repeated myself.

"Bunny? Is that her real name?"

I shrugged. "I have no idea."

His next sentence was too quiet for me to hear.

"What?" I asked, inching closer.

He smiled and pulled me by the hand toward him. I moved onto my side and he adjusted his pillow, offering to share, like we had millions of times in the past.

I shouldn't, I told myself. I should just go back to my own bunk behind the safety of my own flimsy curtain. But I didn't. I lowered my head to his pillow. His eyes seemed larger than life now, his lashes close to brushing his eyebrows.

"I said, our neighbors in Ohio have rabbits. Two big ones."

"Oh." There was something about the energy radiating between our bodies that made goose bumps form on my arms. "Tell me more about your life in Ohio. What's school like there?"

"Indoors. Like the hallways between classes are inside instead of outside."

I smiled. "I know what indoors means."

"It was weird for me at first. We also have lockers because we live in a small town and there aren't as many students."

"Small town, Skyler. Does that mean everyone knows everyone's business and you can't rob the corner mart without neighbor Fred telling his cousin Sue who tells her best friend Lisa who tells your mom?"

His eyes lit up. "Yes, it totally ruined the crime spree I wanted to go on."

"That could make a good video game. Robbing stores without running into a list of characters that are identified at the beginning as being in the nine degrees of separation from you."

"I forget how much you think in video games."

"I know. It's annoying. Willow has banned me from sharing more than one a day."

"It's not annoying. It's you. It's like how musicians wake up with tunes in their heads and writer's keep notebooks by their beds. You're a video game savant."

I laughed a little. "More like I'm obsessed. Maybe I think about it too much. Maybe I'd be more mainstream if I didn't."

"You want to be mainstream?"

"I want to belong, feel like I fit in somewhere. Doesn't everyone?"

His eyes looked past me and around the space. "If we'd had this when we were younger, we wouldn't have had to sit in my sister's tiny playhouse."

"The RV? I know, right? My parents definitely bought it at least a year too late."

"It's nice. Do you ever sit in it at home?"

A smile stretched across my face. "Do I ever just go to the side of the house and chill in the hot RV alone?"

"Are you mocking my question?"

"Yes, I am."

He reached over and squeezed my side. I gasped and grabbed hold of his hand to stop him from doing it again. But then I kept hold of his hand and he didn't pull it away. My body, without moving, seemed to float closer to his.

I took a deep breath and looked around the RV, then answered his question for real. "I never even thought to use it as an escape. I guess I was too busy trying to blend in."

"I was the one who always needed an escape."

"That's not true."

He was silent for a long time and I squeezed his hand, which was still gripping my waist. I decided if we stayed just like this forever I would be perfectly happy.

"Maybe I do play rugby because of my dad. Or at least that's how it started."

"But you like it now?"

He nodded. "It didn't help anyway."

"Your dad is still just as hard on you?"

"Yeah."

"I'm sorry."

"It doesn't matter," he said. "I don't know why I let it bother me so much."

"Because he's your dad and he should be proud of you no matter what."

"We're both old enough to know that we don't always get what we want."

I rolled onto my back, the heaviness of that statement weighing on my chest. "True." *But we can sometimes, right?* I wanted to yell. Instead, I just held on to his hand tighter.

CHAPTER 24

"WHAT THE CRAP?" THE WORDS WOKE ME UP FROM dead sleep. I blinked against the light, then squinted through my lids to see Paisley standing there, mouth slightly ajar.

It didn't register for several moments that she was above me, not the perspective I'd have had if I were in my bunk. It took another moment to feel Skyler up against my side, the weight across my stomach *his* arm, not mine. I nudged him with my elbow. "Good morning," I said to Paisley. "We must've fallen asleep talking last night." Which was absolutely true but I was trying to say it in the most casual way possible so Paisley didn't make a big deal out of it.

Skyler shifted next to me, then turned onto his other side, still asleep. I took the time to look around and see if Paisley was the only one awake. She seemed to be. I picked up my phone from where it sat next to me and saw that it was five in the morning. "It's early," I said.

"Yeah, I had to pee."

I swung my feet to the floor and stood. "Thanks for waking

me up." I pointed to my bunk. "I'm going back to sleep for another hour or two."

She looked between me and Skyler, suspicion in her eyes, but her bladder must've taken over because she just nodded and went to the bathroom.

I walked around the couch bed and just as I went to climb into my bed, I looked back at Skyler. He was sprawled out, mostly on his stomach but a bent leg kept him partially on his side. One arm hung off the bed, his friendship bracelet was on his wrist, and his cheek was scrunched up against the pillow. He was adorable. I wanted to climb back in bed next to him and cuddle up against his back.

Nope, not happening, Norah. I crawled into my bed and eventually fell asleep.

* * *

"Spokane, take two," I heard Ezra announce as the RV rumbled to life. I stretched and reached out for my phone before even opening my eyes.

Eight a.m.

A text from Willow was waiting for me. *Do I get to call these two an official couple or what?* Below those words was a picture of Skyler and me. This was from the same day as the last picture she'd sent me, close to when he'd left, us sitting on the couch. But where the last one was of me looking at him with loving eyes, this was the opposite.

No, but we are friends again.

Just friends?

I thought about the night before, lying in bed with him, whisper-talking until we fell asleep. We'd moved on from talking about his dad to talking about my mom. He'd assured me that everything was going to be okay.

I decided since we're both going to our separate states in a week and a half that I would save us both some heartache.

Lame. Also, why haven't you found more of my notes? They're not that hard to find.

Oh! I did. I found the friendship defies death *one. It was very time appropriate.*

I didn't send you a friendship defies death note.

I was paraphrasing.

Yours sounds cooler.

It is.

The curtain moved aside and Skyler's smiling face was on the other side. "I thought I heard you texting in here."

"I'm a loud texter?"

"Yes, super loud."

He held up the notebook and I nodded. Instead of getting up, which I should've, I scooted over, wanting to feel him next to me again. I really wasn't doing a good job of stomping out these feelings I couldn't afford to have.

He climbed up and lay down beside me. "Where did we leave off?" he asked, flipping pages.

"Hiding Ezra's charger." The pressure of Skyler's shoulder against mine made me happy.

"Oh, right." He ran his finger along a date on the corner of the next entry. "The year we turned twelve."

"Why did you say it like that?" I asked.

"Like what?"

"Like there was some significance to the year we turned twelve."

"I did?"

"Yes."

He shrugged. "I didn't mean to. I was just pointing it out."

"Okay, carry on, Mr. I Make Unnecessary Observations."

"It's for context, Norah. Context."

"Okay, I have the context in my mind."

He started reading the entry, which was written by him. "We need to think of ways to make money because I want to go to the movies. The theater with the reclining seats and good sound system. Do you think we can talk our parents into some kind of allowance? What other ways are there to make money?"

My laugh grew from a giggle to a full-on laugh as he read.

"What?" he asked.

"I remember that summer. You were so obsessed with going to the movies. Why did you want to go so bad? I don't even remember what movie you wanted to see. Was it an Avenger one or something? You loved those."

"I don't remember," he said.

"Really? You were so obsessed but don't even remember which movie was so important to you?"

"All I remember was you did not support this plan so every time you got your allowance, you made us walk to the gas station to buy slushies."

"An excellent use of funds. Yummm. Coke freezes. Too bad that gas station yesterday didn't have any."

He flipped the page.

"Did you ever earn enough to go to the movies that summer? I forget."

"No," he said.

"Huh. All that obsession for nothing."

"Yeah . . ." He handed me the book because it was my entry and that's how we'd been splitting up the reading—each reading our own.

I cleared my throat and began. "Do you think people buy teeth? Maybe you can pull out your molars and get something for those. You hardly use them anyway."

"You were so unhelpful," Skyler said.

"And super weird."

"That was the best part."

I rolled my eyes and kept reading. "You know what I want to save money for? A cell phone. This is the year our parents will let us have them, right? This is the age Austin and Ezra got theirs."

"Why didn't we get them that year?"

"Because I had to pay for half and I kept spending my money on Coke freezes, apparently."

I couldn't see her but Paisley's voice came floating into the bunk. "Are you two really going to hole up there all day? You never hang out with me anymore, Norah. Skyler's hogging you."

"I totally am," Skyler mouthed to me, a twinkle in his eyes.

"You're right, we're being antisocial," I called out. "We'll be right down."

Skyler didn't move. I gestured toward the edge to encourage

215

him and he put his hands behind his head like he had all the time in the world.

"I love that you don't think I'll climb over you," I said.

"You're right, I don't."

"Oh please, that's easy." But really it wasn't. The ceiling was low and he wasn't thirteen years old anymore so he took up more room than I'd been anticipating. As I hovered over him in an attempt to exit the small cubby, he was laughing at my effort. "You're the worst," I said.

He reached up, took me by the waist, and helped me finish my exit. Standing on the floor, my insides fluttering, I tried to gain my head before I joined Paisley on the couch.

"Hi," I said. "What are you up to?"

"Why do you have a goofy smile on your face?" she asked.

"Do I?" I tried to force it away but could only manage to turn it into a regular smile. At least I hoped. I nodded to the book in her hands. "Do you need me to draw some of your findings?"

"Yes, please."

* * *

"You are so good!"

I handed Paisley back the sketchbook. "It's a flower."

"A good one!"

"You just want me to draw more."

"So true."

"Too bad you can't just draw in your interview," Skyler said from the captain's chair. "How could anyone deny you entry into their school when they see how happy you are drawing?"

I wished I could just draw in my interview too. Or just spout off video games I'd spent hours playing. It would make my life a whole lot easier.

That thought must've registered on my face because Skyler said, "Don't listen to me. You'll do fine."

"She didn't say anything," Paisley said.

I held up my bracelet. "Best friend powers."

Skyler held his up as well from across the RV and made an exploding sound.

"You two are weird," Paisley said.

According to Skyler, that was a good thing. I smiled. Maybe it was.

CHAPTER 25

MOM HUGGED ME LIKE WE'D BEEN GONE FOR MORE than just eighteen hours when we arrived at the campsite in Mount Spokane. "Everyone okay?" she asked.

"Yes, are you?" I looked her straight in the eyes, willing her to tell me what was happening.

"We've had a relaxing morning."

Skyler and I would have to find the right time to confront our moms. I started to sit down at the picnic table when I realized I had forgotten my phone in the RV. I went back up the stairs to see that Ezra had already moved suitcases from the side storage and they sat right inside the door. I pushed them out of my way and caught a movement up front, in the driver's seat.

"You want to drive four more hours or what?" I asked.

Ezra quickly lowered whatever he'd been holding out of my view.

I narrowed my eyes. "What was that?"

"Nothing."

As I rushed up front, he shoved something behind his back.

I immediately wrapped my arms around him, squeezing my hands between the seat and where he was pushing his back firmly against it.

"Stop, Norah."

"What are you hiding? Why don't I get to know?"

"It's literally nothing."

I felt the edges of a crumpled paper and pulled it out, ripping it a little; then I took off running to the bathroom where I locked myself inside just in time for him to slam against it.

"Norah, seriously, you're being dumb."

I caught my breath and smoothed out the paper in my hands. A note. It was a drawing of two stick figures hugging, their eyes hearts. Above it were the words *I miss you tons!* That little punk! He stole one of my notes from Willow!

"Did you go through my suitcase?" I asked, shoving open the door. "Why? I don't know anything! You do! Or mom. You should go through *her* suitcase."

"You already did, right? You'd tell me if you found something, if you knew something, wouldn't you?"

"Would you tell me if *you* knew something?"

"Yes."

"Same. I know nothing." I held up the note. "So stop going through my stuff."

He held up both hands in surrender. "Fine. I'm worried about her, though."

"Me too."

My phone buzzed from my bunk, reminding me of the reason I came inside. Willow's name scrolled across the screen.

"Hello," I answered. "I'm not alone," I quickly added because we hadn't actually talked since she found out I was crushing on Skyler and I was worried those would be the first words out of her mouth.

"Who are you with?" she asked.

"Ezra," I said. "Tell him to stop stealing my notes from you."

"Why is he doing that?"

"Because he's a punk." I put her on speaker. "Ezra, apologize to my best friend for being so nosy."

"Hey, Willow," Ezra said.

"Hey, punk," she responded. "You owe me a perusing of your diary."

"I don't have a diary," he said. "But I will write a page just so you feel vindicated."

"What will it say?" she asked.

"It will say, I'm an emo with lots of emotions that can only be written on this super-secret page that nobody will ever find."

She laughed. I rolled my eyes and took her off speaker. To Ezra I said, "You shouldn't make fun of people trying to sort through emotions. Writing them down is a healthy way to deal. Maybe you should try it."

"You're right, maybe I should," he said, obviously just trying to appease me.

Back on the phone I said, "Sorry about that."

"It's fine," she said. "It's not like my notes say anything earth-shattering or secret for that matter."

"True." I tucked the note into my book under my pillow and left the RV to find a better place to chat. I ended up walking to a bench I saw in the distance, surrounded by tall pines.

"By the way," she said. "I told everyone you were throwing a pool party at your house when you get home."

"How nice of me."

"Yes, everyone is pretty excited. Where are you, anyway? Have you made it to Seattle yet and seen the school that is going to take you away from me?"

"We're in Spokane. Seattle is our next stop. I've been practicing like crazy."

"You'll do great. I wish we liked the same things so we could go to the same school."

"You know there are plenty of medical programs in Seattle. We can rent an apartment in between our two schools and be roommates."

"I know, I know, you've told me that before."

"Just think about it," I said.

"Your opinion has been noted and rejected," she said.

"Rude." Some sunlight filtering through the trees left a splotchy pattern on my foot and I moved it around, making the light dance. "Did you ever find out who that guy at the party was? The one you took a bad picture of?"

"I did, actually! He goes to North." North was one of the other high schools in town.

"Nice. Are you going to call him?"

"I'm thinking about it."

"You should do more than think about it."

"So should you."

"Not even close to the same."

"You're right. You have a much deeper connection with the guy you should be doing more than thinking about."

221

I groaned. "I can't, Willow. You know how bad it hurt when he left last time? How much worse would it be if I actually fell for him?"

"Pretty sure you already did."

"No, it would be so much worse if I knew what it felt like to kiss him and I didn't get to for months at a time."

"You could write about your angst in a journal. I hear it's a healthy way to deal."

"Funny."

"I get what you're saying, Norah. I really do. I just feel like you two are different. It's not some fleeting, new thing. It's something real, something that doesn't come along very often, something you shouldn't just let go of because of some temporary inconvenience."

"You're assuming this isn't one-sided. You're assuming he feels the same way. That's a big assumption. I'm assuming he doesn't. I'm grateful that we're friends again."

"Fine, whatever. I'll leave you alone about it . . . for now. But just don't do that thing you do where you overanalyze everything. Sometimes you just have to let things happen how they're supposed to happen."

After we hung up, I sat there on the bench looking at the trees that surrounded me. I could hear water trickling and I wondered if there was a stream nearby. I leaned my elbows on my knees and watched a beetle crawl through the dirt.

I was jealous of Willow. I didn't want to be but I was. I was jealous that she was interested in a guy who lived in the same town as her and if she ended up liking him there would be nothing complicated about it.

"You're going to think I'm stalking you," a voice said from behind me.

I turned to see Ty. "Yes, actually, I am."

"I told you last leg we were on the same route."

"I know. It's funny," I said. "Apparently our parents have the same taste in campsites." Which reminded me ... "Do your parents print out the receipts for each place you stay?"

"You want to compare prices or something?" he asked with a curious head tilt.

I scooted over on the bench and he sat down. "No, dates."

"I don't understand."

"Do you know how long ago your family booked this place?"

He shrugged. "A couple months, at least. Do you want me to ask my mom if you can look at the receipt?"

I sighed. "No." I didn't need him to confirm what I already knew. My mom hadn't planned this trip months ago. It had happened weeks ago and I had no idea why she felt the need to lie about it.

A piece of tall grass tickled my ankle and I rubbed at it with my opposite foot.

"You left without saying goodbye at the dance."

"It was a ... strange night."

"You want to talk about it?"

"It's a long story." One that started years and years ago.

Ty's attention turned to something behind me and I followed his gaze to see Skyler walking up.

"Hey," he said. "Ty, right?"

"Yes, hey again," Ty said.

"I take it you all got your route off Roadtrippers too."

"Yeah, Norah and I figured that out last time."

Skyler raised his eyebrows at me. "I'm sure you did."

I wasn't sure what that was supposed to mean so I didn't say anything.

"We're prepping for lunch," Skyler said. He was giving me an out, because it wasn't my turn to prep for lunch. I appreciated it, but I was busy feeling sorry for myself when it came to Skyler.

"I think it's Ezra's turn," I said. "Let me know when it's ready?"

He was surprised by my response, I could tell. Last time I'd been around Ty I hadn't wanted to be, but being around Skyler right now felt more torturous.

"Yeah, sure," he said, then left me there. Maybe that was the wrong decision. Maybe I *should* just tell him how I felt and let the chips fall where they may, but that could end with Skyler not being in my life at all. I didn't want to lose him after just getting him back.

I turned to Ty to ask him if there was a good clubhouse at this RV park when he leaned in and kissed me.

CHAPTER 26

"WHOA," I SAID, TRYING TO BACK UP BUT BEING stopped by the arm of the bench.

"I'm sorry, I thought . . ."

"No," I said. "I hardly know you."

He looked at the ground. "I'm sorry. You were giving all the signs. I thought I'd take my chance."

"I didn't mean to give signs. I'm actually super bad at signs."

"You're better than you think."

"Well, obviously not, if you got that idea." I pointed to my mouth to indicate the kiss.

He laughed. "True. You're not going to punch me in the face or anything, are you?"

"If I was going to punch you, it would have happened immediately following the kiss. Now I'm just going to awkwardly stand and walk away to go eat lunch."

"Then I'm going to awkwardly stand and be grateful we live in different states."

I smiled. "That sounds like a good plan."

We both awkwardly stood and each took two or three steps backward.

"Bye, Norah."

"Bye." I was trying not to feel stupid as I headed back to camp. Why should *I* feel stupid? He was the one who kissed me without asking. He could've at least done the thing where he went in halfway and waited for me to follow his lead. That was a thing people did, right? I wasn't sure; I'd only kissed one guy and our first kiss happened after I'd said, "Are we ever going to kiss?"

I had just talked myself out of the need to feel embarrassed when I entered our campsite and Paisley announced to the entire meal-prep group—which apparently was *everyone* today—"Did I just see you kissing Ty? I thought you didn't like him."

What could I say out loud in that moment that wouldn't make all three guys, who were now staring at me, go give Ty a talking-to? "Sort of" is the stupid thing my brain landed on before I rushed into the RV.

I flung myself on my mom's bed and slid the door shut. Before long there was a knock and Paisley's voice. "Norah? Are you okay?"

"I'm fine," I said.

"Can I come in? I want to show you something."

I honestly just wanted her to go away, but saying that would make everything worse. "Sure."

She opened the door and sat on the bed next to me. In her

arms was her sketch pad. She wanted me to do more of her homework right now? "Can we work on that later?" I said.

"Will you just look?"

I held back a sigh and reached out for the book.

"Hold on, let me find the right page."

"Okay," I said.

She flipped to somewhere near the middle and gently handed it to me.

At first, I didn't quite understand what I was seeing. My brain was trying to make sense of Paisley being responsible for the drawing in front of me. The style and technique felt so familiar. Then my mouth dropped open. "You didn't . . . Is this . . ." It was a sketch of me. A super-detailed, hyperrealistic, picture-like drawing of me.

"It's Skyler's," Paisley said. "I found it in his stuff."

I practically threw the book across the bed. "You took that without his permission?"

She shrugged. "Yeah, so. I was looking for clues about our moms."

"In Skyler's stuff?"

She shrugged. "In everyone's stuff."

"That's not cool."

"You did it," she said.

"I . . ." She was right. I had done it. Ezra had done it. We'd all turned into suspicious thieves on this trip, apparently. "Only in my mom's. And I didn't take anything." My voice was scratchy because my throat was tight. Aside from the fact that his art was breathtaking, even better than it had been four years ago, I was shocked that he had drawn me. And by memory? Or maybe while looking at a picture? But I couldn't think of which picture he could've used. "You need to go put that back before he figures out it's missing."

"You don't want to look at any more? They're mostly people. He has a couple more of you."

I held up my hands as she started flipping pages. "No, I don't. If he wanted me to see them, he would've shown me." As I said that out loud, my throat became tight for a completely different reason—my feelings were hurt. He didn't trust me enough to even *tell* me he was still drawing let alone show me his art.

"Skyler is private. He doesn't share anything with anyone," she said. "He needs some extra encouragement sometimes."

"Just put it back, Paisley."

"Are you going to tell on me?"

"I don't know yet." How would Skyler react if he knew both Paisley and I had looked at his book? She hadn't even known he could draw until this trip. He had talked about the extreme pressure that came with people's expectations of his work. I didn't want him to feel any pressure to create because of me.

"Hello!" Skyler's voice filled the RV as he came into view.

Paisley panicked and hid the book behind her back, then slid it into the crack between the bed and wall. "Hi!" she said.

"What are you doing? You look like you're definitely guilty of something," Skyler said to her. He seemed to be avoiding my eyes altogether.

"We were just talking about Norah's kiss," Paisley said, wiggling her eyebrows.

"No, we weren't," I said. "At all. Because that kiss was completely one-sided."

"Well, I hope there was at least *some* chemistry," Skyler said. "Because your brother went and invited Ty to lunch."

"He *what*?"

"Is that a bad thing?" Skyler asked. He was still hardly looking at me.

"Yes! Did Ty accept?"

"He's sitting out there right now."

"If you kiss a guy," Paisley said in her matter-of-fact voice, "he's going to think you want him to come to lunch."

"I didn't kiss him," I said into my knees. Why would he accept an invitation to lunch? Did he think I had changed my mind and sent my brother after him? This was going to be one hundred times more awkward than the kiss had been.

"Hey, Paisley," Skyler said. "Will you give us a minute?"

Paisley looked to the crack where she had hidden the sketch pad and then to me before scooching off the bed and out of the RV.

"What's going on?" he asked.

"I don't want him here."

"Ty?"

I nodded.

"Did he . . . What did he do to you?" His voice was hard now, exactly what I didn't want to happen.

"Skyler," I pleaded. "Nothing. He was nice about it, but I

can't go out there. Will you just privately tell him to leave? He'll realize that it was a misunderstanding." I was having second-hand embarrassment for him and I wasn't even out there. I couldn't be the one to tell him. That would embarrass us both even more.

Skyler gave a short nod and exited the RV. I hugged my knees to my chest and stared at the edge of the bed. I rolled my eyes, then stretched forward and fished my arm down the crack for his sketchbook. I had to tell him.

Skyler came back into the RV, a huge smile on his face. "I am so smooth . . ." His words and smile trailed off as his eyes locked on the book in my hands. "What's that?"

"It's not what you think. I mean, it is, but I didn't look at it. Paisley found it and—"

"Found it?" He was angry.

"Obviously she was being nosy but don't be mad at her. I don't think she understands—"

"Privacy? What about you? Do you understand privacy? I'm beginning to think you don't." He narrowed his eyes and snatched the book from my hands. "Wait, is this why you sent me out there to send poor Ty away? To hide that?"

"*Poor* Ty?"

"So you're not denying it?"

"What? No, I was going to tell you. That's why I was holding it."

Paisley poked her head into the RV. "Everyone is waiting for you guys." Her eyes went wide when she saw what Skyler was holding. "You told him we looked at it?"

His head whipped over to me. "You said you didn't look at it."

"It was just one sketch and I didn't know—"

"Don't be mad at her. It was my fault," Paisley said.

"Don't worry, I'm mad at both of you." With those words, he left.

CHAPTER 27

THE AUDIENCE WAS CLAPPING AND PAISLEY AND Olivia were smiling and I felt good for the first time since the day before when I'd gotten into the huge fight with Skyler over his sketchbook. I'd tried to talk to him once since and he gave me the silent treatment, which made me yell, "The silent treatment is my thing! You're just supposed to be mad and then get over it!" In hindsight that probably wasn't the best reaction, but I was frustrated. I'd done nothing wrong and he refused to hear me out. Plus, he was supposed to help me confront our moms and now I had no idea if that was going to happen. I'd probably have to do it myself.

But for now we stood, the four of us—Mom, Olivia, Paisley, and me—clapping for a band I'd never heard of at the Bing Crosby Theater in the middle of Spokane.

"That was so amazing," Paisley said as we filed out of the theater. "I want to do that one day. Perform in front of a live audience."

"I thought you said you were in theater at school. And choir."

"I mean I want to get paid for it."

I laughed.

Mom was scrolling through her phone. "I'll get an Uber."

"Wait," Olivia said, putting her hand up. "Maybe we should get some ice cream first?" She pointed across the street but all I saw was a ramen noodle place.

"Is it too late?" I asked.

"It's only ten," Paisley pointed out. "And we're on vacation."

"Yes!" Olivia said. "We're on vacation."

"What's your favorite ice cream flavor?" Paisley asked me.

"Mint chocolate chip," I said.

"That's a good one. Have you ever tried mint cookies and cream?"

"I have not."

"It's magical," Paisley said. "You have to try it."

"If they have it, I will." We had stopped in the middle of the sidewalk, people pouring out of the doors of the theater behind us. "Is there a place nearby?"

"A few blocks that way," Mom said, holding up her phone as if I needed proof.

We started walking and Paisley asked softly, "Is Skyler still mad at you?"

"Yes. You?"

"Well, he refused to come to this concert tonight. But I don't think he's super mad anymore. It took a lot of nonstop talking to crack him."

"He's talking to you now?"

She cringed. "Yes."

Olivia spoke up from my other side where I thought she and Mom were having a conversation. "Skyler is mad at you?"

"For something really stupid," I said, before she worried. "He'll get over it." It actually wasn't that stupid. I understood why he was mad. I wouldn't want someone looking at my sketchbook without permission, either, but I had tried to explain to him that I hadn't looked through it. It hadn't worked. He didn't believe me. We'd come a long way, but he obviously still didn't trust me.

We arrived at the ice cream shop, which did not have mint cookies and cream. I was more disappointed than that fact warranted.

* * *

A note on the door to the RV when we got back read: *Bonfire at the lodge tonight. Don't wait up.*

It was past eleven and I wondered if either of our moms would go collect the boys from the bonfire. Or at least the underage boy, but neither of them seemed too concerned.

"To bed," Olivia said to Paisley.

"But that's not fair. I want to—"

"To bed," she said.

Paisley gave a huge eye-roll and disappeared into her RV.

"Good night, you two." Olivia surprised me with a hug. "It's almost interview day."

"Yes."

"You'll do great." Why did everyone think I needed convincing? "Good night."

Mom was collecting some items off the picnic table and tucking them away in storage when I turned her way. She smiled. "You can go."

"Go where?"

"To the bonfire," she said, like I was playing innocent on purpose. "I know you want to."

I wasn't sure I actually did, but I nodded anyway because if cracking Skyler required nonstop talking, I might as well get started on it.

*　*　*

I was surprised at how crowded the bonfire was. It was like everyone in the entire RV camp under the age of twenty-five had decided this was what they were doing tonight. It was a cool setting, so I understood why. The fire was massive and set in the middle of a huge brick patio. Wooden chairs and benches filled the area. A path led from the fire down a small hill to a second patio next to the lake, lights strung through the trees.

A large hut sat between the two gathering areas where snacks and drinks were sold. That's where I first saw Ezra. I walked past the fire and around loud-talking guests. Music was flowing through mounted speakers and became louder or quieter, depending on my location.

"Hey," I said, stopping next to Ezra.

"Oh, hey. How was the boring music concert thing?"

"Not boring at all. You should've come."

"I think you're lying, so I'm certain I made the right choice."

"I don't lie," I snapped.

He lowered one eyebrow. "Okay, grump face. Is it past your bedtime?"

"Whatever. Where is Austin?"

"Went to talk to some guy up there. He told me to leave. I was radiating too much straightness."

"Smart man. Have you seen Skyler?"

He squinted toward the lake. "Last I saw him, he was down there."

"Okay, thanks."

He bowed, grabbed his pretzel and soda, and headed in the opposite direction, back toward the fire.

The lake was gorgeous and I could see why so many people had chosen this patio over the fire one—the lights overhead reflected in the black, glassy water. Even farther, the stars did the same, and the moon, a sliver in the sky, had its mirror image shining below as well. I wondered if Seattle had places like this close by or if the city extended for hours in all directions. This trip had helped me realize how much I appreciated nature. I peeled my eyes away from the lake and searched faces for the one I was looking for.

When I found it, I wished my mom had made me stay at the campsite, told me to go to bed like Olivia had told Paisley. Because sitting on one of the benches staring out at the lake was Skyler. And he wasn't alone. A girl I didn't recognize was cuddled up into his side, her arm hooked in his. He wasn't giving *her* the silent treatment, like he had me for the last twenty-four hours. They seemed to be deep in conversation, in fact.

I took several steps backward, walking blindly, unable to

take my eyes off them. I bumped into a body and was about to apologize when I heard, "Hi, Norah."

I cringed and turned around. "Hey, Ty."

"We were supposed to never see each other again."

"That was definitely the plan."

"Is fate trying to help us out?"

"Do you believe in fate?" I asked.

"Sometimes," he said. "What about you?"

"Maybe." My eyes drifted to Skyler on the bench with the pretty girl. "Maybe fate is helping me out right now. Letting me see something I need to see so that I can move forward with my life in a week and a half."

Ty looked over his shoulder and must've seen Skyler because he said, "Or maybe fate is giving you some motivation."

I sighed. "To do what?"

"March over there and claim what's yours."

"I've analyzed every single scenario of how that could play out and there is only one that is slightly decent."

"Did you just quote *Doctor Strange*? Are you telling me you can see the future? Is Thanos going to destroy all versions of your love life?"

I laughed. "I didn't mean to quote him, but I did, didn't I?"

He smirked and then said, "Could you at least let me save a little dignity and pretend you rejected me because you wanted to go after him?"

"Oh, yes, that is definitely what you should tell yourself. And I'm going to tell myself that he doesn't want me because we live way too far away. You can use that excuse for us too."

"That's a good one."

"But what we should really be telling ourselves is that we don't need another person to complete us."

He pointed up toward the food hut. "I'm going to get something to eat and try to find my other half."

I laughed. "Good luck."

He started to walk away.

"Ty?"

He turned back. "You really are a nice guy. Thanks."

"For being a nice guy?"

I nodded.

He jerked his head toward Skyler. "Living too far away is not a good excuse if you really like someone. Just saying." He smiled at me, then turned away.

My eyes found Skyler again. It was a good excuse for not starting a *relationship,* but he didn't get to let go of our friendship so easily. I let my indignation fill me up and I walked until I stood in front of the bench. "Hi," I said when Skyler looked up at me.

"Hi," he said.

"Can I talk to you?"

"I'm a little busy right now," he said.

I looked at the girl, who had sat up straight at my arrival, but her arm was still hooked in Skyler's. "Hi," I said. "I'm Norah."

"Heidi."

"Good to meet you." I pointed to Skyler. "This is my best friend and I just need to borrow him for a second and then you can have him back."

"That's up to him," she said.

"I'll talk to you tomorrow, Norah," he said.

"Will you? Because you didn't talk to me at all today. And I'm kind of over it. Your sister stole your sketchbook and you're talking to her. I looked at one single picture before I realized it was your sketchbook and this is what I get?" I took a deep breath and barreled on. "Well, just in case you were wondering, your sketch was brilliant. It made me question my entire existence as an artist because I'm nowhere near that good." Out of the corner of my eye, I could see Heidi giving me that look people gave me when I didn't edit my thoughts but I was on a roll now and kept talking. "It also made me question my friendship status in your life because I thought we were gold-level best friends but maybe we got more than two questions wrong, maybe we're not even bronze-level best friends. Because your sister assumed that the secret question was right, but I realize we've both been keeping secrets. Our friendship didn't even medal. We barely qualify for a participation ribbon."

"What secret are you keeping from me?" Skyler asked after my rambling speech that he seemed to follow perfectly fine.

I was surprised Heidi was still sitting there, her expression unchanging, like she was taking mental notes for a report she'd write later. She must've had that thought at the same time I did because she suddenly stood. "I'll just let you two work this out."

Skyler stood as well, as if he were about to stop her but then he didn't.

I pointed up to the snack hut. "You see that cute, dark-haired

Latino guy up there? His name is Ty and you should introduce yourself, Heidi."

"Seriously, Norah?" Skyler said.

"Yes, seriously."

Heidi squeezed Skyler's arm. "It was good to meet you. Hang in there." And then she was gone.

"Hang in there?" I asked. "What does that mean?"

"Nothing. Are you done with your speech or did you have more to say?"

"I want you to stop being mad at me."

"I can't just flip a switch, Norah."

"I'm going to be mad at you, too, then."

"That's not how it works."

"Yes, I'm mad at you for being mad at me. Now I'm going to go back to the RV and give you the silent treatment for *two* days."

"You're not going to walk back there alone."

"I walked down here alone. Did I suddenly become less capable since talking to you?"

"Do you know how many creeps there are in RV parks?"

"Probably the same amount there are everywhere else," I said, not wanting to admit I'd said that same exact sentence before.

"I'm going to walk you back," he said, holding out his hand like I needed not only his presence to walk me back but also his guidance.

My stupid hand betrayed me by grabbing hold of his. "Fine," I huffed.

"Fine," he said, wrapping his fingers around mine. That's

when I noticed he hadn't taken off the friendship bracelet I gave him. That seemed like a good sign.

"Once I'm safely tucked away, you can come back and talk to Heidi," I said as we started walking.

"I don't want to come back and talk to Heidi."

"But she told you to hang in there," I said. "You must've been spilling your guts." Jealousy was a dumb emotion, I decided.

"Sometimes it's easier to talk to strangers."

We both went silent after that.

When we stopped in front of the RV, he pulled away and went inside without even a goodbye. The abruptness of the exit startled me. Apparently he was even madder at me than I realized. I looked back at my RV, its windows dark. Mom had obviously gone to sleep. The thought of navigating to my bed in the dark seemed completely depressing in that moment. Or maybe it wasn't that thought that was depressing me.

I took a single step toward my door when the one behind me opened. I turned to see Skyler reappear with his sketchbook in hand. Without a word, he walked toward the bench by the stream. I followed him.

When I sat, he said, "Which sketch did you see?"

"One you did of me."

"What was brilliant about it?" He started flipping pages, a flashlight above the book, shining down.

"Your realism is incredible. But not only that, when I looked at it, I felt something."

"What did you feel?" He kept flipping pages. My eyes could hardly take in one sketch before he was on to the next.

"Stop it!" I whisper-yelled, grabbing his forearm so he couldn't flip another page. "Don't angry-show me your art."

His tense arm relaxed under my grip.

"I don't want to see this just because you're angry. I want you to want me to see it." The page I'd happened to stop him on was a sketch of me. Not the one I had already seen. A different one. Me sitting with my own sketchbook, drawing Old Faithful. The only place Old Faithful could be seen on the page was on the drawing in my lap, because it was a full front view of me. "I'm sad you don't trust me."

He closed his eyes and his chest rose and fell. "I trust you. I don't trust my art."

I continued to study the page in front of me. "There's so much emotion in my expression. You managed to capture the joy I was feeling that day and you drew this after the fact, from memory. I've never been good at people. And making them look so natural in a setting. I swear you're a master of that."

He laughed. "I forgot how good that felt."

"What?"

"You believing in me."

"I wish you could believe in yourself."

"I wish the same for you."

I chuckled a little. "We were always better at believing in each other, weren't we?" I held up my finger. "Stay right there."

He nodded and I ran to my RV and grabbed my sketchbook. I held it against my chest as I returned to my spot next to him. Then I held it out.

"Are you sure?" he said. "I can wait until after your interview in a few days."

"I'm sure."

As he turned back the cover, my chest tightened so much that it felt like I couldn't breathe. I'd started a new book for this trip so it was only a quarter full. He hadn't seen my work since he left and suddenly I felt like a kid again who needed his approval. He studied each of the drawings carefully. He smirked at the one of me throwing cactus needles at his retreating form. He knew that was him; it was pretty obvious.

"Your brain is like a well of creativity, I swear," Skyler said in nearly a whisper.

The way he said it made it clear he thought that was a good thing.

"These are incredible, Norah," he said. "You're like a pro now."

My chest, which was still tight, made my laugh sound strained. "Yes, a real pro."

"I'm serious. You are amazing."

My lungs expanded with pride.

He closed the book and set it on the bench on top of his book. "I'm sorry I got so angry about this yesterday."

"I'm sure it was shocking to see me with the book. To see me literally holding this secret you've been keeping for years."

"A year," he said. "I only started drawing again a year ago."

"And you didn't want to tell your family because of the pressure it made you feel?"

"The pressure wasn't the only reason I stopped." He turned

off the flashlight. He'd been facing me before, and he adjusted his position so he now looked straight ahead. "Drawing reminded me too much of everything I'd given up when we moved."

In the silence, I could clearly hear the sound of flowing water that I had heard the day before but forgot to explore its source. My eyes were trying to adjust to the darkness, the sliver moon not helping much.

"I have another secret," he said, his voice still soft. "I've been keeping it for years and these past few weeks have made it hard to hold on to."

"What is it?" I whispered.

There must've been a full minute of silence, crickets chirping, water flowing, cicadas high-pitched echoing, before he said, "I'm in love with you."

"What?" I asked, my brain not initially processing the words that he just threw out there so casually.

"You heard me," he said. "And while I appreciate you making me feel like this really was a secret, it's time to finally put it out there so we can get past it."

My throat was dry, so I swallowed several times to try to remedy it.

"You knew, right?" he said. "Otherwise I just screwed everything up."

"I didn't know," I said in a hoarse croak.

He cursed under his breath. "Tell me we can still be friends. I obviously haven't done a stellar job of that on this trip, but I was excellent at it when we were thirteen."

"Skyler." I reached out and took his hand. I breathed in and out four times. "That was my secret."

"That you knew?"

"No, that I'm in love with *you*."

"What?"

A smile spread across my face. "You heard me."

He blinked. Once, twice, then a third time. He tugged on my arm ever so slightly and that's all it took. Our lips crashed into each other in the darkness. He pulled me closer and I swung my legs over his lap and wrapped my arms around his neck. For a millisecond I allowed myself to think about how weird it was to be kissing Skyler Hutton. But the fluttering in my stomach and the racing of my heart and the tingling of my lips easily over-powered those thoughts. And as his tongue found mine and his palm cradled my cheek, I was struck by how amazing it was to be kissing Skyler Hutton. My best friend. The person who knew me better than anyone else in the world. He felt the same way about me that I felt about him.

His heart beat against my chest, fast and hard. It felt like the only tie to reality in that moment. I placed my hand over it, let his energy radiate through me. He tasted like mint gum and Skyler.

I kissed the corner of his mouth, then his cheek, then his neck before I buried my face there, overcome with happi-ness.

"Was that okay?" he asked.

"No," I said into his neck. "That was pretty great, actually." I pulled away to look at him. "Wait, did you think it was weird?"

"No. It was . . . perfect. I'm glad we didn't do that when we were thirteen. I would've been terrible at it."

"Are you saying you've gotten lots of practice in the meantime?"

"I mean, not lots, but definitely some."

I laughed and then I stopped laughing and sat back as what he was saying finally sunk in. "Wait . . . you wanted to do that when we were thirteen?"

"Yes," he said. "But I was very aware of the fact that the feeling wasn't mutual back then."

"But now? Were you not so aware of it now? Is that why you told me tonight?"

"No, I thought I was still aware of it now, but I needed to tell you because I thought maybe you'd stop being so . . . physical if you knew. And I could squash my feelings better."

"Physical?"

"You know, holding my hand. Sitting up against me on the couch. Sleeping in my bed. Just small things like that." He smiled. I could see his white teeth in the darkness. I wished I could see all his expressions better because I knew he was teasing me right now and I loved his teasing eyes.

"I wasn't really hiding my feelings, was I? And here I thought I was doing such a good job."

"Oh, you did a good job. I had no idea. But why did you feel like you had to hide your feelings from me? Why didn't you just tell me? You're usually pretty honest about how you feel, the reason I wasn't reading too much into your actions."

My eyes stung as I thought about him leaving in a week and leaving me alone again. "I . . . I just . . . I . . ."

246

"What's wrong?"

I didn't need to say it out loud. He was well aware of the fact too. Instead of answering, I pressed my lips to his again. He kissed me until my skin felt like it was going to burn down all the trees around us.

CHAPTER 28

THE NEXT MORNING, I LAY IN BED STARING UP AT the can light in the ceiling, trying to convince myself that the night before hadn't been a dream. *I kissed Skyler. Well, he kissed me. Or we kissed each other simultaneously. Whatever. We kissed!* I texted those words to Willow to make them more real. Plus, she was my best friend and we always told each other who we were kissing.

YOU KISSED HIM?!?! I KNEW IT!! Was it my note that finally convinced you?

What note?

The one that said "kiss him already."

No, I didn't find that note. I only found the one that said I owed you two dollars for the slushy you bought before I left.

Well, that's true too. How was it?

The slushy?

The kiss, dork.

Amazing!

I smiled, then reached over to the windowsill for my flash

cards. It was now my habit to flip through them when I woke up every morning. That afternoon we were leaving Spokane and would be one day closer to my interview. I bit my lip as my smile got bigger. My past and future had come together in a magical collision. I hadn't thought it was going to be something this big, but it felt good.

I dropped my cards back by the window, too distracted to look through them, and rolled out of bed. After rushing through my morning routine, I went outside to see if Skyler was up yet. His mom was by the portable grill taking the covers off the burners, but he wasn't with her. She looked my way when I stepped down from the RV.

"Good morning," she said.

"Hi, good morning. Are we the first ones up?"

"We are."

How early is it? My phone showed it was seven in the morning.

I sent off another quick text to Willow: *Why are you up at seven in the morning?*

You woke me up, loser. Now let me sleep.

I tucked my phone away and sat at the table.

"How was the bonfire last night?" Olivia asked.

I felt the smile on my face that I couldn't control.

"That good, huh? Did you meet someone?" Her eyebrows moved up and down, making her look a lot like Paisley.

"I . . ." Were we telling our parents? Skyler and I hadn't discussed next steps the night before. We were too busy making out. If we told our moms, would they make us drive in separate

RVs again? Not give us as much alone time? Constantly monitor us? I wanted all the time I could get with Skyler before the trip was over. "Yes, I did."

"Fun!" She moved a skillet to one of the burners.

"Can I help with breakfast?"

"Of course. Thank you."

As I was digging through the ice chest a couple minutes later looking for the eggs, Skyler walked out of his RV. My heart doubled its speed, making it hard to breathe. He gave me his adorable half smile and started walking straight for me when his eyes focused on his mom. His cute smile turned to a questioning look and I shook my head. He gave a single nod as if he had assessed the pros and cons of parental involvement as well and completely agreed with me. Yes, I was relying on my best friend mind-reading powers in that moment, but all evidence pointed to that conclusion when he changed direction and ended up at his mom's side instead of mine.

He kissed her cheek and said, "Good morning. What can I help with?"

She said something too quiet for me to understand.

He laughed a little. "What? I'm not."

"That's not what I heard."

"I'll fix it," he said.

I had no idea what they were talking about. I lifted the eggs out of the ice chest and moved the other items back into place so it would close.

"Good morning, Norah," Skyler said in an overly friendly voice. He came to my side and opened the ice chest I had just closed, retrieving a couple of peppers.

I nearly laughed. I hoped this wasn't the way we were going to play this off the remainder of the trip when other people were around. "Hi," I said.

His mom scoffed. "Skyler, I said nice."

He looked at his mom. "That wasn't nice enough?" Back to me he said, "My mom thinks I'm mad at you and she wants me to be nice."

His mom thought he was mad at . . . Oh! I had told her the night before that he was. I had forgotten about that.

"Skyler," she scolded.

He took the carton of eggs from me and put them on the table, then set the peppers he held on top. Then he scooped me up in a hug. "Good morning, Norah, you look amazing. Did you sleep well?"

I hadn't been expecting the hug, so my arms were trapped between our bodies, but I immediately breathed him in. "Think you can somehow play off kissing me as well?" I said under my breath.

He set me down, his eyes sparkling with humor.

"I'm sorry, Norah," Olivia said. "I hope you can forgive his sarcastic attitude."

"We're not fighting, Olivia," I said. "We made up last night."

"Yes, we really made up," Skyler said. "In a big making up kind of way."

"You're on one this morning," Olivia said to him.

"Yes, I am," he said with a quick wink at me.

She rolled her eyes. "Cut up some peppers, son."

I pulled a bowl from the box of kitchen supplies and made sure to set up my egg-cracking station right next to his pepper-cutting one at the end of the picnic table. Our elbows brushed as we each did our tasks.

"Here, I'll throw those away," he said, reaching past me to pick up the shells I'd been setting on the table. The back of his hand brushed across my stomach as he returned to his side. I held in a gasp and shot him a look. He gave me an innocent smile.

"Is the salt over there?" I asked, leaning in front of him to look on the opposite side of his cutting mat. "No? I thought I saw it." I trailed my fingers along his arm as I stood up straight.

"I have the salt," Olivia said. "Do you need it?"

"Oh, um . . . yes."

Skyler covered a laugh with a cough.

"Mom!" Paisley's voice came from inside the RV.

Olivia went to investigate, and Skyler, as he continued to cut up a pepper, said, "This is fun, but talk quick, why are we not telling our moms?"

"You just went along without knowing why?"

He held up his bracelet. "Backup powers."

"You are the cutest."

"That didn't answer my question."

"I don't know. I figured we'd have no more alone time if they knew."

"Good call." He ate a slice of pepper. "I'm just glad you didn't change your mind."

"No. I didn't. Not even close." I cracked another egg into the bowl.

Out of the corner of my eye, I saw him lean in and just as he was about to reach me, the RV door swung open and his mom said, "That girl is such a grump in the mornings."

Skyler stopped short and pretended to be looking at something on my cheek. "No, I don't see an eyelash."

"I guess it was just my imagination," I said.

"I think the pan is hot if you're ready with the eggs, Norah," Olivia said.

"Yes, so ready," I said.

"So ready?" Skyler teased.

I hip-checked him, picked up the beaten eggs, and walked them over to Olivia at the stove. I handed her the bowl but must've let go too soon because the bowl and all its contents dropped to the ground and splattered all over our flip-flops and ankles.

"Oh no!" Olivia squatted down. "I'm so sorry."

"It was my fault," I said, squatting down with her. "You didn't have it."

"No, it's . . . It was me." She had the bowl sideways like she was going to try to scoop the eggs back into it.

"We should just kick some dirt over them."

"Yes, of course."

Skyler had grabbed the shovel from the back of the RV and gestured for us to step away. When we did, he covered the puddle of eggs with dirt. Then he turned. "Should I get a bucket of water?" His eyes were on our egg-splattered ankles.

"No," Olivia said. "I needed to shower anyway. Tell me those weren't the last of our eggs."

"I think we have one more carton."

"Oh good."

"I'll take care of it," I said. "You go shower."

In her flustered state, she agreed with me and then was gone.

Skyler turned off the stove, then faced me with a goofy grin.

"What?" I asked.

"The lengths you'll go to get me alone."

I gasped. "I did not do that on purpose."

"Uh-huh. Sure you didn't." He stepped forward and scooped me into his arms in an instant.

"What are you doing?" I squealed.

"I'm taking you to the faucet." He carried me the forty steps to the campsite faucet—a crude metal pipe coming up from the ground with a spout on the end—then set me down. He dragged a log over from the fire pit and set it beside the faucet so I could sit. "What else do you need?"

"I'm good. Thank you."

"Soap. Let me get you soap and a washrag." He went to dig through the kitchen box and I slipped off my flip-flops and smiled. I couldn't remember the last time I felt so happy. I turned on the faucet and sat down. I sucked air between my teeth at how cold the water felt on my feet.

When Skyler came back, he didn't say a word, just sat down next to me on the log and began washing my feet.

"You don't need to do that," I said, trying to pull them away. "I'm fully capable."

"Believe me, I know," he said, and after a quick glance over his shoulder, he kissed me.

kissed him back, pulling on the front of his shirt to bring closer.

"What do you think everyone will think about this when we tell them?" he asked thoughtfully.

I smiled. "Our moms will love this. It's a total best friend flex—their respective offspring dating. It's the ultimate bond. Like our friendship bracelets but in physical form."

"You and I are human friendship bracelets for our moms?" he asked.

"Well, you made it sound stupid, but yes!"

"You're right, it sounded perfectly logical before that," he said with a smirk as he continued to run the rag over my feet.

"Never leave," I said.

His hand brushed along my ankle, his smile slipping. "I wish I didn't have to."

CHAPTER 29

"YOU WILL GET TO LOOK AT THAT EVERY DAY IF YOU want to," Mom said as we stood across the street from the lit-up Space Needle, our necks craning to see all the way to the top. After driving half the day, we'd arrived to the RV park late, but Mom wanted to be the first one to see the Space Needle with me, so the two of us took an Uber to Broad Street.

"Will you hang out around here for a little bit?" she'd asked the Uber driver. "We won't be long."

"If I don't get another call, I'll stay parked here."

"Thanks," Mom had said.

Now we stood staring at the iconic landmark. A Lime scooter lay on its side next to a tree. Mom noticed it as well. "I think there's an app that lets you borrow those and zip around town."

"Zip around town?" I said.

"Scoot around town? If you want to do that, we should probably buy you a helmet. You shouldn't ride one without a helmet."

"Are you going to Mom me even when I'm at college?"

"I'm never going to stop Momming you."

My gaze traveled to the Museum of Pop Culture next to the Space Needle. It had wavy walls. "I might not get in," I said, admitting that out loud for the first time. "Maybe I won't be coming here at all."

"Come on, positive thoughts."

I nodded and my eyes were back on the needle. "It would be pretty cool to see this every day."

"It will be." She hooked her arm in mine. "Should we call it a night? We'll see more stuff this weekend; then you'll have lots of things to talk to Dean Collins about at your interview. You'll impress her with all your knowledge of the city."

"She'll be so impressed that I'm a tourist," I said sarcastically.

"People love to hear how much you love their city. Trust me."

We headed back toward the car still idling close by. "Long distance is hard, isn't it?" I asked.

"Are you worried about getting homesick?"

"A little." Even though we were standing at my potential future home, a year felt like forever away. A week was much closer. That's what I was more worried about.

"Long distance is hard. But you can come home for all the major holidays. And summer of course."

"Can we do another trip like this next summer?" I asked.

"Yes! We should. And we need to talk Dad into coming next time."

"Yes . . . Dad." That was a really good sign. Maybe I needed to take that suspicion off the table, the one that she and my dad were struggling. "And the Huttons again," I said.

"The . . ." Her excitement immediately faded. "Oh, we'll have to see. Everyone's schedules are hard to line up. I mean, this trip was months and months in the making."

"Mom, no, it—"

She patted my hand and opened the car door. "Not right now, honey."

"When?" I asked.

"Soon."

That meant there really was something to tell. I could no longer live in the idea that I was just imagining it. I nodded and climbed into the car.

* * *

When we got back to the Lake Pleasant RV Park, our campsite was dark and quiet; everyone had obviously gone to bed. I could hear voices across the way, a different group staying up late.

"I'm going to use the community bathroom to get ready," I said. "You can use ours."

"You going to shower?" she asked.

"Yes."

"Okay."

I gathered my toiletries and a change of clothes, and as I watched Mom lock the door to the bathroom, I was tempted to text Skyler and tell him to meet me outside. But what did I really have to share? I hadn't actually learned anything. I wasn't going to wake him up for nothing. The story could wait until the next day.

The bathroom wasn't far but I was on high alert as I walked to it. I took a lap around the brick building and found a door with a green vacant sign on the lock. The room was fully tiled inside, a shower on the far wall and a toilet and sink on the wall to the left. I set my toiletries on the tiny countertop and hung my clothes on a hook. A towel. I'd forgotten to grab one. Lame. I picked up all my stuff and headed back toward our campsite.

From a distance, I could see two figures standing between our RVs. My heart jumped to my throat, fear shooting down my spine. I slowed down and assessed my options. If I went around the back side of the rental, I could knock on the window by Skyler's bed.

The closer I got, though, I could see it wasn't two strangers at all. It was Mom and Olivia. I froze, torn between making my presence known and keeping quiet so I might finally learn what was going on. It probably made me a horrible person, but I chose to eavesdrop. I snuck around the side of the rental and to the back corner.

"I never thought you should wait and I still don't," I heard Mom say.

"Miranda, please let me do this my way," Olivia said. "They're *my* kids."

"Of course I'm going to let you do this your way. I just want to make sure you're looking at all sides of this."

The wind chimes that Olivia had started hanging up at each stop since Zion rang a sporadic song.

"You don't think I've looked at every single side of this. It's all I do."

"I know," Mom said.

"We only have one more week anyway. What difference does it make?"

"That's my point." Mom's voice sounded pained. "We only have one more week left on the road and I feel like *I've* gotten to spend more time with you than they have. And believe me, I'm so grateful for that, but this should be their time with you. That's the whole reason we did this."

"I just want normal time with them. Where they're happy and we're making memories and laughing and spending time together. If I tell them, they'll worry. They'll watch me. They'll think I should go home. They will no longer be in this moment and then this trip will be pointless."

"There will be more trips," Mom said.

"Yes, of course there will be."

"You have to believe it, Olivia. It's beatable. The oncologist said over ninety percent odds. That's high."

"I know, but regardless, this year or so is going to be hard. It's going to be different."

I gasped and then covered my mouth with my hands.

"Hello?" Olivia said. "Is someone there?"

It was useless to deny it. I stepped out from behind the RV.

Mom gave me her disappointed face. "Norah, it is very rude to eavesdrop. You should've told us you were there right away."

"I know. I forgot my towel," I used as my excuse. My face felt numb, my hands clammy. "I heard you talking . . ." I looked at Olivia. "What's going on? Do you have . . ." I couldn't even say the word.

She closed her eyes and sighed. When she opened them

again, she took me by the hand and led me to the table where we both sat down. Mom sat across from us.

"Norah," Olivia said. "I have stage two breast cancer, which, like your mom said, is very treatable."

I blinked several times to keep my stinging eyes from turning into tears. "I'm sorry."

She squeezed my hand. "It's going to be okay. I start treatment as soon as we finish with this trip."

"Shouldn't you start now? Why are you waiting?"

"This is what I need to be doing right now."

She said it in such a matter-of-fact way that I couldn't argue with her. "Okay."

She smiled. "But I need you to do me a favor."

I nodded. "Of course."

"You can't tell my kids."

"I . . ." I couldn't tell Skyler. She wanted me to keep this from him. How could I keep this from him? "We just regained our gold status."

"What?" Olivia asked.

"I don't want to keep a secret from him."

"It's not your news to tell," Mom said.

"He'll be angry if he finds out I knew and didn't tell him."

"You're right," Olivia said. "He will be angry. But how do you think he'll feel if you're the one to tell him and not me."

She was right. They were both right. It was definitely not my place to tell him. Not my story or my illness to share.

"He's going to need his friend more than ever when he finds out," Olivia said.

I nodded. "I'll be here for him."

"I know you will."

"When will you tell them? Soon?" I asked. "Now that I know."

Her eyes welled up with tears and she pinched the bridge of her nose. "My plan was to tell them after the trip. I might have to rethink my plan now that you know."

"Don't rethink your plan because of me. Or Ezra. He won't tell. He wouldn't even tell me." It would be hard to keep this secret but I wasn't about to let her make a decision based on my nosiness. "Do what you need to do, what you think is best. We won't tell anyone."

"Ezra?" Mom said. "How does he know?" Her eyes shifted to Olivia.

"I didn't tell him," she said.

"What makes you think he knows?" Mom asked me.

"He was talking to Dad about a secret. Does Dad know?"

"Yes, but . . ." Mom crossed her arms. I knew that look. That was the *I'll discuss this with him later* look. To Olivia, Mom said, "I'm sorry."

Olivia's shoulders rose, then fell. "It's okay. Ezra has not treated me any different."

"Maybe that's a sign," Mom spoke up. "Maybe this all happened because you need to tell your kids sooner."

"Because everything happens for a reason?" Olivia said with a bite in her voice I had never heard there before.

"It's your choice," Mom said.

"Yes, it is." Olivia stood and walked off into the night.

I thought Mom would go after her but instead she joined me

on my side of the table, where she immediately wrapped her arms around me.

"I'm so sorry, Mom," I said.

She petted my hair and I could feel her tears on my temple. "Me too," Mom said. "But it will be fine. Everything will be fine."

I wasn't sure if she was saying that to comfort me or herself but I really needed to believe her.

She put her hands on my shoulders and looked me in the eyes. "You think you could do me a favor?"

"Yes."

"Can you encourage Skyler to spend more time with his mom?"

"Of course." I took a slow breath.

After a few minutes, my mom pulled away. "I better go make sure she's okay." I nodded over and over even after she left.

CHAPTER 30

I DIDN'T EVEN CARE ABOUT THE GROSS TILE FLOOR or walls in the public bathroom where I sat, fully dressed, door locked. I meant to take the shower I had planned on taking before, but I just sat there, steam filling up the room.

Olivia was sick.

My chest had been on fire since I heard the news and it still was. I had thought I was worried before but now I was overwhelmed with worry. Was she really going to be okay, like they'd both assured me? People beat cancer all the time. Stage two was good news . . . at least I hoped. But how could I keep this from Skyler?

"Unexpected question number one hundred, Norah," I mumbled. "Would you say that when making out with someone, you should have the decency to be completely honest with them? Or do you not believe in morals at all?" I squeezed my eyes shut. "It's not your secret to tell. It's not your secret to tell . . ."

I shut off the shower, picked up my phone, and dialed Willow.

"Hello," she answered after three rings, her voice sleepy.

"Sorry, I forgot it was so late," I said, my voice betraying my emotion. Tears filled my eyes and I sniffled. "I found out . . ." I couldn't finish the sentence.

"Oh no," she said. "He told you? I'm going to kill him."

"What?" I asked.

"I wanted to be the one to tell you. In person. After your interview."

I blinked slowly, trying to comprehend what she was telling me.

"Do you hate me? Please don't hate me. You're my best friend. I didn't mean to fall for him. It just happened."

And just like that, it hit me, like a slap across the face. Ezra talking to someone on the phone, telling them he wouldn't tell me. Ezra reading a note I thought was mine but was obviously his. Ezra texting in the bathroom. The message preview I saw on his home screen. Ezra didn't know about Olivia's secret. He had his own. "You and my brother?" I whispered. "For how long?"

"I don't know . . ."

That wasn't true. And that meant this wasn't brand-new. They had been keeping it from me for a while. "Is this why you wanted to be my friend?" How come it had never occurred to me before? Everyone knew and loved my brother. He was confident and funny and high school royalty. I thought Willow had been immune to his charms.

"Seriously?" she asked, anger in her voice.

I pulled the phone away from my ear and jammed my finger

against the red circle as hard as I could. Then I pushed the heels of my hands against my eyes. This was too much to process all at once. Olivia and Willow and Ezra. My hands were shaking. I stood up on wobbly legs and turned the shower back on. Then I peeled off my clothes and stood under the stream until the water ran cold. I dried off and pulled my pajamas over my still slightly damp skin.

I gathered up my things and opened the door. A strangled scream escaped my mouth when someone was standing right outside waiting for me.

Ezra put his finger to his lips.

I shoved past him, realizing what this meant: Willow had called him. Because he was someone she called now. She had told him everything. Told him to fix it. He couldn't fix it. "Leave me alone."

"We were going to tell you," he said.

"Ezra, if you keep talking to me, I swear I will be forced to punch you."

"Norah, hear me out. Please."

"No. I just want to sleep."

"I'm sorry you had to find out this way but I'm not sorry about my feelings for Willow."

I whirled on him, poking my finger into his chest. "She's all I have back home, Ezra. You could've had anybody. I only have her."

"One person shouldn't be your everything, Norah. Didn't you learn that when Skyler left? Branch out. Find more friends. That's what normal people do."

I bit down hard on the inside of my cheek to keep myself from crying again and rushed ahead.

The wind chimes were going strong as I reached our campsite. They felt like the soundtrack to a horror movie now. I wasn't sure I could be a wind chime girl after this.

* * *

I had not slept well. Not that I was surprised. It was morning now and the sun was shining around the edges of the blinds, making them glow like a portal to another world. I wondered if everything was screwed up in that world too.

My phone was full of text messages from Willow. I ignored them and reached over to the windowsill, but instead of grabbing my flash cards, I picked up the notebook. We'd left off on a Skyler entry. I ran a finger over his handwriting and then read.

Right now it feels like life is just happening to us, outside of our control. One day we'll get to pick everything about our lives. Where we want to live, who we want to spend our time with. Who we don't. I'll choose you, Norah.

I closed the book and pushed it to the side again. I remembered reading that entry the first time. It was before I knew the Huttons were moving, and I was so confused. I'd pulled on my shoes and ran to Skyler's house. He wasn't home, though.

"Where is he?" I'd asked his mom. I knew his schedule like my own and he should've been home.

"He went for a walk."

I checked all the normal places: the orchard, the neighborhood park, the elementary school courtyard. He wasn't in any of them. Finally, I found him in his own backyard, in his sister's playhouse.

"Hey, dork," I said, peeking my head through the small window. "I've been looking everywhere for you."

"I was walking."

"That's what your mom said. But you don't look like you're walking. You look like you're sitting in a very small playhouse." I stuck my arm through the window, trying to reach him.

He laughed and scooted to the back corner.

"Fine, I guess I'm coming in." We hadn't sat in the playhouse in at least a year and when I opened the door, I knew it would be a tight squeeze.

"Don't come in. We won't both fit."

"Is that a challenge?"

"Why do you think everything is a game?"

"Because I like games."

He rolled his eyes.

I climbed in. "Look at that. I win."

"Win what? The reward of feeling claustrophobic?"

"Am I too close?" I inched even closer to him. "Do you hate this?"

"No."

"What's wrong?" I asked, noticing that he wasn't playing along with my teasing. "Does this have to do with that confusing notebook entry you wrote?"

Skyler's knees were up against his chest, his eyes shining with held back tears. "Mom said we're moving."

"Your parents want a bigger house or something?"

"No. We're moving far away."

"What?" My body went numb. "No. You can't."

"I don't want to." Tears ran freely down his cheeks now. He reached out and grabbed my hand. "It's okay."

I pulled my hand away. "You're okay with this?"

"No, I'm not. I'm scared."

"Of what?"

"Of being alone, of not making any friends, of "—he ran his finger over the faded *B* on my bracelet—"of never seeing you again." He hastily wiped at his tears.

He was right, everything had felt out of our control back then. I was feeling it again, that sense that sometimes, no matter how well we planned or how hard we worked or our very best intentions, life wasn't up to us.

The door opened and Mom's voice said, "You up yet, Norah? Food is ready."

"I'm up. I'll be right there."

When I walked outside after brushing my teeth and hair, everyone was already at the table eating. Ezra gave me a pleading look that made the fire flare up in my chest again. But then my eyes found Skyler. He smiled at me.

I rounded the table and stopped behind him. I put one arm around his neck, hugging him from behind, my cheek against his.

He laughed through a mouthful of pancakes and patted my arm. "Good morning."

"Are you handing out hugs?" my mom said, probably because she thought I was going to give away their secret if I acted like this. But she didn't need to worry. I had so many secrets at the moment that everyone would only be thinking about their own.

"I'll take one," Austin said, and I obliged.

I straightened up and took my place by my mom, across from Skyler.

"So which tourist attraction gets our business first?" I asked, pretending like that was all completely normal. My mom hadn't explained her odd behavior the whole trip; I didn't feel the need to explain mine.

CHAPTER 31

THEY GOING TO THROW THE FISH?" PAISLEY asked. "I thought that was the whole point of coming here." Pike Place Market was a bunch of small shops all under the same roof. Like a farmer's market (with fruit and fresh seafood and flower vendors) and a craft fair (with art and jewelry and needlework) and a bakery (with doughnuts and cakes and cookies) and lots of other mismatched odds and ends, all lined up and stacked several stories deep on the waterfront.

We'd stopped along with the rest of the crowd in front of a fresh seafood vendor, the fishy smell in the air strong, but nothing was happening. I had been sticking close to Olivia all morning, following through with my promise to my mom that I'd encourage Skyler to spend more time with her. Plus, it kept Ezra and his stupid puppy dog eyes away from me.

"Have you been here before?" I asked Olivia.

"No, it's my first time in Seattle."

"Really?" Skyler asked from her other side. "I didn't realize that. What's your favorite place that you've been before this trip, then?"

"I'm not a big traveler," she said. "Haven't had the time or the money. But I'm excited about our San Francisco stop in a few days." She turned to me. "Your mom and I used to do short weekends there."

"I love San Francisco too," I said.

Skyler hummed. "Now that I'm thinking about it, Mom, you really haven't been anywhere in the last four years. You need to get a life."

She laughed, but my stomach dropped.

"Thanks, kid," she said.

"Maybe we should move back to Fresno so Miranda can force you out of the house occasionally." Skyler smirked at me with the comment.

"I'm sure you'd love it if I upended your life again," she said, her voice full of sarcasm. "Right before your senior year."

Skyler's voice went soft. "I wouldn't mind."

I sucked in my lips to keep from smiling.

Olivia was surprised, though. "Really? You'd leave all your friends and go back to Fresno?"

"Yes," he said without hesitation. "Wait. Is that a possibility?"

"No, it's not. You know we moved for Dad's job. Nothing has changed."

"I know," he said.

"But after high school," I said, "you could go anywhere. Like Seattle, for example." But as the words came out of my mouth, they reminded me of Willow. That's what I always said to her. That's what she'd always shot down. Was she so against it because she wanted to go to a school close to Ezra?

"It's true," Skyler said.

Olivia patted his arm. "That would be fun. You and Norah in the same city for college."

"Human friendship bracelets," he mouthed to me.

There was a shout from one of the fishmongers that I didn't understand, followed by a sustained cheer from the other workers. Then a fish flew through the air and into the waiting hands of a guy by the register. The crowd whooped as he held the fish above his head.

Paisley clapped. "Okay, that was cool." Then she cupped her hands around her mouth. "Do it again!"

Instead of a fish, this time the man picked up a giant squid or octopus or something with very long tentacles and chased Paisley with it. She screamed and ran. Olivia laughed and rushed after her.

Ezra said, "I'm going to get some of those seasoned peanuts around the corner! You want some, Norah?" He was trying to make peace. I was not ready to make peace.

"No," I said. "But grab some for Willow while you're there, yeah?"

He widened his eyes at me. My mom would be mad at him if she knew.

"Does Willow like peanuts?" Mom asked.

"Loves them," I said. "Super-salty ones. The kind that make it so you can't even talk."

"Okay," Mom said, obviously not thinking anything about my weird antics; she was used to them. "Everyone meet back here in an hour?"

Skyler didn't wait for more permission than that. "We're checking out downstairs!" he said, then grabbed my hand and weaved us through the crowd and down a ramp. He didn't stop when we got to the bottom but led me down two flights of stairs. It seemed like we were in the basement of a flea market now. There were stacked old chairs along the walls and tables of knickknacks and racks of clothes. There were also rooms with paintings and some with books and comics. There was a dark room with scarves draping the walls and a glowing red light with a sign that boasted of a psychic within.

"Should we get a reading?" I asked as we passed.

He didn't stop. Back in the farthest corner, not a soul in sight, he finally turned me to face him. "Do you want to tell everyone?" he said.

"What?"

"Is that what this morning was about? And the salty peanuts talk? Because I'm not trying to keep you a secret. I would've stood on the table right there next to the pancakes at breakfast and said, 'I love this girl!'"

My heart fluttered. "You would've?"

"Yes, I was waiting for the cue."

"What cue was that?"

"One more second of that hug would've done it."

His arms were folded across his chest and I grabbed hold of them. "No, that's not what this morning was about. Or the peanuts."

"Then what?"

I wanted so bad to tell him about his mom but at the same

time I didn't. Aside from the fact that it wasn't my secret to tell, he only had so many more days left of not knowing this big scary thing. I could see why Olivia wanted to gift her kids a worry-free vacation. "Ezra is kissing Willow."

"He's what now?"

"Yeah."

"Are you okay?"

"No."

"I'm so sorry. Should I go beat him up? Is that my role now?"

Just like that, all the heaviness on my shoulders lightened. I laughed. "No, if anyone is going to beat him up, it's going to be me."

"There it is." He slid his hands along either side of my neck until his fingers were buried in my hair; then he slowly lowered his face to mine. The kiss was soft, his lips barely brushing against mine, but it completely stole my breath away.

"I'm glad you've had lots of practice at kissing," I said with my eyes still closed. "You're very good at it."

"Not lots," he responded, a smile in his voice. "I said some."

"Some. Lots. Whatever. Do it again."

He repeated his kiss. "Should we go check out some art here?"

"Yes," I said, finally opening my eyes. But instead of walking, I tugged on his arms again and pulled him into a hug. I held on to him tight, realizing I wouldn't be able to do this when he found out the news about his mom.

* * *

"Why are we doing this?" Skyler asked the next day. He was sitting on the concrete floor at the top of the Space Needle, his back pushed against the gold metal wall on the opposite side of the wall of slanted glass. "It's like nobody cares about my mental health at all."

Ezra and Austin were standing on one of the clear tilted benches right next to the thick glass, pretending to fall while taking videos with their phones. I had successfully avoided saying a single word to Ezra since the peanut talk the day before. I could tell it was making him angrier by the second.

"Nobody cares about your mental health," Paisley said.

Skyler nodded. "I know, that was my point."

"It would be impossible to fall from up here," I said.

"What if this whole thing tipped in some sort of catastrophic earth-moving event?"

"Yes, I hadn't thought of that," I said.

Paisley went to the glass and pressed her forehead against it. "I can see the whole city from here."

"Pretty sure that's the point," Austin said, jumping down from the bench and patting her on the head.

"Where is your mom?" I asked Skyler. "You should get some pics with her. This view is amazing."

"I don't know where she is." He tilted his head. "Why are you obsessed with my mom this weekend?"

"What?"

"You've been following her everywhere."

"I have not."

"You totally have," Paisley said.

"I don't know. I haven't seen her much this trip. I'm trying to catch up."

"Catch up?" Paisley asked. "She works, she reads, she watches television, she always talks about how exhausted she is. There you go, the summary of her life. You're welcome, I just saved you a couple hours."

"Where does she work now?"

"She's a substitute teacher at our school," Paisley said with a sigh. "Super fun."

"I bet she loves seeing you guys around." I pulled my phone out and took a picture of Skyler, whose head was now between his knees.

"You're right. She does love that. She waves at me every time she sees me."

"That's cute."

"Trust me, it's not."

"Hey, kids," Ezra said, heading toward the doors. "We're taking the elevator down one. There's a glass floor that moves."

"Not happening," Skyler moaned.

"Did he just call us kids?" Paisley asked.

"I'll get Skyler to safety," I said. "You can go with the dads."

"You're really not going to come?" Ezra asked.

"Bye," I said.

He shook his head and went inside.

Paisley looked at Skyler, then at me. Was she starting to suspect something? Much to my disappointment, I hadn't touched Skyler since the bottom floor of Pike Place. But Paisley was smart. Finally, she shrugged and rushed after Ezra and Austin.

I petted Skyler's hair. "You going to die?"

"I might."

"So when I asked you if you'd rather stand on a hundred-story building and look at the ground or show your favorite artist your most recent drawing, you overestimated your ability to stand on a hundred-story building."

"It doesn't matter. I already showed my favorite artist my most recent drawing, so I don't have to do this."

"You have not."

"Did you not look at my sketchbook?"

"I am not your favorite artist."

"Yes, you are. I wasn't kidding when I said that."

I kissed him on the top of the head. "You are the sweetest. You ready to get back on solid ground?"

"Yes, please."

I held my hands out to him. "I got you."

He let me help him up, then walked behind me, his hands holding my waist, his forehead on my shoulder. I led him inside and to the elevators. We waited behind a couple of people. When the doors slid open, a woman stepped out and said, "This elevator is going all the way down, no stops, no return trips. If that sounds like the elevator for you, step on in."

It must not have been the elevator for the people in front of us because they did not step in. That meant we had the ride all to ourselves. The doors slid shut.

"Is your boyfriend okay?" the woman asked. Skyler hadn't changed position.

"He's fine," I said. "He'll be much better when the Space Needle doesn't fall to the ground with him on top of it."

She pushed the button for level one. "You're not the first person scared of heights that I've seen. Not even the worst. Last week some guy fainted."

"Thanks?" Skyler said.

"We'll be down soon." I put my hands over his on my waist, then threaded our fingers together and brought his arms around me so he was now hugging me from behind. He relaxed a bit.

When the doors slid open, we walked through the gift shop and straight outside into the open air. A patch of grass was to the left and I pointed to it. We both sat down and he took several deep breaths. "Better?" I asked.

He nodded. "Did you let that woman call me your boyfriend back there?"

"I did and I'd do it again."

He laid his head in my lap and my hand immediately started playing with his hair.

"Will you?" I asked.

"Will I what?"

"Be my boyfriend?"

He held up his wrist, presenting the friendship bracelet. "Does the title come with an upgrade?"

"It adds kissing privileges to that," I said.

"Deal."

He stretched up to collect one right then and I obliged. As he settled back on my legs again, he asked, "So what are you going to do about Willow and Ezra?"

"Am I overreacting? I should be mad, right?"

"I'd be pissed."

"I am. And they knew I'd be mad. That's why they didn't tell me. But somehow that makes it even worse. I'm embarrassed, questioning everything about our friendship and why it started and if she was using me all along."

"Whoa," he said, reaching up and taking my hand in his. "Norah, that's a jump. She obviously had a relationship with you first."

"I guess. I'm just . . . I don't . . . She fits in. So does Ezra. People just *like* them."

"People like you."

I shrugged. "People like the watered-down version of me."

"I like the concentrated version of you."

I laughed. "I'm glad."

Out of the corner of my eye, I saw my mom exiting the building. I moved my legs, dumping Skyler's head on the grass.

"Ouch," he said.

"Sorry. Incoming."

He sat up, but I feared it was too late. My mom was giving me her mom look.

"Norah, let's chat," she said when she reached us.

CHAPTER 32

MOM LED ME OVER TO A RED METAL SCULPTURE that arched over the sidewalk and grass. A larger-than-life piece of art.

"Is everything okay?" I asked, attempting to play innocent. I knew why she wanted to talk.

She stopped by one of the supporting legs of the statue. "Four years ago when the Huttons moved, Skyler had a really hard time. Out of all the kids, it was the toughest on him."

Or maybe I didn't know why she wanted to talk. "I know."

"Why do you think that is?"

"Because he has a hard time making friends, fitting in." *Like me,* I wanted to add but didn't.

"That might have been part of it."

I waited, knowing she was about to tell me what she thought the real reason was.

"He had a huge crush on you."

My mom knew that and I hadn't? I must've looked surprised and she seemed to think that meant I was hearing this for the first time.

"He did," she said as if I didn't believe her. "I should've told you before the trip but I thought for sure he had moved on."

"Why are you telling me now?"

"Because I'm worried that he hasn't."

"Why would that be a big deal?"

"The news he's going to hear next week is going to be really hard on him. And he doesn't need extra emotions to deal with."

"Extra emotions?"

"If you had a crush on someone and they were thousands of miles away, wouldn't that take an emotional toll on you?"

I nodded because, yes, it would. It was going to.

"Now imagine at the same time, you find out your mom is sick."

My jaw tightened. "That would be hard."

"Exactly. Please, Norah, I know you two are the best of friends, but don't make his life more complicated. Be his friend, but don't hold his heart hostage. He's going to need it in the coming months."

I stood there in shock. It felt like she was saying that him loving me right now wasn't in his best interest. But I couldn't decide if she felt that way because she thought I didn't love him back, or if it was because she thought that regardless of my feelings, loving me would be too hard for him with everything he'd be dealing with. I had been wrong. My mom did not want human friendship bracelets.

"He's not thirteen anymore, Mom," I finally said. "I think he can handle hard things."

"Is that what you want to be? Another hard thing he has to handle?"

"No . . ."

"Good. So we're on the same page."

I wasn't even sure we were in the same book. Assuming she didn't realize we were secretly kissing, I had no idea what she expected me to do with this information. Start ignoring Skyler? Stop hugging him at breakfast? Tell him I didn't like him back so he could move on and focus all his emotions on his mom? I had a feeling she expected that last one and I wasn't going to tell her, at least not now, that I was definitely not on that page.

"Can we go back now?" I asked.

"I'm sorry," she said. "I shouldn't have sprung that on you like that, but you needed to know so you can be a good friend."

"Okay," I said.

By the time we got back to Skyler, everyone was with him, mostly giving him a hard time about his fear of heights.

Paisley held up a plastic bag and said, "Oh, Skyler, I got you something to remember today by." She pulled out a Space Needle T-shirt.

"You're so funny," he said.

"I really am," she replied.

Olivia laughed.

My first snarky instinct when we got back to the group was to walk up to Skyler's side and slide my arm through his. And that's what I did. But as I stood there, having let that instinct win, I began to realize that maybe all my instincts were wrong, selfish. Maybe I really *had* screwed up when I kissed Skyler. I hadn't known about his mom at the time, of course. But I had always known he was leaving. I had always known how hard the first separation had been for both of us. How much harder this

283

second one would be on us with even stronger feelings involved. Had I made a huge mistake?

* * *

"Are you on the debate team or something?" the girl asked me. Her name was Clea.

I tugged at the silky bow at my neck that I hadn't remembered the shirt had until I'd put it on that morning. It had been choking me since I arrived at the college. I had obviously tied it too tight. "No, I'm not."

"My best friend in high school was and I swear she had that exact same outfit." She laughed like we were in on a joke together. She wore jeans and a graphic tee with a character I didn't recognize on it.

I was already feeling anxious and this wasn't helping. Two guys walked by and both stared at me until they passed.

"What's that room used for?" I asked, pointing to our right.

"They're all just classrooms." She'd been giving me a tour for the last fifteen minutes and I could tell she'd never done it before. "I showed you the interesting places first. I should've saved them for the end."

She *had* shown me some cool rooms—the CGI studio, which was all green aside from the tech, and the room that was all computers. Each station had two screens, a keyboard, an electronic drawing pad, and other things I couldn't see. Each room we'd looked at had a class in session, so we really just peered in from the doorway.

"Is there an outside area anywhere?" I asked.

"You need vitamin D? I'm pretty much a vampire."

"I do like the sun occasionally."

"Well, that's good because that's probably as often as you'll see it. You are in Seattle. You're coming from the land of sun, right?"

"I am. Where are you from?" I asked.

"Here. So I'm used to it. But yes, there's the roof, which is a pretty cool place to sit. There are chairs and tables. Some people sit and eat up there."

"You have like a snack bar or something?"

"We're pretty small. There's a food court unrelated to the college downstairs. People buy stuff there or bring their own food."

We passed a room with a handful of guys standing around a computer. "How many girls go here?"

"You mean right now in the summer session? Or in the fall?" she asked.

"Either."

"Summer isn't as full. There are five of us here. But that doubles in the fall. *Go us.*"

"Ten girls?"

"I know," she said. "The industry has a long way to go. But we're helping change it one girl at a time, right?" She held her fist out for me and I bumped it with a smile. Despite her comments about my outfit, I liked Clea. I liked her graphic tee and her nerdy quips. Maybe I would fit in here. The thought made me excited.

"And now we have arrived at your interview. Level two." She bowed and presented a closed door.

"I consider this the big boss level," I said, pointing to the plaque with Dean Collins's name etched in gold.

"Oh, please, big boss level is senior year."

"Or actually landing a job." I gripped my sketch pad closer to my chest.

"True. Good luck," she said. "It was nice to meet you, Norah."

"You too. Hopefully I'll see you in a year."

"Maybe. I'm set to graduate in the spring."

"Oh, right. Congratulations."

She left and I knocked on the door and heard a muffled, "Come in."

CHAPTER 33

THE ROOM I WALKED INTO WAS SMALL. A COUPLE bookcases and file cabinets filled the space and a woman sat at a desk. She smiled a friendly smile.

"Hi, I'm Norah. I'm so happy to be here." I looked around for a chair but didn't see one. Was I supposed to stand the whole interview?

The woman held up a finger and pointed to her ear, where I could see an earbud. "Yes, I see. You have until December."

"Sorry," I whispered.

She pointed across the room and clicked a button on her phone. "You can go on in."

"Go on in . . . ?" That's when I saw the door on the far wall. "Oh."

She smiled again but not in an understanding way that assured me that everyone had done the same thing, but in a way that let me know I was the first. Then she continued her phone call. I bowed my head a bit and walked to the closed door. I offered another knock, then let myself in.

An older woman sat behind a laptop. She wore a pantsuit and had white chin-length hair, styled in a sweeping fashion across her forehead. She looked like a candidate running for Senate, not necessarily the dean of a gaming college. The tie around my neck seemed to tighten, reminding me that I probably looked that way as well. I patted my hair, which I had pulled into a low ponytail, and cleared my throat. "Hello, Leslie—" I stopped abruptly. Why had that come out? "I mean, Dean Collins. Sorry. Nice to meet you."

"Nice to meet you as well. Come in, Norah."

I realized I was lingering by the door. I stepped all the way in and closed it behind me.

"Have a seat."

I gave a curt nod and walked forward. I could do this. I was ready.

I am a professional. A serious professional with experience and talent. These were the words I repeated over and over in my head as she looked over the folder she had open in front of her and I clutched my sketchbook in my sweaty hands.

"How are you today, Norah?"

"I'm good."

"I like your suit. Very professional."

"Thank you." *Take that, Willow.*

"It's not often I see the students dressed up."

"I'm sure it's the last time you will see me like this."

"I'm sure of that as well," she said with a little chuckle. "So tell me a little about you."

"I love animation, I love gaming, and I've been working on coding."

"Everyone here loves those things. Tell me something I might not have already guessed about you."

"I'm optimistic and do well in school."

"What do you do outside of gaming?"

"I do a lot of gaming," I said with a smile. "And drawing. But we're taking an RV tour right now. We've been on the road for a couple weeks. We've hiked and floated rivers and watched geysers erupt."

"And have you discovered anything new about yourself on this trip?"

She was asking for something new when she hadn't even learned about the original yet? "Um . . ." Had I? I'd discovered that the right circumstances could make a liar out of all of us. I'd discovered that I'd been wearing even more of a mask than I thought for the last four years and that maybe I didn't even know the real me anymore. But that's not what she wanted to hear. "That I really like nature," I said. "More than I realized." That was true too.

She nodded slowly and I had no idea what was going through her head. She pointed to my sketchbook. "Did you bring me some samples?"

"Yes, of course." I passed over the book, hoping there weren't sweaty outlines of my hands on the cover.

She flipped it open.

As she studied the pages, I said, "I feel passionately about the generation of girls growing up playing games and I'd love to help provide positive representation for them."

"What do you mean by positive representation?"

"I mean games that feature strong women as leads."

"So are you saying you have a problem with the representation that exists now?"

"No . . . Well, I mean, some of it, but I think it would help to have more women creators so that women can be represented in a realistic way. There are some great women comic creators that I love. And some animators and developers, but not nearly enough."

Her furrowed brow made me wonder if she disagreed with that idea, but she didn't look up, just continued to flip pages.

"There are a ton of male creators that I love as well," I said. "I just think the industry could benefit from a more diverse creative team."

"You'd like to shake things up? Come up with ideas that have never been thought of before?"

"No, I'm not trying to change things. I want to contribute to the already amazing canon that exists."

"Why not?" she asked.

"What?" I returned, confused.

"Why aren't you trying to change things? You said there is not enough representation but in almost the same breath you said you don't want to change things. You said you feel passionately about providing positive role models for girls and yet the moment I gave you a little bit of pushback on your ideas, you backed down. Is that the positive example you were referring to?"

My cheeks were red. I could feel the heat practically radiating off them. "No," I said. "That's not." I pointed at the book she still had in front of her. "That is."

"Your art and ideas are good," she said, closing the book. "This industry can be brutal for women."

"I know."

"I'm looking for women who know who they are so we really can shake things up. I'm not sure you're there yet." She slid my book across her desk until it rested in front of me.

I swallowed hard and nodded. "I understand." The words came out barely audible.

"Everyone has room to grow," she said.

"Yes, for sure." I felt the panic set in. She was all but rejecting me. "Seattle is beautiful," I spit out, remembering what Mom had said about people loving a good hype of their city. "We went to the Space Needle yesterday. And Pike Place Market is super unique."

"I'm not from here," she said. "But, yes, there are some great touristy places. Have you been to the Chihuly Museum?"

"No."

"It's an artist's heaven. You should check it out."

"Right. I . . . yeah . . . We . . . Probably later today."

She clasped her hands together. "We'll be in touch, Norah. It was great to meet you."

She stood and extended her hand, dismissing me. That was it? She knew everything she needed to know about me in less than ten minutes? I jolted to my feet, scooped up my book, shook her hand, and practically rushed the door.

I grabbed hold of the handle. It was cold in my palm, which must've been a thousand degrees. Then something came over me and I couldn't stop myself. I turned around and said, "You're holding me to a higher standard than every guy in every one of those classrooms out there. You're expecting me to come to college fully formed, overflowing with grit and fight, when I'm only seventeen years old? I'm good. I have good ideas and I will only get better. I had hoped this place would teach me things I could use. This industry is going to stay just as one-sided as it is if you force women to jump through hoops to prove themselves but men only have to have basic skills and balls."

I left the room on shaking legs and didn't look back. If I looked back, it would be confirmed that I had said that out loud. I had said the word *balls* to the dean of admissions.

CHAPTER 34

"I'M SURE YOU DID BETTER THAN YOU THINK YOU did," Mom was saying on our car ride back to the campsite.

I was practicing deep breathing because I didn't want to have a breakdown.

"We're always our own worst critics. You'll see when you get your acceptance letter later this year."

I closed my eyes and counted three heartbeats in and three out.

"I mean, what exactly did she say?"

"I don't want to talk about it, Mom." I had told her a few things when I first got in the car but didn't go into detail. I especially didn't tell her about my amazing display of temper, or my word choice, at the end.

"Did you tell her that you still had time to be more confident in your convictions? You have your whole senior year."

"I did not tell her that."

"Hmm. Well, it's not too late. Maybe you could write her a nice thank-you telling her more of what you believe and stand for. I'm sure she loved you. Maybe this is a test. She wants to see how badly you want it. She put the ball in your court."

I coughed out a short laugh at her word usage.

"What?" she said.

"Nothing."

"You are fun and talented and very friendly. I'm sure she saw all that. Take a deep breath and think positive."

"Mom, can you not do this right now?" I just wanted to sit and despair in peace.

"I'm sorry that I'm trying to be supportive."

I held back a groan and pushed my forehead to the side window. I should've insisted on going into town alone. The others were barely getting breakfast started when we left and then were planning to go on a hike. I now wished my mom would've gone with them.

Mom was mostly quiet the rest of the trip. She'd thrown in a few more "helpful" suggestions along the way. I just wanted a huge hug from Skyler but when we got to the campsite, it was empty. Everyone was obviously still on their hike.

Mom paused by the picnic table. "Olivia said there's a plate of leftovers from breakfast in the fridge. Are you hungry?"

"No, I'm fine." I headed for the RV, hoping for a few quiet moments before everyone came back.

"Are you going to mope all day about this?" Mom asked.

"Maybe," I said, unable to help myself.

"Where is your normal optimistic attitude?"

"I'm discovering something called realism."

"I think if you put this disappointment into perspective, it might help you feel better."

"What's that supposed to mean?" I asked, turning to face her again.

"I'm just saying we should be grateful for the opportunity and see what we can learn from it, but not dwell on it."

"Not *we*, Mom. Me. This is my future we're talking about."

"I know, but your future is still there and very bright."

"I'm not allowed to be disappointed about this for one second because of what's going on with Olivia right now? Is that what you're saying?"

"No, I'm saying that sometimes things happen in our lives that can make other things not seem as bad."

"Yeah, well, maybe that thing that has happened in our lives is another thing that had me stressed in that interview today. I shouldn't know this. And I shouldn't know it before Skyler, Austin, and Paisley."

"Yes, the lesson in eavesdropping is a big one too."

"Thanks, Mom," I said sarcastically. "I'm so happy you're deciding that right now is the time for life lessons. Are you done or would you like to teach me about the harmful effects of lies and secrets too? I think we could all use a refresher course on that."

My voice must've gotten loud or maybe it was the sound of my heart beating in my ears, but I had not heard the others walk up until Ezra said, "Did you seriously tell her, Norah?"

My head whipped over to see all the Huttons and Ezra standing off to the side. It was obvious they'd been hiking. Paisley was red faced, Austin was guzzling water, and Olivia was supporting herself on the edge of the table with one hand. Skyler stared at me with concern.

Paisley crossed her arms over her chest. "It's not a big secret when we all know."

Mom and Olivia looked at Paisley in shock.

Wait, has Paisley figured out Olivia is sick?

"You told *her*, too?" Ezra asked.

"No, I didn't," I said. "You're the one saying too much right now and acting completely self-righteous about it."

"Norah," Mom scolded.

"Seriously?" I asked.

"What does everyone know?" Olivia asked Paisley carefully.

She let out a big sigh, rolled her eyes, then pointed at me. "You've been kissing my brother."

I gasped and Skyler laughed.

"She hasn't been kissing *me*," Austin said. "I'm still gay."

"Wait," Ezra said, nodding at Skyler, then me. "You two are making out? And you're mad at *me*?"

"He's not your best friend, Ezra. It's not even close to the same thing."

Mom met my eyes; she was hurt. I wanted to yell out Ezra's secret so she'd stop looking so disappointed over mine. Olivia seemed worried too. And then something occurred to me—she probably thought that if I was making out with Skyler, I had told him the other secret. Her secret. The one I thought Paisley was about to spill seconds ago.

I shook my head. "He doesn't . . . I haven't . . ."

"Yes, we have," Skyler said. "We're kissing."

He wasn't helping.

Olivia wobbled on her feet. She lowered both her hands to

the edge of the table now. "I'm not feeling so well. I think I'm just going to . . ." Before she could finish, she collapsed.

The world seemed to come to a standstill as Olivia fell forward, hit her head on the table, then landed in the dirt. An audible gasp filled the air and I wasn't sure who had let it out. Maybe all of us.

Skyler moved first, rushing to his mom's side. By the time he got there, Austin was kneeling beside her too.

"Is she conscious?" I heard my mom ask.

Was she? I moved forward, but she was surrounded.

"Mom?" Skyler said. "Mom, can you hear me?"

Olivia groaned.

"Should we call nine-one-one?" I asked.

"No nine-one-one," Olivia said, trying to sit up.

"You hit your head pretty good," Austin said. "You should get it checked out."

"I agree," my mom said.

Ezra had joined the brothers, and the three of them helped Olivia up onto the bench.

"I just need to rest," Olivia said.

"Actually," Paisley said, her voice shaky. "You shouldn't sleep. You might have a concussion. You should go to the doctor."

Olivia reached out for Paisley, who rushed to her side and hugged her. "I'm fine, baby."

"It wouldn't hurt to get checked out," Mom said.

"I see it's six against one here," she said. "Fine, Miranda, drive us to a hospital where we can park these things, I guess."

Mom was already heading for the rental RV, which made

sense because she was the only one who could drive that one aside from Olivia. She looked at Ezra as she reached the door. "Pack up the camp and meet us at UW. It's closer than Seattle," my mom spit out as if she had memorized the hospitals near each of our stops. Then I realized she probably had.

"I'm going to go with my mom," Skyler said to me, helping her to her feet.

"Of course, yes, go."

As he walked away, he didn't look back.

All the Hutton kids ended up going, leaving Ezra and me standing by the picnic table, watching them leave. A huge lump had formed in my throat.

"Who knew she would be so upset that you and Skyler were kissing," Ezra deadpanned.

"Don't talk to me." I started picking up a few odds and ends that needed to be put away before we left—two camping chairs, the tablecloth, the big bin of kitchen supplies.

"You seriously need to get over this," he said, adding some things to the side storage as well.

"You need to get over yourself." I was so angry about what he had done to me while in the same exact moment being scared about what was happening with Olivia. "You think she'll be okay?"

"Who? Olivia?" he asked, shutting the side compartment and locking it into place.

I nodded.

"Yes, people fall all the time. She just got banged up a bit. The hike was harder than we all thought it would be. She was probably dehydrated or something."

I don't know why I asked him the question; his answer gave me zero assurance because he didn't know what was actually going on. Would this accident push Olivia to tell her kids what was happening? And if so, how would they all take it?

I moved toward the door so we could leave.

"Do you want me to break up with her?" he asked, stopping me in my tracks.

"What?"

"Willow. Do you want me to end things?"

"Seriously?"

He kicked at a weed that had pushed its way through a patch of grass, like he was thinking about it.

I smacked his arm. "You'd hurt my best friend like that? You're a horrible boyfriend." I smacked him again.

He laughed and folded his arms across his chest, turning away from my assault. "I just want to make things right for you. And for her. I feel terrible."

"You *should* feel terrible. But you can't break up with her. And *you* have to tell Mom and Dad."

He groaned. "I know. Once we get home?"

I nodded.

"So we'll be okay?"

"You chose each other. I'm sure you'll be fine."

"Norah, you know what I mean. You and me."

"Right now, I don't even know if I'm okay with myself."

CHAPTER 35

THE INFORMATION DESK LADY DIRECTED US TO THE emergency waiting room where we found everyone still waiting. My eyes locked with Olivia's.

"How are you feeling?" I asked.

"Just tired," she said. She had a good-sized knot on her forehead from the fall, but no cut or anything.

I took in the others, trying to gauge if she'd said anything. If they knew the bigger picture here. They looked worried but not sad. My guess was she hadn't told them yet, but maybe I was wrong.

Skyler, who'd been sitting next to her, stood, then hesitated. Had we just been friends, he could've given me a hug, but now that everyone knew we were more than that, I could tell he didn't know what to do. And that hurt more than I wanted it to.

I was not going to make this about me. Skyler was allowed to feel however he felt right now. "I saw the cafeteria was open. Can I get anyone anything?"

"I'll come with you," Mom said.

"I'd love some coffee," Olivia said.

The rest of the group shook their heads.

"We'll text you some of their offerings in case you change your minds," Mom said.

As we left the others, I felt like I was leaving my heart behind. As soon as we were in the hallway leading to the main entrance again, and well out of earshot, I said, "Did she tell them?"

"No."

"Do you think she will?"

"I'm not sure. Maybe it will depend on what the doctor says when she gets seen."

"Did anyone . . . Did Olivia say anything about . . ."

"About you and Skyler?" Mom asked, her voice making it perfectly clear that she was irritated. "I think everyone was too worried about Olivia to think about that."

I was just wondering if a discussion had happened and that's why Skyler had been standoffish in the waiting room. "I know you think it's a mistake."

"I *know* it's a mistake. At least right now, but apparently you stopped taking my advice."

"Mom, it's not like that. We were . . . I didn't know about Olivia when I kissed Skyler."

"But now you do. Now you do."

* * *

An hour passed, maybe two, as I sat in the RV and sketched to try to get my mind off everything. I sat out here because I didn't want Skyler to have to worry about how to act around me or feel awkward. I wanted him to focus all his attention on his mom.

So I was surprised when a knock sounded on the door, followed by Skyler's smiling face appearing as he opened it. "You really should use the lock when you're sitting alone in the middle of the parking lot."

"Hi," I said, and then stupid tears sprang to my eyes and down my cheeks.

"Oh no," he said, rushing inside, the door swinging shut behind him. "What's wrong?"

"Nothing, no, nothing. Are you okay?" I tossed my sketchbook onto the couch next to me.

He sat down and pulled me into a tight hug. "Yes, I'm fine. I'm sorry I was a spaz back there. In all the stress, I had forgotten that they knew we were kissing now. It's like my brain forgot to store the two minutes before my mom's fall."

I nodded. "You don't need to apologize. What's happening inside?"

He released me and leaned back, one arm resting along the cushions behind me. "My mom is finally getting seen but they wouldn't let us all in with her, obviously. She only wanted your mom to go."

"Where is everyone else?"

"The vending machines, I think. I came straight out here."

I cuddled into his side, laying my head on his chest and encircling his torso with my arms. It was the first time today I felt any sense of rightness.

"What are you drawing?" He tilted his head to look at my open book.

"Nothing. Just crap." I'd been drawing whatever came to my mind, which in this case was stars and shooting spaceships.

"Your crap is really good."

I shook my head.

"Oh! I forgot! How did your interview go? Did she ask hard, unexpected questions?"

"I don't want to talk about it."

"Not even with me?"

"Let's just say it ended with me basically telling her that if I had balls, she would let me in her school."

Skyler's eyes widened. "Was that on your flash cards?"

I laughed and then groaned. "I thought I was this strong female gamer, ready to change the world. But she was right. I'm not. I'm a person who can't even be myself around half my friends. How do I expect to stand up for myself to people who won't want me there?"

"You just told the dean of admissions that she was being sexist and you're saying you don't know how to stand up for yourself?" he asked. "Sounds like the opposite to me."

"But before that," I said. "I was unsure, trying to say the right things."

"Understandably. But it sounds like you showed your true self by the end, the one you try to filter more than you should."

I shook my head. "I shouldn't be thinking about all this with your mom and stuff."

"How could you not be thinking about it? You've been preparing for this for months. You're allowed to be upset."

He wouldn't be saying that if he knew what was really

happening with his mom. This thought made me sad. "I'm sorry we kissed when you have to leave again."

"You are?"

"I don't want to hurt you."

"Norah," he said. "I know this next year is going to be hard. But I hope you aren't sorry we kissed."

"It's going to be harder than you even know," I said.

"And if we hadn't kissed it would be easier?"

"I don't know." I was feeling restless, sad, and uncertain all at the same time. "Let's read the notebook."

"Yeah?"

I nodded.

He went to my bunk and retrieved the book. He flipped through it as he took his seat next to me again. "It's your entry."

"Will you read it?" I asked.

"Sure." He held the book up close to his face. "People think I'm weird. I know they do. But I've decided that creative people have to be. Otherwise how are they going to think about the same things differently than everyone else. Or create things that the rest of the world hasn't already created?"

He paused.

"I was smarter at thirteen," I said.

He smiled. "You were pretty smart."

I tilted my head to look at the entry. "Is there more?"

"Are you hoping your thirteen-year-old self is going to tell you what to do now?"

"Yes, did she leave a template to an apology letter? To whom it may concern, I know I've said or done something stupid, but despite the way I delivered the message, it was very true."

"Is that for the dean?"

"It's really sad that you have to ask. That I could write that letter to so many people right now."

He chuckled.

"Yes, my mom thinks I should write an email to the dean."

"What do you think?"

"I don't know."

"It's okay not to know."

I nodded to the book.

He held it out for me. "It's your entry, you should read it."

I played with the bottom of his shirt, twisting it around my finger once, then unwinding it. I looked at him. His gaze was unwavering. I took the book from his hand. The words were written in my even strokes that seemed so confident and sure. I read, "You're already gone so maybe you'll never read this. Or you'll read it when you come back to visit. Or maybe, if I remember to, I'll read it to you over the phone. Or maybe four years will go by and I'll read it out loud to you in an RV in a hospital parking lot."

"Wow, you were so oddly specific," he said.

"I often am."

He smirked.

I continued. "I already miss you. And since you've been gone I've been thinking about this. The creative thing. You helped me discover that because you never made me feel stupid for being me. And you never made me feel stupid about what I thought up or created. You always told me that art is meant to be shared so that it connects with the people who need it most." The smile left Skyler's face, turning it serious, thoughtful. "It sounds so

305

cheesy now that I'm writing it down but I don't think I'd be the artist I am or even the person I am if I hadn't known you. Yeah, I'm not going to read that out loud to you. I'd be too embarrassed. But maybe one day you'll read this. And maybe you feel the same way."

A horn blared on the street outside and I jumped a little. I closed the book and set it aside, then hugged my knees to my chest.

Skyler was my person. He always had been. My thirteen-year-old self knew it and my seventeen-year-old self knew it even more. It didn't matter what my mom said, or the hard things we were going to face in the coming years. I knew we'd face them better together.

"I feel the same way," he said.

"I'm not sorry we kissed," I whispered.

"I'm not sorry either."

"I love you," I said.

"I love you too."

"Skyler, there's something . . ."

"What?" he asked when I didn't continue.

"Your . . . Never mind."

"Never mind?"

"Just remember you love me later, okay?"

"You think I'm not going to remember that when I'm gone? I've loved you for half my life. I'm not going to forget."

CHAPTER 36

I AWOKE TO THE SOUNDS OF COMMOTION. INSTEAD of my head resting on Skyler, it was now resting on a pillow. I sat up and rubbed my eyes. "What time is it?" I asked my mom, who was riffling through her suitcase.

"It's eight o'clock," she said.

"In the morning?" I asked, still groggy from sleep.

"No, at night. We're leaving in the morning."

"Olivia is okay, then?"

"Just our family. The Huttons are flying home from here after the doctors observe her overnight."

"Wait, what?" I stood up and immediately got light-headed. I sat back down again. "Is Olivia not doing well?"

"She has a low-grade fever, but she's doing fine. The doctor here and her doctor from home agree that all this travel and exertion is taking its toll. It's time for her to rest before her treatment starts."

"Oh." I wasn't mentally prepared for that development. We were supposed to have a week left.

"They were always going home at the end of this trip, Norah. It's just happening a little earlier than expected."

I watched my mom refold a stack of clothes, avoiding eye contact with me. "Are you ever going to not be mad at me?"

"What?" She looked up.

"I know I didn't take your advice, but maybe your advice was wrong, Mom."

She sighed, then came and sat next to me. She took my hand in hers. "I'm not mad at you. I'm worried about you. I'm worried about him. I'm worried about Olivia. I'm just this big ball of worry right now."

"I love him. And we're good for each other. Maybe having more love in his life this coming year will actually help him, not hurt him."

"You could be right," Mom said. "Love is a pretty powerful thing."

"It doesn't take away all of life's disappointments, but it can provide a nice place to fall."

* * *

I knocked on the open door to Olivia's hospital room. She was watching the television in the corner and looked my way with a smile.

"Skyler isn't here," she said.

"I wanted to talk to you. I know it's late. Is it okay if I come in?"

"Yes, come in." She pointed the remote at the television and turned it off.

I sat in the chair next to her bed, not quite sure what I wanted to say. "I'm sorry that I hogged Skyler this trip" was the lame sentence I decided on. "I'm sorry if it wasn't the amazing family bonding time you were hoping for."

Olivia took a sip of water. "The only thing I hoped for at the start of this trip was for my kids to have some fun before having to face hard things."

"What about you, though? Did you want to have some fun before facing hard things?"

"You don't think I had fun?"

"No, well, I don't know."

She smiled. "Your mom is my very best friend. We've had some disagreements these past couple weeks over how I'm handling things, but we've had so much fun. Best friends are important."

I nodded, thinking about Willow. I missed her.

"Plus, I have spent time with each of my kids. Learned more things about their lives and struggles, learned more about what makes them laugh and what scares them. I haven't had uninterrupted time with my kids in a long time and this is exactly what I needed."

"I'm glad."

"I heard your college interview didn't go how you expected it to."

"Skyler told you?"

"Yes."

"I felt like my brain went missing right when I walked through the door." I was trying to be everyone but who I was. "It's okay, though. It's all about perspective, right?"

She smiled. "Was that for me?"

"What?"

"You pretending not to be disappointed."

I looked down. Saying what I thought people wanted to hear and not what was truly on my mind was going to be a hard habit to break. "I'm disappointed."

"And now what?" she said.

"I guess I look more seriously at some other options. And I work on being my most authentic self."

The blood pressure cuff on her arm began to take a reading, filling up tighter and tighter, the machine beside her beeping. We both watched it until it had deflated again. My eyes went to the digital number it produced: one-thirty over ninety-two. That seemed high, but Olivia didn't even glance at the number.

"Have you heard the saying that when God closes a door, he opens a window?" she asked.

"Yes."

"Sometimes we have to go looking for those windows ourselves, but they're there. And maybe they turn out better than the door we were about to walk through."

"It's hard to see it that way right now. I just feel like a failure."

"I get it. But failure in life is inevitable. It's only a problem if we let it keep us from progressing."

"You're right. I know that."

"You don't have to know that right now. You can be disappointed for a while longer."

I held up the bag I had carried in with me.

"What's that?"

"A present for you."

"You didn't need to get me a present."

"I know, but I figured I owed you one since I've been kissing your son behind your back."

That made her laugh. "Your mom is more upset about that than I am."

"My mom worries."

"She is very good at that."

Olivia put the bag on her lap and pulled out the tissue paper I had packed it with. She peeked into the bag first, then lifted out the wind chimes I had bought her at the hospital gift shop. They were made to resemble the blown glass at the Chihuly Museum close by.

"They're beautiful," Olivia said. "Thank you."

"I hear you're flying home tomorrow," I said.

"Are you mad at me for taking my son home a week earlier than expected?"

This time I laughed. "I mean, it's not my favorite thought, but no, of course not. I want you to take care of yourself."

"You want me to tell him before I leave, don't you? So you can be there for him in person."

I nodded.

She looked around the hospital room, her eyes pausing on each of the various machines, then coming to a stop on the IV in her arm. "I can't tell them here, Norah. Not when this setting will make it feel that much more daunting. I have to wait until we get home."

"I understand." And I did. She was right. More than that, this wasn't about me or what I wanted. It was about her.

She lowered the wind chimes back into the bag and replaced the tissue paper. "Skyler . . ." She paused as if she had changed her mind in the middle of a thought. "I was going to say he'd understand why you couldn't tell him. But I actually don't know how he'll feel. I guess this will be your first long-distance test."

"Let's hope we ace it," I said.

She reached out for my hand and I provided it for her. "I'm rooting for you."

"I'm rooting for you."

CHAPTER 37

I WALKED THROUGH THE WIDE HOSPITAL HALLS and rode the elevator that smelled like disinfectant down to the first floor. I hadn't seen Skyler since I'd woken up from the nap I hadn't intended to take. I pulled out my phone once I got outside to see if he'd texted me. Nothing.

I bit my lip as I stared at the dark screen; then I scrolled to the missed calls I'd been declining for the last three days and clicked on Willow's name. It rang two times.

"Please don't hang up on me" is how she answered.

"You think I'd call you just to hang up?"

"You'd have every right to," she said.

"I'm not going to hang up." I sat down on a bench that bordered the sidewalk.

"Do you know when I first knew you were going to be my best friend?" she asked.

"No," I said.

"We were at school, in PE, all crammed in the gym because it was raining. The teachers were asking everyone what activity we should do and everyone was just saying the normal stuff like homework or dodgeball or whatever. And you screamed out *the floor is lava!*"

"Everyone laughed."

"They did?" she said. "I don't remember that part. I just remember thinking that sounded fun. And I was surprised when we didn't immediately do it. I knew I wanted to be friends with someone who thought up fun, different ideas like that. So the next day, I found you at lunch and I never left you alone after that."

That story, the one I'd always remembered as the moment in my life when I began shrinking myself, was the moment Willow saw me. "Why didn't you tell me about Ezra?"

"Because I knew I was being a bad, selfish friend and I didn't want to lose you."

"You haven't lost me."

She took a relieved breath.

"But I only got you one souvenir. So there."

She let out a choked laugh. "I miss you."

"I miss you too." A family walked down the path toward the parking lot, a couple and a little girl, all holding hands. I watched them until they were gone. "I bombed my interview today and Skyler is leaving tomorrow."

"What?"

I filled her in on everything that had happened since I'd talked to her last.

"Norah, that's awful," she said when I was finished. "I'm glad you called, but if you only have one more night with your boy, you better go find him."

"You're right. See you soon." I stood. "Oh, and don't tell Ezra we made up. He needs to sweat it out for a couple more days."

"I like this idea."

"Bye."

The RVs were in a dark corner of the lot, so I didn't see Skyler until I was rounding one vehicle. And then I jolted to a halt. He sat on top of our RV, his back to me. I climbed the ladder carefully, not sure what state I'd find him in. The fact that he was up here voluntarily had me wary.

"Hi," I said as I crawled across the RV toward him.

His gaze turned from staring at the windows of the hospital to me. A smile stretched across his face. "Hi. Look what I did."

I laughed. "Are you stuck up here now?"

"No, thank you very much."

I finally reached him and plopped down beside him, facing the hospital as well. "What are we doing?"

"I was watching the different windows light up." He nodded toward the hospital. A lot of the windows were dark, but as I stared, a soft glow shone from a square that had been black before.

"It's like that brain challenge game we did when we were little," I said. "Where we had to memorize the pattern of lit squares."

"Oh, yeah. I forgot about those brain game challenges." He stared at the windows some more. "I guess I just thought they'd all be lit up all night long. But I don't know why I thought that. Even people in hospitals have to sleep or go home."

"True," I said.

"It's weird when you realize something you haven't before or when things turn out different than you expected."

"Like my school interview?"

"Or my move four years ago."

I laid my head on his shoulder. "Like us."

"Well, no, I always expected us."

I pinched his side, and he laughed. "Some of us are slower than others," I said.

He sighed and another window lit up. "Like my mom," he said.

My smile slipped off my face and I went very still.

"There's something more going on with her, isn't there? We were focusing on your mom, but it's really my mom."

"I can't . . . ," I said.

"She doesn't want you to tell me."

I sat up, wondering if he was going to beg me to tell him and if I'd be able to resist. Or if he was going to be upset that I knew and he didn't. "I'm sorry."

He smiled a soft smile. "I won't ask you to tell me, but is she going to be okay?"

"I really believe she is," I said.

He squeezed my hand. "I'm leaving tomorrow."

"I know."

"I don't want to. But we're going to be fine."

"I'm not scared," I said.

"Neither am I. We'll see each other soon."

I stretched up and kissed him.

"Am I interrupting something?" Paisley asked from the top of the ladder.

"Yes!" Skyler said at the same time I said, "Come on up."

She crawled over and sat beside me. "You left your sketch-book wide open on the couch, Skyler," she said around me.

"I know," he said. "What did you think?"

"I was allowed to look?"

"I know you looked, but yes, you were allowed to."

"I mean, it was wide open," she said. "Was it for my project?"

"Yes, an elderberry plant from the hike this morning."

"An elderberry plant? Are you a plant expert now? Mom would be so proud that her project is educating one of us."

I put my chin on his shoulder. "I'm so happy other people get to see your art now."

"Art is meant to be shared, right?"

"Your thirteen-year-old self was pretty smart," I whispered.

This time I heard the footsteps on the ladder and then Austin's head appeared. "What's going on up here?" He was followed onto the roof by Ezra.

"Scoot down," Austin said. Unlike the rest of us, he and Ezra didn't crawl across the roof, they walked.

"I'm not moving," Skyler answered. "There's plenty of space."

I laughed, I couldn't help it. "I won't let you fall."

His eyes softened and he looked at me and said, "I won't let you fall either."

EPILOGUE

One year later

I WAS HOLDING ON TO THE SIGN SO TIGHT THAT THE edges had crinkled into a misshapen mess.

"Chill yourself," Willow said from where she stood next to me at the San Francisco airport. San Francisco was one of Olivia's favorite places, and it was one of the stops we didn't get to make when our RV trip was cut short a year ago. So we all decided it would be the perfect place to celebrate her remission.

My parents and Ezra were behind us, sitting on some chairs next to baggage claim.

"I cannot and will not chill myself," I said with a smile in her direction. "Ms. I Get to See My Boyfriend Practically Every Day of My Life. You have zero room to use those words on me."

"I take it back," she said. "In fact, I wish I had brought a handful of socks to throw in the air so we could replay the last time you were waiting on Skyler." Willow was holding a sign

318

too. It had a picture of the devil on it and said *We would like to welcome one of our own.*

I nodded toward the sign. "Good thing he already likes you."

"*Everyone* likes me, remember?"

Ezra walked up behind her in that moment, wrapping his arms around her waist. I had gotten used to the two of them in the last year. It was hard at first, but Willow made sure we still had friend time without my brother around.

I stood on my tiptoes, trying to see over a crowd of people walking our way. Skyler had taken the news about his mom hard, as anyone would, but he'd been mostly upbeat and hopeful over the last year. I'd seen him exactly three times. Once when I flew out to surprise him for his birthday in September. Once when he came my way for New Year's. And finally, when we met up for spring break. That was three months ago, and I hadn't seen him since. We'd talked and texted and FaceTimed, of course, but I couldn't wait to actually see him IRL. And to not stop seeing him.

He was coming to California for college, and I decided to stay too. I'd found another window that ended up being way better than that door that had been closed. We had both been accepted to the University of California, Santa Cruz. They had a game design department and it was close to the beach and the sunshine and Willow, and I was so happy.

I saw someone in the distance walking faster than the crowd around them and I knew it was Skyler.

"Go," Willow said from beside me.

I dropped my sign and ran, weaving through bodies and

around rolling luggage. I knew I had a goofy smile on my face, but I didn't care. His huge smile matched mine. I rushed forward and threw my arms around his neck. He lifted me into a hug.

"I missed you," he said against my neck.

"I missed you too."

"This is a better way to show that you miss someone than ignoring them, yes?"

I laughed. "Yes, you've gotten much better at reunions."

He kissed me, then returned me to the ground. "You ready to start being in control of our own lives for a change?"

"You have no idea."

ACKNOWLEDGMENTS

Thank you, first of all, to my readers, who allow me to continue doing my dream job! I am so happy that you love to read about love. I love to write about love! And I hope I can continue writing about it for many years to come. Thanks for reading my books and sharing them and reaching out to me and leaving reviews. All of this makes me so happy and grateful! This book was so fun to write. I want to go on a summerlong RV trip. It's one of my dreams. I'm still trying to convince my six-foot-eight-inch husband that cramming into an RV for longer than a weekend is one of his dreams too. I definitely need to work on my convincing skills. He is fully supportive of me taking friends on said trip, though, and I have a strong feeling my friends won't need much convincing.

Thanks to my amazing editor, Wendy Loggia, for pushing me to make the story the best it can be. I feel like you understand the heart of my stories, and that means the world to me. And thanks to the whole team at Delacorte Press: assistant editor Alison Romig, cover designer Casey Moses, designer Cathy Bobak, associate director of copyediting Colleen Fellingham, copyeditor Carrie Andrews, production manager Tracy Heydweiller, SVP and publisher Beverly Horowitz, president and publisher Barbara Marcus, managing editor Tamar Schwartz, and publicist Lili Feinberg.

As always, thanks to the best advocate an author could hope for, Michelle Wolfson, my agent. I've said it in fourteen books before this one and I hope to say it many more times: You're the best, Michelle, and I'm so grateful to have you in my corner.

A big thanks to my awesome husband, Jared, and my kids, Skyler, Autumn, Abby, and Donavan. You are all my favorite people (even after quarantining together for a year). No, but really, I love you all dearly and am so happy you're mine. I gained a son-in-law this year too! Joe, thanks for being so good to my girl, and welcome to the family.

I'm blessed with awesome friends who love me even when I become a hermit. Thanks to Stephanie Ryan, Brittney Swift, Emily Freeman, Mandy Hillman, Megan Grant, Candice Kennington, Renee Collins, Jenn Johansson, Bree Despain, Elizabeth Minnick, Misti Hamel, Rachel Whiting, and Claudia Wadsworth.

I have a big family, which always helps me write families. I'm grateful for all of them. My mom, Chris DeWoody, and her husband, Mark Thompson. My dad, who passed in 2006 and who I think about and miss often, Donald DeWoody. My brothers and sisters, Heather and Dave Garza, Jared and Rachel DeWoody, Spencer and Zita DeWoody, and Stephanie and Kevin Ryan. My husband's parents, siblings, and spouses: Vance and Karen West, Eric and Michelle West, Sharlynn West, Brian and Rachel Braithwaite, Jim and Angie Stettler, Rick and Emily Hill. I also have thirty nieces and nephews. Plus great-nieces and great-nephews! And I love all these people with my whole heart. I feel so lucky to have them.

ABOUT THE AUTHOR

KASIE WEST is the author of many YA novels, including *Sunkissed, The Fill-in Boyfriend, P.S. I Like You, Lucky in Love,* and *Listen to Your Heart.* Her books have been named ALA-YALSA Quick Picks for Reluctant Readers, JLG selections, and YALSA Best Books for Young Adults. When she's not writing, she's binge-watching television, devouring books, or road-tripping to new places. Kasie lives in Fresno, California, with her family.

kasiewest.com

DON'T MISS THESE STORIES OF
SECRETS, LOVE, AND FRIENDSHIP!

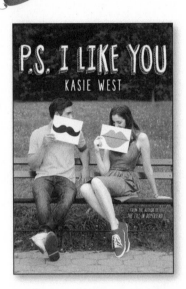

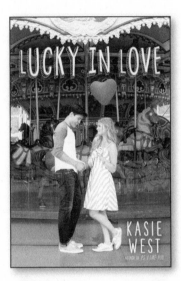

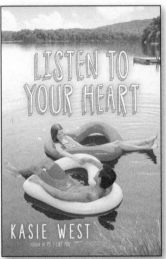

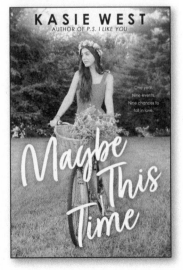

IreadYA.com

SCHOLASTIC and associated logos are trademarks and/or registered trademarks of Scholastic Inc.

KWEST4

**DON'T MISS ANOTHER
SWOONY SUMMER ROMANCE
FROM KASIE WEST!**

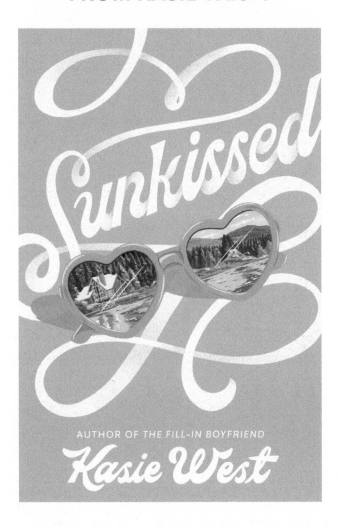

AUTHOR OF *THE FILL-IN BOYFRIEND*

Kasie West